CHARGING THE DARKNESS

J. RODES

This book is a work of fiction. Names, characters, businesses, organizations, places, events and incidents either are the product of the author's imagination or are used fictitiously. Any resemblance to actual persons, living or dead, events, or locales is entirely coincidental.

For information contact :
http://www.authorjenrodewald.com

Cover design by Roseanna White @
RoseannaWhiteDesigns.com
Images from Shutterstock.com and
Lightstock.com
Party Seal by Kailynn Rodewald

ISBN: 978-0-9978508-4-0

Published by Rooted Publishing
McCook, NE 69001

First Edition: September 2017

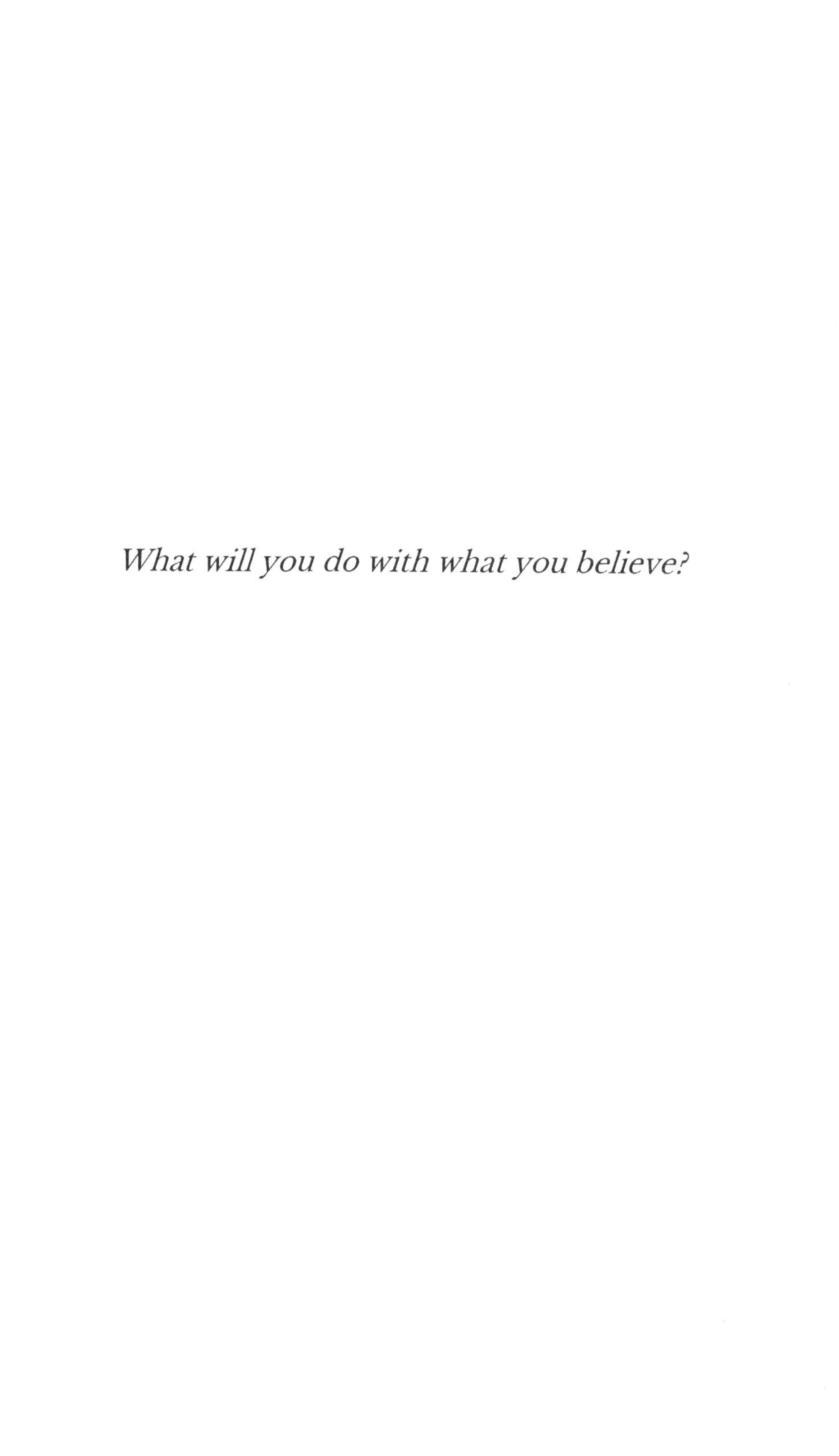

What will you do with what you believe?

J. Rodes

one

Quinn

AM I AWAKE? IS THIS A DREAM?

The questions swirled through my foggy consciousness, and I wondered if it was possible to leap dimensions. To be outside of yourself, looking at what was on the inside as if from a far-off view. Because what I was seeing, hearing, I couldn't piece together. It was reality—what had happened—but then it wasn't. The events kept shifting, changing slightly, as if a different filter had been layered overtop of reality, and then a new layer was added, and then another...until I could no longer tell fact from fiction.

But I did know one thing.

The girl I saw was the girl I'd loved, and I'd thought she'd loved me too.

It is necessary. A voice hovered from a distance. As if imagined. Unreal. But familiar. *The girl could be our undoing.*

Hannah...

"Quinn." Mother's calm whisper redirected my mind. "My delight and hope..."

Numbness overtook my brain, warm, and for a breath of a moment, welcoming. I yielded to it.

White blindness overwhelmed my senses. After a high-pitched ring, my vision returned and the scene repeated. I'd lost track of the number of replays. But it looped again, and I saw Hannah's face moving away from me.

"Hannah!" I cried out. Had I said that? Had I called out for her? "Hannah!" I must have, because I did it again in this memory, my voice desperate. Confused.

"Quinn." Her voice answered me. But...

No. That wasn't right.

"There he is. Quinn Sanger," she said, pointing to me.

The boy who held her—who was that? His eyes hardened as he focused on my face.

He'd been there, yes. I knew he'd been a part of that scene. Had he held her? Like that? Had he looked at me with hate?

My chest collapsed as I processed the memory. Hannah pointed me out to the people who had been chasing us. "Quinn Sanger. That's him."

"Hannah?" Panic edged my voice as my heart sank under an agonizing weight. "What are you doing?"

The boy scooped her into his arms and ran. Leaving me. I watched them scramble into a chopper, Hannah's expression cold.

And then...

Darkness. A blow to my head stole away the scene, and for a heartbeat I was thankful because it eased the crushing pain of her frigid rejection. But in the next moment, the bright whiteness came again, and with it, that fierce ache hooked deep into my soul.

She'd betrayed me. I loved her, risked everything for her, and she'd set me up, sold me out.

As the blank white space receded, the searing split ravaging my heart consumed all the questions I'd been asking. It *had* happened—the memories were vivid and clear.

Hannah had betrayed my heart, used my position, and made me an enemy of the state.

The agony of her duplicity was only outweighed by the black mass of bitterness oozing in to take its place.

I let the anger fill every cell of my being, rooting it deep into my soul. I had no reason not to.

***

Eliza

Hanging, but not really. Pressed to the ground, and yet floating. The contradiction of sensations blurred the thoughts in my head.

I couldn't process the sounds around me...whispers. Cries. Silence.

I tried to shut my eyes but found they were already closed. What was this light that ripped through my cocoon of darkness?

The light faded. Something clicked in the distance, and the sporadic hint of voices was suddenly cut off. I drew a long breath and exhaled. A moan shuddered through the black stillness. Mine?

An odd sensation covered my arm. A touch—but not human. Maybe human? A hand, but not skin. Warm, but clammy and rubbery.

"I'm here, Liza."

Not possible. He was only a memory. Gone from my life. Or perhaps my life was gone.

"Keep fighting." His whispered voice cracked. "We need you to keep fighting because now it's your turn to save our people."

My mind was everywhere random, but not in reality. I was dying. Trapped in the Quarantine. A dying girl could save no one. And honestly, I wasn't sure life was worth saving anymore. Charcoaled souls, so much evil. The beauty of living I'd once clung to had been stained with inky cruelty.

Was I still in the Quarantine? Fragments of memories tried to surface.

"Don't be afraid, sweetie." The lips behind the mask moved, and as if delayed, the voice registered moments after. "We're here to help. You are free."

I tipped my head back, waiting for a sense of relief. Of joy.

Neither came.

Free? For what? I'd never be free. Not from the memories. Not from the anger.

Shame followed the ungrateful thought. Forgive me, Father...

Perhaps the Party had thought of a new way to torture us. They would make us well only to be turned out again. Maybe completely naked this time. Chained to the walls...

I blocked out the darkness of my thoughts.

A hum from outside hung overhead, the strength of its buzz growing with every passing second until it became a roar. Suddenly a thunderbolt-like crash cracked the sound waves around us, the booming loudness shaking the earth on which we traveled. Another boom shattered the air, making my ears ring with a high-pitched squeal.

We held our breath as the van still trembled along the quivering road.

And then...silence.

The memory cut off, leaving me hanging in the dark, unsure of this present reality. Pressed down and yet floating, not knowing where I was.

With Braxton's voice haunting my confusion.

***

Braxton

Staring across the hallway of the dilapidated farmhouse at the shut door of Eliza's room, I wrestled in my spirit.

I didn't know what to ask God for.

Eliza lay in the tiny darkened room we'd converted for her recovery, her fragile, starved body ravaged by smallpox. Annyon kept a close watch on her, as he had the other patients this makeshift hospital had housed. His face contorted with the anguish of guilt. They weren't surviving.

This monster had been his—well, not all his.

He was not alone in the genetically mutated strain project. Actually, I believed he was telling the truth—that he'd thought they were messing with death only to find the key to ensure life. A safeguard against the threats of biological warfare from our enemies.

More twisted lies elegantly packaged and delivered with pleasant poison, compliments of the Progressive Party. Why would Annyon have ever suspected that they'd secretly tested this GMS smallpox on our people at a camp the Party had claimed was similar to a high-dollar recovery center?

These thoughts twisted through my mind as I slipped into the room, careful to only let in a sliver of light. I slid onto the stool near Eliza's head. The yearning to brush her hand, skim the skin of her face pulsed within my fingers—but I dared not. Not only was she still contagious—forcing me to wear this awkward hazmat suit every time I sat with her—but the sores coating her thin, sagging skin would ignite furious pain at my touch.

She'd moaned when I'd entered the room. Probably because the light that had slipped through the opened door burned her blistered eyes. I didn't need to inflict more pain because of my selfish desires.

Which was why I sat there, not knowing what

to pray for. Death would be kind. Life would be a sacrifice.

But the reality was that we needed her. Not just me.

"Keep fighting." My hand rebelled against knowledge, the desperate need to touch her, for her to know that I was sitting there fighting with her, overwhelming me. Lightly, gently, I laid my rubber-gloved hand over her arm. "We need you..."

Her life could save many others. And she was the final proof that could change everything. She could destroy the Party.

We all needed Eliza to live.

two

Quinn

"Quinn."

That voice I knew. It wasn't the voice that I'd wanted. Though anger had taken what had been warmth and trust and turned it to cold hate, I still longed to hear my name on Hannah's whisper, tinged with the blooming beauty of emotions I thought she'd once cultivated for me.

She didn't. The voice wasn't hers.

"Quinn, fight through this. Come back to me."

The woman who spoke, her voice both calm and familiar, didn't spark a sense of safety or a yearning to fight out of the blaze of dreams and memories and pain. Instead, hearing her made me want to bury deep within the hazy comfort of unconsciousness. Because I didn't trust her either. I couldn't define why, except there was something—had always been something—between us that didn't fit right.

My mother scared me. With her calm, well-kept exterior, her practiced manners, her prestige—power, in our world—she struck me as off. Our relationship, though she worked for closeness, was strained. There was something false about it.

I had dreams about that too. Had ever since I was a small boy. And unlike the dreams that continued to repeat in the white agony of my current struggle, those dreams didn't shift. New layers were never added, giving new detail or confusing what I'd thought I'd seen before. Those dreams were consistent. Terrifying.

Unexplained.

I'd told her about them once, when a boy. She, with her placid voice, confident posture, personal yet distant touch upon my shoulder, firmly assured me that my dreams were only that. Dreams. Provoked by the tragedy I'd witnessed when I was only four. Made personal only because of my tender heart and unparalleled compassion.

"But," she would reassure. Firmly. With almost a hint of warning. "They are not dreams you own. You have always been safe at my side. My son. My delight and hope."

She would smile then, but her eyes never did.

Her eyes were ever a command. To me or to anyone on whom she set them. Compliance. Unwavering loyalty. These were her silent demands. Even upon Uncle Kasen.

This was why I feared my mother. Why I didn't want it to be her voice calling me out of the abyss.

In my perfect vision—a vision I'd glimpsed before the betrayal—I'd seen Hannah as my salvation. And I thought she had been—she'd given me proof of what I'd always suspected. That my mother and her Party were not what they seemed. The seemingly spotless white of their claims was toned with darkness beneath.

That proof was false. Hannah was false. Which meant my intuition had also been false.

"Quinn, my delight. My hope..."

That voice, still calm. Still cultured. She called. Perhaps beckoning me not only from this restless sleep but from all of my misgivings. She'd proven me wrong—proven herself right about Hannah.

Perhaps she'd been right all along. Those dreams were not mine to own. I was her son. It was shameful that it took a girl's devastating betrayal for me to learn where I could truly place my trust.

But proof I had. It was time to awaken. To take the place she had prepared for me.

To embrace my mother's hope.

Straining my eyelids open, because the pain still singed into my head, I sought her face. There, beyond the gauzy cloud of semiconsciousness, she sat. That mechanical-like smile waiting on her glossed lips as she looked down at me.

"There you are." The smile still didn't reach her eyes.

The world slowly came into sharper focus and began to spin. The liquid burn of pain glazed beneath my lids, and I shut them against the dizzying turn of the room.

"Do not worry, son." She leaned nearer as her whispered words feathered against my ear. "We will right the wrong done to us."

I fought against the images her words provoked. That of Hannah wrapped close in the arms of another boy, cold indifference in her eyes. I couldn't brush them away, and my heart burned.

The pad of Mother's thumb brushed over my cheekbone, and then her palm rested on top of my forehead. "Do not doubt it, Quinn. Let it give you strength. With it you will find the power to do what must be done."

My limbs, stiff and cold, lying against the bed at my back, trembled as the memory rolled through my mind again.

I blinked, preferring the whirling room to the replay that became clearer, more piercing, with every rewind, and found Mother still gazing down at me. Her smile had changed ever so slightly.

No longer painted, her lips curved in satisfaction.

Because I'm alive. Hannah didn't win.

I gripped those thoughts and clung to them, fighting away the fragile voice declaring them to be untrue. Hinting that her grin held a sinister hue.

Clearly Mother wanted me alive. Proof enough of her sincere maternal love. A love that I would finally embrace.

***

Braxton

I stood at the edge of the burial ground, my eyes on the unturned soil behind two more fresh graves. Wouldn't remain untouched for long.

We were down to only three. Of the twenty-seven infected victims Jude's rescue party had been able to pull from the Quarantine, only three still fought against death. Most died within twenty-four hours of transfer. The other two still clinging to a wisp of life were certain not to make it through the night.

Eliza was our best hope. She was the closest to winning the struggle. Part of me raged against that. It was unfair. What would her scarred life be after the horrors she'd survived? And yet she lived, and that made my heart glad.

More evidence of my selfishness.

"Jude has a job for us." Tristan's calm voice wafted from behind me.

I didn't turn, my attention still glued to the mounds of freshly turned dirt checkering the ground. The markers were rustic at best. Carved planks of wood pounded into the ground. Name—if we had a name. Date of last breath. Cause of death: *Smallpox. Unleashed by our benevolent Party.*

Jude's eyes had frowned when that last inscription had been read out loud. Strange how, even in his awkward posture—bound to a chair, unable to even hold his neck up straight—he could clearly communicate his thoughts with one look. When he chose to. The look he'd employed said, *This isn't right, and we will not be better for it.*

After the remembrance, the burial of yet another soul who didn't survive the plague released by the Party, I had challenged him.

Because still, at nearly twenty, I hadn't grown up enough to realize all that I didn't understand.

"It's merely the truth, Jude," I'd whispered at his side.

"Words carry power, young Luther." In a hushed but unnatural voice, he responded with a remark frustratingly similar to something my father would have said.

"And what do you fear this power will produce?"

He studied me in the strange, quiet way that was uniquely Jude, his eyes gentle yet commanding. Intelligence written on his face, though it was scarred and misshapen.

"Resentment will not be a servant." His mechanized voice somehow still carried the impact of passion, concern. "And it will prove to be a vicious master. We must practice the difficult task of forgiveness—or when it comes our turn, we will be the ones standing in shame."

The layers of his wisdom dove deep within me, and my thoughts turned to Eliza. The weight of his implication took me down, made me feel as though my lungs were being crushed.

If she knew the truth...

Forgiveness was truly more than I could ask for. I shriveled in the toxic muck of guilt and wondered if it would be nobler to ensure she never found out the truth.

The question seemed presumptuous. She had to survive smallpox first.

More heaviness. I turned away from the graveyard, dragging my thoughts from the darkness as I faced Tristan.

"What is it he wants?"

"Supply run." Tristan stopped next to me, his eyes filtering over the disturbed ground I'd been studying. "North this time."

"Was there a hospital there?"

Tristan nodded. "Smaller than the last town, but he says there's still a chance supplies will have been left. And even if not medical, with the new refugees from camp, we need anything we can find. Canned goods. Grains. Whatever we can scavenge."

I nodded, not looking back to the graveyard. I'd spent enough time wallowing there for the morning. "Hannah will come."

Tristan tipped an eyebrow at my *it's not optional* statement. "Jude didn't mention her. You, me, Miranda, and Skye. That's our normal."

"Hannah needs to keep moving. And I need to keep an eye on her." I steadied my gaze on him for one full second and then turned to go speak with Jude.

Certainly Tristan understood what I didn't say. Hannah was reckless and unpredictable. She was also my unspoken responsibility. The last thing I wanted to have to tell Eliza—well, next to the truth about the Persuasion I'd left in the mill two years before—was that I'd let her sister get in harm's way.

Explaining why Hannah was in love with Quinn Sanger was going to be hard enough.

"You clear it with Jude. Miranda and I will wait for you at the van. Skye might be glad for the break."

Halfway to Jude's lab by that time, Tristan cut a path away from mine toward the hill opposite Jude's bunker. Another steel-framed building sat at the base of that rise, though it was not buried into the earth's gut. Three vehicles, and the precious supply of fuel kept in a huge tanker truck, waited within that structure. Our connections to the world beyond the Refuge. The reason Jude was able to rescue so many from the Reformation Camp before the Party had flown in the bombers.

Scarred earth. That was all that remained as testimony to the Party's inhumanity. Except those who had been rescued before the bombs dropped. Our community had more than doubled the day the veil tore, and we had yet to find a new normal, a balance, among so many desperate and disillusioned.

I stopped at the entrance to Jude's lab and turned back to look over the village. A hint of green seeped under the prominent brown of dried grass that swept over the curves of valleys and hills. The whispers of spring. A brush of hope. From death came life. The struggles of a long, cold winter, dark and haunting, were giving way to the gentle touch of light, the soft warm breath of the sun as we tilted a little more toward it every day.

But a shift in weather didn't really indicate a shift in life. The Party was still very much in power, though the rise against it had broken free with stunning force. People were no longer blinded by what Jude had named *social capital*—giving or doing something with the intent to gain something for yourself—and many had taken a stand. Some, a violent one.

The tension didn't bring comfort.

As the knots in my shoulders tightened, I turned back to the underground lab and passed through the door. The dark halls had once felt confining. Scary. Now they welcomed me with a promise of purpose. Finally, I could do something. Start becoming what Eliza had wanted me to be.

Jude was where I'd expected him to be. Scanning one of the screens tipped at an angle just right for his lower line of vision.

"Tristan said you had us on mission?" I spoke while walking toward him, not fearing that I'd startle him. For all that Jude lacked physically, his acute senses more than made up the loss. He likely had heard my footfalls the moment I'd entered the underground.

"Yes." He continued to watch the monitor. "You didn't need to confirm with me. Tristan knows the route."

"I want Hannah to come."

He hesitated. And then, "So be it."

No discussion. No asking me why? This was not what I'd expected. Jude remained captivated by whatever was playing out on that screen. I tipped, one shoulder pointing toward the ground, so I could better make out the action.

A fireball erupted near the White House. The spire of what had been the Washington Monument toppled, slowly at first but gaining speed as it crashed tip first into the green beneath.

My breath became thick and stuck in my throat as my pulse throbbed hot and hard. "What is this?"

Jude's garbled, low voice answered. "War."

The scene replayed again. An orange explosion that vibrated the earth into a momentary blur. The monument split, tottered, and then plowed the ground below.

"Did you..."

"No." Jude flung his head, and it flopped so

that his eyes drilled into mine. "This is not my work."

Jude would not want that on his conscience. It wasn't how he lived or thought. He fought for the hopeless—but hopelessness came in many forms. Exhibit A: me. Exhibit B: Hannah Knight. Exhibit C: Eliza. Exhibit D: Quinn Sanger.

With that kind of diverse lineup, there were no easy answers. The human experience was simply too complex to blanket problems with a one-size-fits-all solution.

I stared at the screen, unable to turn away from the replay. "What will happen?"

"I don't know, Luther." The drop in Jude's tone said defeat.

"They'll blame us."

"Yes. Already have. Hannah's name was mentioned—as was yours."

So, they had confirmed our identities. Wanted by the US government for treason. Now, terrorism? Acts of war?

All I'd ever wanted was the American dream. A comfortable life. Success. Public enemy? Not ever on my bullet-point list of hopes and dreams. I pushed away the sharp stab of disillusionment. This was the life I had, and there wasn't any changing that.

"What about Quinn?"

"His mother is adamant that he'd been used.

Tricked. He has yet to make a public showing. They say his recovery is slow—the blow to his head was severe."

Had Jude shared any of this with Hannah?

"Luther, you were sent on a supply run. Go. This is not something for you to shoulder."

It would be though. Eliza had been right. There wasn't a place to hide. Eventually they'd even find us here. And then...

War. We were defenseless. Truly and completely defenseless. The only thing we had going was Jude's brilliant Umbrella—the shield that kept the digital eyes off our village, that made us vanish on the uninhabited Vacant Plains.

It wouldn't last forever. I only needed to glance at Jude's calculating eyes to know it for a fact.

"Go." Jude spoke louder, his switch from encouragement to command pronounced.

My Jackal life kicked in, and I almost flung a salute as I stood straighter. "Yes, sir."

I pivoted and took two steps before Jude's voice stopped me again.

"Hannah?"

Her name was a question. A challenge.

"What about her?"

"She could stay with her father. She would be safe."

Not from herself. Not from her impulsive actions and her lingering resentment. Especially since Evan's stability had slipped. Jayla had died, and Eliza was barely hanging on to life. With the shattering of his family, Evan had folded inward, becoming only a wispy shadow of the man he'd been.

"She's better off occupied. Useful."

With a small movement of his index finger, Jude moved his chair, spinning to face me again. "You worry about her?"

"Yes."

He studied me, his eyes calculating. And then he angled his chin in an awkward nod. But before I could redirect my steps out the door, he spoke. "Are you sure this concern is about Hannah?"

The undertones of his question were clear. Not about Eliza? Not about my need to prove something that had never been true—that she'd been right about me?

My shoulders sagged, and I looked to the ground. "I don't think you need me to answer that."

three

Quinn

The stale air of the bunker was maddening. I hadn't seen real sunlight in days. Mustard yellow had tainted the skin under my closely shaved whiskers. The need to feel the real warmth of the spring sun, to smell air washed by rain, to view real life rather than still life pushed me past the throbbing reminder of my fractured skull.

For two weeks I'd been on my back, first at the hospital, a private room sectioned off for me. To keep away the protestors who still raged against the Party on the streets of our capital. Then at our bunker, where we'd been relocated, along with Uncle Kasen, for our safety while the unrest pulsed throughout the nation.

It was time to face DC again. To see what my actions had wrought.

The tunnels, secret from all but the select few of the Party who guarded, worked, or lived within the vaults, wound in a circular pattern. I wasn't sure from which building I would emerge, but the extensive hallways and size of the quarters indicated it must be large.

The halls were mostly unpopulated, with an occasional military guard posted near a mechanized door of some sort of importance, none of which affected me until I reached the final exit.

"Mr. Sanger, you're about."

"I am." I nodded to the armed man standing guard, blocking my exit.

"I was not aware."

I arched an eyebrow. "Well, now you are."

"Sir, my apologies." He didn't budge his *you shall not pass* stance. "But I cannot let anyone in or out without prior notification or clearance."

"Are you kidding?"

His solemn, tight-lipped expression sufficed for an answer.

"Am I in prison here?"

His Adam's apple bobbed. "You are restricted—for your own safety."

"My safety? I'm fine."

"Sir, perhaps you have not been made aware

of the gravity of the situation above."

"Of the protests? I'm aware."

His eyebrows collapsed into a scowl. "The violence of the new resistance cannot be classified as mere protests, sir. We are, in fact, on the brink of war."

War? Judging by his all-business, *I don't mess around* expression, the man in uniform was entirely serious.

Had I truly incited a civil war? Had that been the design all along—had Hannah honestly used me to provoke a *war*? My jaw clenched as the blood sizzled through my veins.

"I must see," I growled.

"I cannot allow you past, Mr. Sanger, without clearance. There are still suspicions about you, and for your own good, I would advise you to stay where we can keep you out of harm's way. Losing you completely would be devastating to the Party."

His words set off a subtle sense of exaggeration. I couldn't possibly be that important.

With a long, drawn-in breath, and the beginning stirrings of a fresh headache, I squared a look on the stubborn soldier. "Does this order originate with my mother or with my uncle?"

Again his lips sealed.

No matter. I did have connections. With my mouth twisted in irritation, I reached for my All-In-One, always at the ready near my belt. In less than five seconds, I had Uncle Kasen's number on my screen. Benefits of being related. I had an ever-ready direct line to the president himself.

"Quinn." Kasen's smooth, deep voice spoke into my ear after only two rings. "How are you?"

"I'm quite better, thank you, Uncle. Except I need to get out of the bowels of the earth." I eyed the soldier still standing guard as I spoke. "Seems, however, that I must have permission to surface."

"Yes. A standing order, son."

In the silent beat between us, I raised an eyebrow. Was he really going to keep me down here? "One I'm sure you can amend, yes?"

He failed to give me an immediate answer.

"Uncle Kasen? I'm not a badger, and I need fresh air."

"Son, I don't think you're ready—"

"I can handle it," I interrupted, my irritation stamping my voice. "Just let me out."

Another pause. Then, "Just a moment, while I consult with your mother."

My mother? The president of the United States had to seek permission from my mother to allow me to the surface? Yet another odd piece to this relationship between them...

He had the position. She, it seemed, had the power. He rarely made a move without consulting her, and never did he go against her directives. The upside-down nature of the arrangement fingered an odd sense of alarm through me as I stood there waiting for my *mommy* to say I could go outside to play.

"President Kasen, surely you don't need—"

"Quinn." My mother's voice cut off my disrespectful challenge to my uncle. "You should be resting."

"I'm tired of resting. And I need to see the sun. Tell the guard to stand down."

"I beg your pardon?"

Had I ever directly defied my mother like this? Yes. Once. Because of a girl. That hadn't worked out well.

"Mother."

She sighed. "I'll meet you at the tunnel entrance. Don't proceed without me."

I pictured my prim-and-proper mother in full military dress, armed with an automatic weapon, escorting me around the National Mall grounds. Absurd. The image made me snort. No doubt my mother was a powerful woman, but her strength lay in her persuasion, her ability to bend others to her will. Not in combat.

The next moment the guard placed a hand to his ear, listened, and then nodded. He eyed me with a hint of disapproval before he stepped aside, punching a code into the keypad that would open the door to my freedom.

"Your fresh air, sir." His voice carried a thread of mockery as he addressed me.

Couldn't blame him. After all, I'd had to call my mom to let me out.

"Thank you"—I glanced to the embroidered name on his pocket—"Larson."

He saluted. Because he had to, I guessed.

A set of stairs led me up one direction before it turned a forty-five-degree angle, and then I was climbing in a different direction. The stairs continued to cut one way and then another at unpredictable intervals, and as I climbed I not only became disoriented, but I wondered how deep, exactly, the bunker was.

When the light shifted from a jaundiced yellow to a more natural shade, the muscles in my shoulders and chest untangled. I hadn't realized how wound up I'd been, kept underground like a bat. My lungs expanded as I took in air that felt...real, not fouled by intake machinery and the fuel required to run them. Illegal fuel, I thought. I tipped my head one way and then another, encouraging the unwinding of the tension that had knotted in my neck.

When I finally emerged from a roughhewn tunnel in the earth, I found I was nowhere near the National Mall or Capitol Hill. Eight-foot fencing, topped by penitentiary-style barbed wire, surrounded the abandoned hill from which I'd just emerged. A sole road extended beyond the fencing, not well maintained and unnervingly soulless.

A rise of panic jolted my pulse, and when a hand brushed my elbow, I raised a fist, ready to backhand whoever had sneaked behind me.

"Be still, my boy. It's only me." Mother chuckled, though the sound hardly sounded tickled. Irritated, more likely. "I told you I would meet you here."

I took in my unfamiliar surroundings again. "What is this, Mother?"

She made a show of looking around, then spread her hands as if it should be obvious. "Fresh air. Isn't that what you wanted?"

I steadied a humorless stare on her. "Where am I?"

"Standing on a hill. Such a view, yes?"

I didn't blink. "Mother."

She hitched a brow, her silent demand for my compliance made perfectly clear with the look she leveled on me.

Compliance had become overrated.

"You told me we were in Kasen's bunker. I assumed that was beneath the east wing—which you certainly understood. Clearly we are not.

Where. Are. We?"

Disapproval darkened her eyes. "You're not ready to see Capitol Hill. And you're safer here. That's all you need to know right now."

I was done with secrets. Done with being manipulated by the female attachments in my life. Unfolding my arms, I clenched my hands as they fell beside my hips. "Fine. Keep your classified information. But you're not keeping me here."

I took a step toward the lone, empty road leading down the mountain. Mother intercepted my progress before I could take two.

"You still don't trust me. Don't understand that what I do is for your own good." She scowled, measuring me as if she could weigh the strength of my shoulders, the resolve of my intents. "Fine, son. Perhaps it is for the best to see the fruit of your slip in loyalty. Perhaps it is time for you to understand the cost of your betrayal."

A sour burn turned inside my stomach. *Betrayal.* I had been the one deceived. But then again...

"Stop speaking in riddles, Mother. Just say it to me straight."

"Straight?" Her mouth slipped to a grim line. "You've incited a civil action bordering on war. By helping that little witch, you ripped a gap through our nation. Stymied our progress. And, dear boy, you've made yourself a target for all sides. We've kept you here for your safety. But you might be right. It is time for you to see." Her hand locked on my elbow, tugging me back toward the tunnel in the earth.

I jerked away. "We were going to Capitol Hill, yes?"

An exaggerated sigh preceded her frown. "Yes. Not that way. It'll take much too long, and you'll be far too vulnerable. We will go back to our quarters and change, and then we shall go by way of the underground."

The underground. Conspiracy theorists had littered rumors throughout the decades about a government underground—a literal city or stronghold—that reached at least seven stories below DC and fingered through most of the territory. It was claimed to have been created for the political and military elite, in case of the worst, to *preserve a continuity of government.* Didn't sit well with those who didn't fall into those two slim categories, and the loudest of sideline whistleblowers made their perceptions of injustice known.

Hardly mattered, because the rumors had not been believed. While a few hillside bunkers—described much like the one I was reentering—had been found and named over the years, an entire network worthy of *city* classification had seemed ridiculous.

Which was probably why it was ignored.

Mother's heels stamped a *don't get in my way* rhythm against the stone-earthen floor as she strode back the way I'd already come. I followed, resentful that I didn't see an option *not* to tag along. As we passed through the hydraulic doors and around the soldier I had to beg passage past only fifteen minutes before, I felt the fire of humiliation consume my face.

I was not a man on my own terms, commanding my own decisions, carving my fate. At the moment, I was a prisoner on friendly standing.

Because of Hannah.

Mother didn't speak until we reached the semicircular entry point hosting the door to our quarters. She stopped near the marble table, which held a glazed topaz bowl of planted succulents. Odd finery for the underground. That had to be her doing. She did not live beneath her pristine standards. Ever. Even several stories below the surface.

"You will find a pair of jeans and a Blue Devils T-shirt in your room."

Her command was clear. I didn't like feeling like a dog on a leash. "I'm already dressed."

"You're not going to the capitol dressed like

that."

Three months before she would have been mortified if I'd gone anywhere in public dressed in jeans and a T-shirt. I waited, holding a silent challenge to her imposing demands.

"We will go incognito. You can't be recognized. So change. Now. And wear a hat."

My eyebrows lifted, and I barked a laugh. "Incognito, Mother? Really?"

Her frown spanned her lips, lined her brow, and dimmed her eyes. "Would you like to remain under house arrest?"

At least we were being honest.

"I would like to be in command of my own destiny. Starting with my wardrobe."

Eyes narrowing, she took on a look that seemed nearly...dangerous. Dread clamped in my chest, and I felt my resistance to her tremble.

"Your destiny has profound importance, Quinn Sanger. The likes of which you cannot fathom. I am fighting to keep it for you, since you have been so careless—almost eager to toss it to the gutter for a girl who was never even worth your notice. Would you rather I throw you to the mercy of the vindictive rebellion? Or perhaps you'd like to take your chances with the stiff justice of the Party?"

A shiver slithered over my arms as I

considered the justice of the Party. Swift. Exacting. Almost harsh.

Because the glory of humankind could not be achieved without unwavering loyalty along with firm and unquestioned justice for those who failed in that demand.

***

Eliza

Life seemed obscured. My thoughts and vision swirled with a sense of discord. As if I wasn't where I thought I was. And yet, the view was clear. Every picture understandable, as if I'd done this all before.

The wind cut a shiver through my coat, unhindered by the openness of the Vacant Plains. There would have been an *other* kind of beauty here—the vision extended for miles upon miles all the way to the hazy horizon, beckoning the imagination to create in the empty spaces. But really, I couldn't get past the stirring of dirt, the hopelessness of every face, and the reality of where I was.

Reformation Camp.

I swallowed against the sting in my dry throat, the movement of my mouth pressing my lips together. The bruise on my jaw throbbed, and I brushed my fingertips over it. I'd never been struck across the face like that before. Hulk's knuckles had left a deep impression.

But I didn't want to focus on that. On how he'd found me—for some reason I'd stayed in the woods near the mill instead of going back to the cellar. On how I couldn't remember walking back to town, but somehow, he had me standing on the platform, waiting for the LightRail that would bring me here. How his back hand flew hard and the impact left black smudges and white lights blurring my vision.

My fingertips moved to my mouth, and I picked something else to remember. The lips that brushed mine. The deep, emotion-threaded voice that claimed me as his own.

I held on to the memory of Braxton Luther, lashed him tight to my heart as the line in front of me shuffled forward.

A girl three places ahead of me stumbled, her exhaustion and hunger buckling her knees. She'd been on the railcar when I'd been tossed in. Her shaved head had caught my attention before I looked into her hollow eyes. The blackness in her vacant stare made the hollow dark spot in my gut expand.

Miranda flitted through my mind. She'd said she was a Purge girl. Fed to the desires of the boys in the Den and then sentenced to the stacks of the Purge. Standing in that line, I could imagine what that meant, especially when I lifted my eyes to the mushroom of black smoke belching into the long sky.

"Get up, you piece of trash." A young man stomped toward the girl in the dirt, the butt of his weapon raised as if ready to crush her thin body.

She scrambled to obey, her limbs shaking, head tucked into her bony, thin shoulder.

I didn't think before I moved. Just stepped forward until I was at her side, my hand slipping around her waist.

The boy in the Jackal uniform leered, his eyes making me feel naked and ashamed. "New girl." His lips quirked in a way that made me think of Satan. "Welcome to hell."

Again, his eyes traveled over my body, making the burn of nausea press into my throat. I looked away, tucking my chin down just as this Purge girl had and holding her secure to my side.

"Don't let them break you," she rasped. Her bottom lip trembled, and she blinked several times. No tears formed in her eyes.

Probably too dehydrated to cry.

I looked past the check-in station, the point where this line was destined, toward the scattered steel buildings dotting the depressing scene of my new home. Shaved heads. Burlaphewn clothing. Drooped shoulders. Downcast eyes.

Still, they stayed. Unbroken. Even in this hell.

"Has she woken up at all?" A voice, distant, unfitting, shifted reality. I knew him. Loved him.

The line where I had stood dissipated from my view. The scene before me smeared and then vanished. A sensation of falling drew me backward, blackness taking over what had been vivid and hopeless. Suddenly my body felt as if it were burning, and white-hot pain crawled across my skin.

The Purge?

"No. But she's still fighting." Though similar to Braxton's, I didn't know this voice. He didn't sound cruel. Actually, hope cradled his tone.

Something cold touched my mouth, and my lips parted, welcoming the relief. A drop of water doused the fire on my tongue, and I swallowed.

"See if she'll take more." That same unfamiliar but kind voice spoke again, muffled, as if coming from behind thin glass.

Another cold brush of liquid grazed my lips.

More. I swallowed, trying to find the strength to form the word.

"Aren't you a scavenger today?"

"Yes."

The voice I loved responded, even as another

cool drop of water seeped into my mouth.

"We leave in a bit. Hannah's going."

Hannah? Braxton and Hannah? I worked to sort the information, to make sense of where I was, what was happening, but the ache in my head and the sizzling pain scraping my skin wouldn't let me focus.

"I'll give you a few minutes," the other voice said.

More. Again, I concentrated on making my voice work, desperate for another cooling drop. My tongue felt swollen and unusable.

The cold relief slid across my lips again.

"Keep fighting, Liza." His whisper seemed fierce, even though the words wobbled. "I know it's not fair, but we need you to live."

Were there tears in his voice?

A featherlight warmth slipped over the skin above my ear. The touch didn't feel quite like his—but it soothed some of the fire from that spot on my head.

More.

The glide of water slid over my mouth one more time, and the tension of my body drained. Black nothingness wrapped around me, and I surrendered to it, my last coherent thoughts dwelling on the touch I hoped had been his. Letting it take me elsewhere.

***

Quinn

The bunker went deeper into the earth's crust than I'd imagined. Two stories below our quarters, a system of tunnels connected the entire underground, and I was dumbfounded to find a miniature subway hidden in the dark belly. The mystery—and impressiveness—of this elaborate system gnawed at my curiosity as I stepped into a subway car behind Mother.

"This cannot be all of our work." With a wave, I indicated the car we'd entered, the tunnel we'd walked through, and the bunker beyond.

Mother's ominous look of disapproval melted into her more typical grin. Confident, not really happy. As if she possessed a secret.

I found no real comfort in her mood shift.

"No, the Party cannot claim all the credit, although restoring and updating the remains of what had been started long before our time took much effort. Alas, we are not the first to have conceived of this. Impressive, yes?"

I tipped one nod as the car launched into motion, forcing me to grip the bar above my head. "It is. Who paid for it?"

Unaffected by the motion propelling us through the bowels of the earth, she blew a soft snort, as if that little detail was irrelevant. "Son, remember your education. Remember the struggle of humankind to progress to what we ought to be, to realize our full potential. And remember that sometimes we are our own stumbling blocks. Humankind's greatest enemy has not been nature—the forces of weather, time, and earth. Our worse foe has been man himself. Liberate your mind from it. Draw back the curtains shadowing your vision, and look upon the possibilities. We are on the cusp of it, standing at the edge. You need only the courage to grip—"

"Mother, there is no crowd gathered here. Only me. And I do not need your persuasion." I'd heard this all before. Many, many times. Though her passion was unavoidably stirring, I didn't latch on to it blindly. Not the way the masses did.

The corners of her mouth drew tight. "On the contrary, I quite believe you do. Your loyalty has been questioned during your recovery. Time and time again. While I defend your misstep—excuse it, lamely, I might add—I cannot tell you honestly that I don't have my doubts."

"You've made that abundantly clear." I met her frown with one of my own. "And yet here we are."

"Indeed. Here we are. About to glimpse the fruit of your actions." She lifted her face at an angle. "And then we shall see what you will do with it."

"I'm willing to address the people. Give my sincere apologies. Make my allegiance to the Party clearly known. What else would you have me do?"

The high-pitched whirling of the subway car filled the silent tension between us. Mother looked away, the angle of her chin determined. The set of her mouth confident. "We shall see, my hope."

Back to that again. Any other son would have found strength in his mother's endearment. I found it unsettling—and pretty much always had. It was as if she wasn't actually speaking to me, the man, but to something else entirely, which made me feel more like a pawn than her son.

My jaw tightened, and I looked away. Light flicked by, followed by blackness until, after a full second, another light passed outside the blocked window. The streak of motion indicated a high speed of travel, but I couldn't guess how fast the subway moved. Neither could I pinpoint where we were in relation to the capitol—a foolish hope since I hadn't a mental map of where we'd started to begin with. The sense of blindness, of lack of control, pushed panic upward in my chest.

Maddening. A sensation I'd been familiar with my entire life.

The high hum of motion suddenly became an ear-piercing squeal, and my balance shifted forcefully toward the front. My grip strengthened on the bar, and I noticed yet again Mother seemed almost not to notice the change in motion.

She'd expected it. Not her first ride.

The door buckled open, and Mother led the way forward. Breathing deep, burying that irritation, I followed, tugging on the rim of the hat she'd insisted I wear. She stopped at a wall in between two lights strung near the curve of the tunnel and thrust her hand against the dark wall. A greenish glow slowly warmed from the wall, surrounding the palm she'd laid flat against what I'd first thought to be earth. A beep, the click of a lock, and then the whoosh of a pair of doors came in rapid-fire succession.

Without a glance toward me, Mother stepped to the side and then forward, the semidarkness folding her within as she slid away from me.

"Come, Quinn." She beckoned from the shadows. "Time to face the truth."

I studied the wall that hadn't seemed to change from my vantage point and then sighed. The lack of information given to me was still infuriating. But I didn't want to live trapped below the surface forever. I stepped forward and passed through the earthen wall as if it wasn't there.

Because it wasn't.

"That's a new trick," I murmured.

"Fun, yes?" Her satisfaction lifted her voice.

"Sure."

She moved beside me, and again I saw the greenish glow come alive in the darkness. Not wanting to miss the opportunity, I looked around to see what I could in the small amount of light the glow afforded.

"It's just an elevator, son." Mother chuckled and then changed her tone. "Surface," she demanded.

As with everything and everyone, the elevator complied. A whoosh and then a click, and then the ground beneath my feet pushed upward, and the sense of blind motion spun in my head.

Seven stories below ground took a while, it seemed, to climb. By the time we surfaced, the dizziness in my head had turned my stomach sour. My time in recovery continued to have an effect. When the doors opened to a steel room, daylight streaming in from skylights pricked my eyes, burning the back of my skull. I blinked as I shuffled forward, finding my balance iffy at best. Mother gripped my bicep with one hand and guided me forward.

"That was a hard blow to your head. You see, now, why I kept you in our quarters for so long."

Quarters she'd led me to believe to be something other than what they were. Secrets. Facades.

The thought beckoned me back to the moments I'd spent with Hannah, before I'd aired that video. She'd said things weren't what the Party had claimed—that secrets lay hidden beneath their facade. I'd believed her. And, curse it all, there was a tiny fraction of my brain that still wondered...

Yeah. She was totally reliable. The girl who'd left me to die for her treason. I banished the traitorous thoughts that had tiptoed into my head. Hiding a safe place below ground was very different from accusing the Party of mass murder.

What if... A turn of nausea cramped my stomach.

No. *Be gone, little witch.* She was lies. All lies. And the stomachache was a lingering result of being bedridden—Hannah's fault—and then being put onto what amounted to a roller coaster in the dark. Motion sickness was not a true symptom of reasonable suspicion.

"Deep breath, son," Mother whispered as we approached another reinforced steel-armored hydraulic door. "This isn't pretty."

As if hardwired to obey without thought, I drew in that deep breath she'd just commanded. The doors opened, and I took my first step into the mess I'd made.

My pulse seemed to slow dangerously, throbbing through my limbs and head as I looked at the scene opening to my view. The building I'd just left had once been a part of the Smithsonian, but that particular museum was now barred from the public—had actually been repurposed.

Because of the ill tension that still reverberated from the Bloody Faith Conflict, it had been determined that some history was inflammatory and not worth remembering. Only that which was glorious and a tribute to humankind's forward achievements had been allowed to remain—which, granted, afforded quite a bit of museum space. But wars, conflict? The Party had determined that nothing of those blotches on human history were allowed to cast shadows over our people anymore. The next generation would not be burdened with such a past, such memories. They would only be inspired by good, and by such measures they would continue the Party's launch into the glory of humankind.

Trajectory was determined by focus.

But something had gone very wrong with that

plan. Something...me.

I felt my insides, my posture, my whole being shrink as the enormity of what I'd done crushed against me.

The Spire of Glory—once known as the Washington Monument—had been toppled, the pyramid tip of the great tower now buried in a gash struck deep in the green earth, broken in half by what must have been a missile launch.

Armored police wielding full-body shields lined the entire length of Independence Avenue. Constitution Avenue mirrored the military scene, and the emptiness of what was once a vibrant, ever-moving, ever-populated scene was barren but for a few suited members of the political elite or military.

I dropped my gaze to the ground, letting the bill of my hat provide hiding. Cringing at what I would see when I looked toward the capitol, I stole a stuttered breath before I followed Mother's tug on my arm, her silent command to face what I'd done.

The lack of noise roared in my ears. No blaring horns, screaming sirens, rumbling crowds. This was not the DC I'd known. The eerily still air pulsed with a melancholy strain, a silent tune telling me of the chasm I'd carved deep into our nation. One as deep, as jagged and jarring, as the gash the toppled spire had dug.

A gouge that seemed to have no mending.

Mother guided me to the corner, and I couldn't fight against the demand to look up. The dome of our White House echoed the story of the broken spire. Gashed and blackened by something large and powerful, what had stood as a symbol of American pride and hope and progress now cried against the blue sky. A large scoop had been removed from the dome, as if a massive angry fist had blasted through it, leaving jagged marks of rage dangling from the pieces that refused to fall.

I stopped. My feet refused to carry me forward, and my eyes refused to stop seeing. Even when I blinked them closed, the destruction continued to stare at me.

"Ugly." Mother's voice came soft yet unwavering. "It is ugly." She turned me to face her, and I opened my eyes again. "And we must face it."

"What happened?" I stammered.

"After the video, the rebellion gained strength. They found a way to capture some of the military bases scattered throughout the less controlled states. Here is the result of their rage. This is what happens when people refuse to conform. This is why we created the Reformation Camps in the first place. They are not what Hannah claimed. This is the rebels' doing—not ours. This is why the Progressive agenda must prevail—if we fail, we will be cast backward into darkness. Our hope will fade. We will not become, as the human race, what we could be. What we have always been destined to be. You will not become what you should."

Mother paused, letting her passionate claims swirl through me. I still stumbled over things like *conform, Reformation Camps, agenda...* Words that refused to settle in my mind. But I took in the ravaged scene around me, and suddenly, perhaps for the first time, Mother's position made sense. She saw a vision of our future, and it didn't look like this. Conflict. Damage. Darkness.

What if she was right—what if conforming to the Progressive agenda was the only way to become a civilization of peace? Of real progress? This strong central leadership the Party pushed for—had gained—if they saw this future and a way to seize it, then didn't it make sense to hand them the lump of power they'd sought?

Didn't it make sense to join them?

The agreement in my head gained ground. Peace was better than this. Security was worth the price of independence. My suspicions of Mother's thirst for power for power's sake burned to ashes as I took in the rebellion's destructive fingerprints. I turned to her, my jaw set hard.

"What must be done?" I asked.

One corner of her mouth lifted, and pride gleamed in her eyes. "Hannah's last name is Knight. Her family is known for their stubborn rebellion." She held my scowl with her own intense gaze. "And she's still out there."

"Where?" I nearly growled my response.

"That is your task, my boy."

She didn't blink, and I felt the full weight of her demand.

Find her. Bring her and her family to justice. And by doing so, I would topple the rebellion.

I could regain the ground the Party had lost. By my hands.

***

My heart thundered violently, my head pounding with the same cruel rhythm. Pain flooded the darkness.

The flames seemed more intense this time.

Heat blistered against my face and hands, and the smell of fuel stung my eyes and nose. The cries, screams.

They were from a woman, coming fragmented, and accompanied by sobs.

Remember, son. Remember me.

And then it all vanished.

I sat up, my head pounding, my heart surging

wildly. The dream always ended there, and though I knew the sequence by heart, I always struggled to breathe after seeing it play out again.

Those words. They felt like they were for me. Every. Time. Spoken to me.

But they couldn't have been. The voice was unfamiliar beyond my dream, spoken by a woman I could not summon an image of nor remember in any other context.

Swinging my feet to the thick carpet on the stone floor, I brushed a palm down my face and then pinched the bridge of my nose. This dream...it was as disturbing as it was persistent. But I knew better than to share it with Mother. She would twist her expression into sharp disapproval, tell me that it was not a dream I needed to take ownership of, and to let it go.

"An unfortunate product of your deep compassion, son," Mother would say. "Do not let it rob your peace."

I had no choice in the matter.

four

Braxton

Though only the wind occupied the abandoned street, I could hear the strain of a whistle and the twang of an acoustic guitar in my mind. We parked in front of a two-story building, on a straight bricked road in a literal ghost town. Dust stirred down the length of abandoned road, alongside a tumbleweed and a scrap of old newsprint. Trees, once cultivated and well-kept along this charming Main Street, Smalltown, USA, bloomed in the early April sunshine, wild and unpruned. The residents had long since relocated. Their lives, no doubt, uprooted. Changed by force. Made better?

Possible, but not probable.

I wondered what the people who had lived there thought back when the transportation limitations went into force. Did they protest? Fight against the removal of their way of life? If they did, did anyone hear? Care?

Thoughts I never landed on when I was sixteen and life was all about me. My future. My success. My security. How small my vision had been, and yet I'd been perfectly confident I saw things right.

"Get moving, Luther." Tristan nudged me forward with his elbow. "We'll meet up at the hospital. You and Hannah check the storefronts. Get what you can and get out."

If we hadn't been in a hurry, I would have stood there and let my imagination play. Hollywood couldn't have created a more perfect set for an old western gunfight. Billy the Kid could have been tucked behind any second-story window, ready to make his rebel escape yet one more time.

Funny that. Here we were, rebels ourselves. Different times, different reasons. But nothing really new.

"The hospital is on the edge of town." Tristan nodded toward the east, apparently the direction we needed to be going. "Take anything that might be useful for the village. Twenty minutes. That's it, so spread out and work quickly.

Miranda and I will go search for meds. We'll meet at the ER doors."

What exactly was it that had us in a rush? We'd done several of these scavenger hunts over the past couple of months. There wasn't a reason to hurry. These were, after all, ghost towns. Meaning, there wasn't anyone in them. Nothing to hide from. No reason to run.

But arguing with Tristan...not worth it. He'd glower at me for five full seconds and then show me his back, his mind zeroed in on his mission. Unless I wanted to walk back to the village—over one hundred miles away, and without the protection of Jude's Umbrella coin—I had to shut up and get to work.

Hannah hadn't said much of anything during our two-hour drive from the Refuge. In two months, I'd heard a grand total of five words from her: *Yes. No.* and, *Shut up, Braxton.* Granted she'd said those words several times over, but a conversation beyond those curt responses seemed impossible with her.

She still hadn't gone to see her sister either.

Regret consumed her. Maybe it wasn't regret, but that was the only word I had for it. Hannah was obsessed with Quinn, with what happened back in DC. Her vow that this wasn't over? She absolutely meant it, and I had no doubt that every spare moment she could find, she was working on some kind of scheme. Not that I could blame her, but as always, she was too much like me. We weren't good with forming coherent plans. Too much emotion clouded our judgment. The both of us really needed to learn to find wisdom outside of ourselves—and to figure out whose guidance we should follow and whose we should completely ignore.

No easy task for two jump-in-without-looking kinds of personalities.

I eyed her as she marched away from me. Stiff back. Deep frown carving her profile. Pretty much like she'd done back in the forest of Glennbrooke before she'd gotten herself mixed up with Quinn Sanger.

"Hannah, stay close."

"Shut up, Braxton."

See? Still stuck on that. I double-timed until my stride matched hers.

"We gonna get past this?"

She graced me with a two-second glare and then turned her face toward a small grocery store.

"Crikey, Hannah." I snatched her shoulder before she could put it to the front door and shove. "I know that you're upset about Quinn. I get it. But this?" I spread my hands out in front of me and then motioned between us. "How is this helping?"

Her jaw worked, but she said noting.

"We'll figure it out, okay, kid? You just need to trust—"

"You?" she snapped. "Trust you? You let this happen. You practically made it happen! Now I don't even know if he's alive, and it's your fault!"

Irrational. So not surprising. But still irritating.

"Fine. I saved your life—because *Quinn* told me to—but, sure. It's all my fault."

She flinched and looked down to the crack-riddled sidewalk. Several flutters of her dark eyelashes told me she was battling tears—which I'm sure she resented.

I slid a half step closer. "Look, kid. I get it, and you've got to believe that Jude does too. Quinn's sacrifice didn't go unnoticed by anyone. But now just isn't—"

"Save it, Braxton. I don't need your help. And I've got my dad back, so you don't need to fill that spot either." She shoved her shoulder into the door and grunted as she pushed. The rusty hinges screamed against the disturbance, but they gave in to her pressure with slow resolution. "Just stick to your pining for Eliza, and leave me alone."

I followed close behind her, clicking on the LED flashlight we'd brought as we moved toward the dark, unlit back part of the store. "When are you gonna grow up?" I spoke in a low bark. "When will you see that this is bigger than just you? Bigger than just me? Look around, Hannah. We live among people who have been starved, stripped, beaten, neglected. Completely dehumanized. Can't you spare a moment from your sulking to see that there's so much more at stake here than just you? Just Quinn?"

Hannah spun, her sudden stop-and-turn catching me off guard, and I ran into her. With a huff and a mighty shove, she sent me a step backward.

"You got Eliza back, didn't you?" She moved a step forward, filling the small space between us. "You did everything that came into your stupid head, and you still got her back, so you can just stop with the big-brother-know-it-all crap. What makes you think my story can't turn out all right in the end?"

"I never said that." I scowled, trying to laser-beam sense into her crazy head with my stare. "And all right? You think everything is all right? Eliza is still fighting for her life, and even if she survives, she'll bear the scars of the pox for the rest of her life, not to mention the burden of the nightmare she's lived through in the camp. Do you really think that's all right?" I crammed a hand through my hair, the weight of my own words washing like cold lead over my heart. "You love to point out all the dumb stuff I did, all the selfish choices I made, but you refuse to learn from them. Instead, you justify yourself with all my stupid crap. Does this make sense to you? Don't do what I did!"

Hannah's face crumpled into some sort of hurt-defensive-angry concoction, which meant she was listening. At least there was that.

"Quinn knew what he was doing back in DC. By your own claim, he's not stupid." Forcing calm back into my voice, I fisted my hands at my side, resisting the urge to shake her. "Maybe you need to honor his sacrifice by looking to others."

"You don't understand." Her bottom lip trembled, catching me off guard and cooling the heat of frustration in my chest. "You don't know his mom. What she's capable of."

A sigh rolled through me, and I brushed her elbow. "I've seen her work, Hannah. So has Jude. He'll figure something out."

Brown eyes searched mine, digging for a promise. One I really couldn't give. But I slung an arm around her shoulders and tucked her into a hug, because I really did understand. The thought of losing Eliza had made me crazy too. Hadn't made me smart though. That was what I needed Hannah to see. Crazy-dumb didn't work out so well.

We broke apart and turned back to the task we

were supposed to be working on. Canned goods. Grains. Anything still edible or useful. I snapped the burlap bag Jude had sent us out with, the faded Earth's Bounty Potatoes emblem catching my attention. Irony. That was what that was. Scavengers sent out for food with an Earth's Bounty Potato bag.

Dust tickled my nose, bringing my attention to the musty smell of the dark building. Orange-brown watermarks marred the drop-tile ceiling, and rust stains smeared the white-tiled floor. Everything, it seemed, wore the scars of the Party.

What would the nation look like on the back side of this?

"Found pay dirt."

Hannah's soft call drew my attention from the stains and deeper reflections. I rounded the aisle that she'd put between us and found her squatting in front of the shelves.

"Fruit. Cans are still sealed, and looks like they're in good condition."

I nodded, the stirrings of a grin tugging on my face. Look at Hannah. Participating. Helping. And almost excited about it.

"Enough to fill both bags?" I asked, kneeling next to her.

She shook her head. "Not even close. But it's something at least."

At least. I wrestled with ingratitude. Last week Tristan and I came back with two bags of weevil-infested rice and a box of powdered milk. Considering that scurvy was a real threat and we were still several weeks from any hope of *earth's bounty* appearing in the wild, canned fruit was a good thing.

"Good find, Hannah." I squeezed her shoulder and stood. "I'm going to check farther back."

She nodded, and I left. I passed shelves scattered with plastic kitchen utensils and moldy rice cakes, and an empty freezer that smelled like dead fish and an old gym sock. My stomach turned, and a gag closed my throat. I moved on. Quickly.

Careful to scan every corner, every shelf, I made my way back to Hannah. She finished loading the last of her cash and stood. Her potato sack was almost three-quarters full. If we were careful—meaning skimpy—the supply might last the village two days.

Two stinking days.

God, we need help.

* * *

Quinn

The halls were dark and clammy, and my tolerance for living like a mole was becoming like a frayed fishing line. One good snag and I was going to snap.

Mother was still hiding me. Sheltering me? Or keeping me out of the way?

Still, those doubtful, traitorous thoughts persisted. *Hannah had lied. Used me. Let this suspicious doubt go.*

I could have, especially in light of the destruction I'd seen above ground. Except for that persistent childhood nightmare. It'd been plaguing me every time I slept, playing overtop of the memories of Hannah leaving me to die on the street. How was that possible—I thought you dreamt of whatever you were thinking of right before you slipped into slumber?

The fire, the screaming, the call for me...they all seemed so vivid. Real. And they were consistent. What did that mean?

Why wouldn't Mother want me to know?

A dull throb knocked inside my brain. Leftover damage from the kiss I'd been given from the butt of a gun. *Thanks, Hannah.*

This was real. The Party, our vision of unity and greatness. The place my mother and Uncle Kasen had carved for me. Those were important. Demanded my full attention and energy. Dreams were just stupid stirrings of imagination and fear.

I shook my head, pushing away the remnants

that still nagged at me while rounding to my left at an intersection in a dimly lit hallway. Voices stirred the air in that direction, and curiosity propelled my feet.

I followed the strains of conversation. It sounded...official. Urgent. And maybe secret. Or maybe my imagination had shifted into overdrive. Too much time in the ground.

Still, when I reached an opening to my left, I stepped to the shadows near the wall, pushing my back against the chilled stone that made up the cavernous hallway.

"There, sir." A young woman spoke, her voice clipped. "That's not expected."

Interest beckoned me to look at whatever was unexpected. I craned my neck to peek around the doorway that had been left open. Though the space was small, a bank of screens covered the front wall. Three officers sat at a control board, and a man—the commanding officer, I assumed—stood behind them.

"Zoom in." Mother's voice answered, rather than the man, and then she stepped to his side.

The woman in the middle of the three at the control board responded without looking. "Yes, ma'am."

The center screen changed, the image of a wide plain dotted with a few buildings enlarged until only one building filled the screen.

"Wait." The female officer spoke again. "Something happened. I swear there was—" She didn't finish.

"What?" Mother snapped.

"I guess nothing."

"No." Mother stepped directly behind the operator. "What did you see?"

A pause. The woman leaned closer to the screen in question. A building. Large—likely a school or hospital. On the Vacant Plains, which would explain the deserted parking lot, the lack of movement or life anywhere around it.

"There was a vehicle, I thought..." Her voice trailed off, but her index finger indicated a clearly empty spot on the screen.

"Probably a deer or other wild creature, Lieutenant." The officer in charge, who hadn't moved, spoke with a deep gruffness. Almost annoyed. "Move along."

"No." Mother didn't turn from the screen. She paused, leaning closer, and then stood rigidly straight. "Erase it."

"Stateswoman Sanger, that is extreme. And unnecessary."

Mother turned to face the man who would dare challenge her. Cold eyes. Unflinching stare. Fully in command.

He didn't back down either. "Do you want to draw unnecessary attention this close to our near unraveling?"

"I won't take chances. No one is supposed to be there anyway. Erasing a ghost town costs nothing."

My chest knotted, and my eyes flickered back to the screen. Likely, no one was there. No one should have been there—the Vacant Plains had been mostly evacuated because of toxicity concerns after the Bloody Faith Conflict. And then the explosion a couple years back had chased out those who had resolved to stay. But what if...

"We are on the verge of civil war." The officer argued with my mother. "Do you really want to give the rebels any more cause?"

"If someone is there, then they are hiding. Which is why we are hunting, is it not?" Mother's eyebrow cocked, as if it were a trigger on a gun.

Pull it, and you're dead.

Apparently not suicidal, the commanding officer said nothing.

"Erase it." Mother didn't shift her cold stare away from him as she gave the order.

A chilled hesitation filled the room. Then, from the young woman at the panel, "Yes ma'am."

Keeping to the shadows at the corner of the door, I watched while the screen changed again. The image switched to real time, and we were swooping back to take another pass over the tiny abandoned town. Drones. The operators were flying remote drones.

Lower we flew, until the brown blur became dormant grass, the dots became houses on a grid, and the smudges became buildings on a main street, two schools, and finally, a hospital.

People's lives had been centered there, once upon a time. Their work. Their play. Their joys and sorrows.

"Do it." Mother's command came cold and emotionless.

The lieutenant nodded.

One one thousand. Two one thousand...

Impact.

A ball of fire consumed the screen.

Suddenly I was back in my dream. Clammy sweat seeped from my neck and forehead, and my hands shook. My knees threatened to buckle, and black dots fuzzed my vision until I had to squeeze my eyes shut or collapse.

It was real. This was real.

Was the dream?

***

Braxton

A hum tickled the back of my ears, prickling the hairs on the back of my neck. Hannah and I had finished our search of the main street and had run over to the hospital. We were about to push through the slightly opened sliding doors at the marked emergency room entrance. But that hum...

I stepped away from the crumbling overhang covering the entrance and tipped my chin up to examine the sky. Clear blue and as deep as any ocean I could imagine. The bright April sun glared almost directly overhead as I searched for the source of the noise.

That hum. It wasn't good. Couldn't be good. Where was it coming from?

A black dot escaped the blinding intensity of the sun's glare, its travel slow and disconcerting.

Hot panic flooded my veins. Air travel had been restricted since our little tearing the veil stunt. That wasn't a passenger plane, and we weren't anywhere near a commercial flight pattern. That only left one possibility, and it was bad news.

I pushed Hannah through the crack of the sliding doors, ignoring her stiff arm shoving me back. "Go. Now." I gulped, glancing back at the drone overhead. It remained steady, straight over us, but that could mean anything. "Get Tristan and Miranda and tell them we're in trouble. They have to get back to the van. Now."

Her eyebrows pinched, and in typical

Hannah-questions-everything-and-refuses-to-cooperate fashion, I fully expected her to argue.

I didn't give her enough credit. Instead, she spun into the building and took off at a sprint, her body tight and clearly well trained as she whipped around a corner and out of my sight. My heart was a booming baseline as I slipped out from under the awning covering the door, squinting into the sunlight, my sights set on that drone.

It dipped. Turned. Came back toward us.

"Hannah!" I shoved at the cracked opening of the ER doors, ensuring it'd be wide enough for Tristan to edge his bulky body through. "Tristan, now! We have to go now!"

Footsteps pounded, and Hannah, still sprinting, was the first to reappear around the corner. Miranda trailed her, and Tristan's wide frame emerged behind them.

"What?" he barked, hardly winded at all.

"A drone. It just turned around. It's coming back."

"Then get in here." He scowled. "Don't let them see you."

I jerked my head toward the parking lot. "The van!" I watched while understanding drained the fire from Tristan's eyes. "You didn't leave the coin in there, did you?"

We weren't supposed to be here. No one was

supposed to be here, and a van parked in an empty lot was a sign saying, *Here we are. Come and get us.*

"No." His jaw worked, and a wild panic lit his eyes. "I can get there. It's not too late."

"They're coming back. They wouldn't have turned around if they hadn't already seen something was off."

"Could just be a double check. If I get there now, the shield will cover us. They could think it was a fluke. A blip on the screen."

"Or they could drop the same fire ball they dropped on the camp."

Tristan pushed between the two girls and then crammed his broad shoulder through the gap in the doors. "It's the best chance we've got right now."

Bulky was apparently not always better. He wasn't going to fit. Not in time to get the coin to the van. Palm up, I held out my hand. "Give it to me."

Stuck, now midchest deep, Tristan nodded, tugging the Umbrella coin from his cargo pants pocket. "Activate it now, before you get there." His palm smacked mine, the cool of metal in the center. "And move those beanpole legs, Luther."

Funny guy. Always making the skinny-boy jokes, even though I'd finally filled out to almost half my father's massive size. Leaving the cool shade of the awning, I pressed the face side of the coin with my thumb and hoped the digital mirage would cover my sprint to the van before the approaching drone had us in visual range again.

Likely not. The hum grew persistently louder, overcoming the thud of my boots pounding the pavement.

God, help.

Why exactly had Tristan parked clear on the opposite side of the lot from the building? Like anyone would actually have need of the *ER Patients Only* space right next to the freaking door. An irritated growl rumbled from my core as I slammed against the side of the van, hoping—praying—frantically that Jude's mobile Umbrella worked, that the drone's digital cameras only saw the mirrored surroundings of the land, effectively erasing our presence from the Party's view.

I looked back to the ER door, working to control my staggering breath, panting more from terror than from the run across the parking lot. Having muscled his way through the stubborn crack of the doors, Tristan held a zeroed-in gaze on me, on the van, his arms blocking the girls' passage out of the hospital. I understood his intent. If a whistle pierced the air, the warning sound of an impending explosion, the girls would at least have a chance within a building that might be structurally strong enough to withstand impact.

Might. Probably not. What else could we do?

Now flying low enough to take my picture, the drone seemed to hover as it crawled across the sky above the town. Searching.

On purpose.

They'd seen us—the van.

The muscles in my neck locked hard as I kept pressure on the coin with my thumb. Tristan continued to watch me, and I tipped my chin toward the sky. The belly of the drone slid over the top of the parking lot, its shadow a chilled kiss of death. My arms trembled. I squeezed my eyes shut, forcing the sting of sweat from my lids. Breath held, I looked back to Tristan.

His lips moved, words silent but clear. *Don't. Move.*

When all is said and done, and you stand before the King, what will you say?

My father's voice, calm, sincere, and strong, filled my mind.

Why would He let you into His kingdom?

His challenge was no longer abrasive to my rebellious spirit. My eyes squeezed shut, and I imagined bowing low. Seeing nail-scarred feet. Feeling the hands that had been punctured for me land soft upon my head.

"I am yours," I whispered, breath calming, the thud of my own throbbing pulse slowing. "Save me."

A gust of wind surged across my face, warm and carrying a hint of rain, of life, and then the light of the noonday sun blazed through my tightly shut eyes.

The drone lifted, passed.

Still we held frozen until the tail of the aircraft became black against the deep-blue sky. Tristan turned to the girls, pulled them each through the door, and the trio raced to the sides of our van. I held the Umbrella coin secure, popped through the door that Miranda had yanked open, and scrambled inside behind her. Tristan and Hannah took the front, and within five beats of my heart, Tristan had the engine running and the vehicle in drive, and then he peeled away from the hospital and onto the road. Miranda crawled to the back of the van and pressed her face to the darkened window of the back door.

Silence. Tense. Relieved. Terrified. Silence.

"No." Miranda's voice was a plea. A strain of panic. A hushed cry for mercy.

Tristan pounded on the steering wheel, likely his foot weighted with enough pressure to bust through the floor. "Go, go, go," he muttered, each word in sync with the thrust of his hand.

"It's coming back." Miranda's voice gained

volume. "It's coming back." Dread made her words tremble.

They'd seen us. And they weren't coming back for a second look.

"Go. Go. Go." Tristan's shouts were pure adrenaline.

I shut my eyes again. Picked a memory. The sweetest one I had.

Eliza. Her eyes soft. Full of hope. Love.

She'd made a hero out of a cockroach. I still couldn't understand how. But I was glad I'd die as something closer to what she'd believed me to be. Glad for the chance to be something more than a sellout.

A whistle screamed through the clear spring air, the warning before the boom of impact overcoming the roar of the van's engine. The earth beneath us shook, and a reverberating thunder accompanied the quaver. The road before us shivered, then buckled, and Tristan slammed on the brakes. Squealing tires joined the high-pitched scream of my eardrums being shaken to their limits, and the van spun, giving us a front-row view of the explosion. A brown cloud of earth threw itself skyward, blocking the light of the sun. Even before the dust settled, a ball of fire grew from the ground, filling the space on the horizon where a town had once been plotted.

Erased.
But we were still alive.

five

Quinn

"You seem distracted, my delight. Are you still unwell?" A delicate click chirped from Mother's china cup as she set it onto its saucer. Ever proper.

"No. I'm much better now, thank you."

She studied me. Her gaze seemed more calculating than concerned. "What troubles you then?"

I swallowed. The scene I'd witnessed the day before prickled in my mind. Might as well speak it. "I saw what you did yesterday."

She sat, expression unmoving.

"To that town, on the Vacant Plains."

"What were you doing wandering around?"

"Needed a walk. I'm not a prisoner, am I?"

Her controlled smile smoothed her lips. “Of course not, my boy. We are only here for your safety. And yesterday, what you saw was only a precautionary measure. No one was in that town, so there is no harm done.”

“How do you know?”

Her eyebrows dipped inward ever so slightly. “No one is supposed to be there. That’s how I know.”

“And so you simply erased it from the face of the earth?”

She failed to respond.

“Why?”

Her lips thinned, and then she lifted her coffee for another sip. Measured response. “We have reason to believe the rebellion is centralized on the VP. Something didn’t look quite right when we flew over that town, and we couldn’t risk being wrong.”

The rebellion base camp out there on the wide-open plains where any drone passing over could see them? Not likely. Somewhere in the Rockies. Hiding where they could actually hide, that made more sense. Mother was being subversive. Again.

“What if there were people—other people there? Simply trying to survive?”

Her eyebrows lifted, as if I just said the most ignorant thing of my life. “They were not supposed to be there. That is not our problem."

A throb pulsed in my forehead, drumming a fresh wave of pain and doubt into my skull. If only I could see things clearly. Swipe away the haze that seemed to ever cloud my understanding.

"Quinn, I cannot fault you for your ever-loving heart. It makes you who you are—a rare treasure. But if Hannah taught you anything, it should be this: some things cannot end with a happily ever after. We have this vision and a responsibility to go with it. Sacrifices must be made, for the good of the most. That is what we are doing."

For the good of the most. Not for all. The most. Sacrifices? Were we the ones making the sacrifices?

Questions stirred up confusion. That sense of being lost swept me within its swirling storm again. A sensation Hannah had provoked in me.

Hannah was not my friend. Hannah had nearly destroyed me. Hannah...

"Do the dreams still come?" Mother repositioned herself across from me, her back erect in the chair placed just so at our gleaming, polished table.

I swallowed, the feel of discomfort against the button-up shirt I'd donned that morning strangling.

Divided. Violently severed, this America had become. Because of what I'd done because of Hannah's lies. And while I struggled to heal, my head severely concussed from the blow I'd taken while Hannah and the boy had escaped, the country plunged into the stirrings of civil war.

But here, in the bowels of our safe house, Mother remained herself. Her practiced manners, firm command of every moment in every situation. She had it all in hand, even in crisis.

Something I should admire and work toward.

"Quinn, do you need to lie back down?" One perfectly shaped brow lifted against her forehead. "Your presence at the conference would make great strides toward righting that which went wrong, but if you're not ready..."

"I'm fine." I straightened, matching my posture to hers and pushing aside the dizzying unbalance of doubt. "I'm ready."

Her satisfaction lifted the corners of her mouth as she tipped a nod. "That's the man I raised."

Indeed it was. Duty first, above all things. What was a headache when our future could yet be righted?

"But you did not answer me, and I would like to know." Folding her manicured hands, Mother rested them upon the table. "Do the dreams still bother you?"

She meant the dream about Hannah, about what had happened. And yes, that dream still repeated, knifing through my skull and into my heart. Seemed like the pain should have dulled by now. I shouldn't have been shocked to see the scenes after so many replays. But they still cut anew every time. And still felt...

The other dreams had returned too. Just two nights before. I saw the blaze consuming the building. Heard the frantic screams for help.

Saw a woman whose eyes had always captured my full attention and heart. Blue, like mine. With a look that—

"Don't let her treachery weaken you, son." Mother interrupted my thoughts. "If she still haunts you in your sleep, let it be your strength. Let her betrayal fuel your resolve. Today we will begin to make things right. And this time, Quinn, you will be sure of your path."

I lifted my gaze to Mother's, absorbing the determination radiating from her impassioned speech, her set expression.

She stared back at me. Hard. Heated. Commanding. "This you must do so that you may take the place for which you were born. We will yet unite this nation, and by doing so, bring the glory of humankind to perfection. You, my son, my hope and delight, will lead us toward the destiny we have long sought. And as a nation transformed, we will then guide the world to the ultimate goal. Humankind will finally take the final steps to completeness. We will at long last go where evolution has been propelling us over the millennia."

My mind wound around her fervent words. Similar speeches I had heard for years. No one could fault Mother for lack of devotion. Her ideals were deep rooted and unquenchable, and she had a clear vision for what must be done. For herself, for the people of our nation. For the world. And yet as I silently fingered the implications of all I knew of her convictions, an unsettled wariness quivered deep within. As always.

The resolute stand of Pastor Luther suddenly eclipsed my wonderings. He had opposed the Party and all of its "forward progress," claiming that "compassion with an agenda is not compassion at all. It is bondage." His position intrigued me then. Still did now, because with Mother...

This mistrust...

I couldn't explain it. And I'd lost the evidence I thought I'd had to support it.

The silence between us stretched, and Mother's expression hardened. "Quinn, we are responsible for progress. You must see—"

"I've heard this before, Mother." I held her disapproval for a moment and then looked down to the table. "And I know that you're right. I just have a small headache."

She lifted her cup and tipped a delicate sip of coffee past her lips. "Of course. Take the medication the doctor prescribed. It will help. We will leave directly. Have you memorized what you must say?"

I shut my eyes. The speech I'd prepared was simple compared to the passages of philosophy, political treatises, and progressive ideological theses I'd spent years poring over, dissecting, memorizing. Mother knew I'd have no issues with the assignment.

Except, perhaps those that I would not let her see. The doubt that still nudged beneath the bitterness toward Hannah. The twist deep in my gut every time I thought of what Mother had done to that ghost town on the VP.

The chair across the table moved, and five delicate footsteps tapped the floor, and then Mother was behind me. Her hand warmed my neck before her fingers massaged the tension at the base of my skull.

"You, my delight and hope..."

My eyes slid shut. Warm numbness oozed through my mind, taking away the lingering headache and nagging doubts.

The erased town on the plains floated across my memory, triggering no resistance. It must be done. I must do what must be done...

Destroy them.

The thought surged strong, and for a moment, I wondered if it was truly my own thinking or something silently, strangely imposed by her.

I pushed away the disconcerting sensation, yielding again to the comfort of the numbness. This hesitation—concern—was left over from before Hannah revealed her true self. Emotions that had not served me well and that I must now outgrow. Destroy.

"I have the words committed." My voice rumbled low, determined.

Mother stepped away, removing the pressure of her thumb against the back of my neck. Immediately missing the relief that sensation had brought, I glanced up to her standing at my side.

Again, an eyebrow cocked on her steady face. "Only the words?"

I met her challenge and held, clutching the determination that had just rooted in my mind. "I am ready, Mother. I will do what must be done."

***

Eliza

"The other two didn't survive. She's all we have left."

The voice swirling above me was the one that sounded like Braxton, but wasn't him. I wanted to open my eyes, to see who continued to speak in the space above me, filling my senses with confusion and making me stay when I wanted to go.

Not into the darkness of memories. Into the promise of beyond.

I still craved death.

Forgive me.

"We need you, Liza..." That breathy whisper, spoken much nearer than the first voice, was Braxton.

The pain in my chest... I was sure it was my heart tearing.

"She's in pain again," he said.

I wondered how he knew.

"Can't you give her something?"

Their words jumbled, a low swirl of male voices that must have been discussing me. Before they were done, I felt a cold surge wash through my arm, and then warmth sank through my body. The numbness washed over me, and my mind sailed on the tide I could not control.

It would take me there again. I didn't want to go. But I was helpless against the current.

"Hang on, Liza..."

No. I don't want to...

His voice drifted away. Darkness enclosed me, held me in its firm grip until it delivered me to the scenes of the camp.

Scenes that would not let me go.

They selected a group of us. About a hundred of the most "healthy" among our abused and starving people. They pushed us into the big hangar, using the butt of their weapons, their fists, their boots. Whatever they wished. They herded us into the building like cattle and shut the big steel doors. Light filtered through the cracks of the aged building, narrow shafts of yellow pushing through the doom of our prison. We circled together in the middle, unsure what we should be afraid of next.

"Do not let the fear consume you," an older gentleman rasped. "The One who gives light has not forgotten us. He will send His deliverance when the time is right."

"When the time is right, we will all be dead," cried a woman bitterly.

I hoped so. I didn't want to live with this place burned into my mind.

"Do not lose heart, sister. He sees every sparrow that falls..."

Do you see us here?

A flicker of light near the place where the horizon outside would be caught my eye. It danced, drawing my attention closer as it pushed into the darkness through a narrow slit of damaged metal.

Don't lose heart.

Something clunked in the corner of the building, startling us and snapping my attention from the light. The whir of a machine stirred the air, and a cool mist drifted over us. Like a fog nestling into a shallow valley, it filled the building, blurring the bits of light that had teased me with a sliver of hope.

We stood huddled together, trembling. I wished I hadn't paid attention during the history classes I remembered from childhood. Didn't want to think about things like Auschwitz, and gas chambers, and experimental medicine...

The whirring stopped. The mist settled.

The doors opened, and we walked back into the bleak setting of the courtyard.

We didn't understand. Not until the first victim fell sick the following week. The woman who had cried just before the mist had been turned on fell in the middle of evening slop time seven days later, a rash bubbling along her neck and chest. Her body burned to the touch, and none of the Jackals guarding us would come near.

They shouted for us to drag her to the big hangar. She died four days later. By that time, more than half of the group who had been exposed to the mist were also sick. Dying.

I wondered why I wasn't among them. But I'd done a research project on the deadliest viruses known to man. Smallpox looked just like this.

And it could take almost three weeks for the virus to incubate in my system.

* * *

Quinn

The room felt vast and bleak, though it was crowded. Men and women, whose positions of leadership should have intimidated me, watched as I approached the podium, their solemn faces melting into the darkness that rested beyond the bright lights focused on the front. Resentment hung thick among them—an emotion I shared. And I would show them, through this delivery, that I was exactly where they were. Betrayed. Even if they thought, at the moment, that I was their betrayer.

I drew a long breath before taking the final steps to the mic, clasping on to the anger that roiled through me as I allowed that scene one more replay. The one where Hannah glared at me with hate as she left me on the street.

Mother was right. It did fuel my strength.

"Ladies and gentleman of our benevolent Party." I gripped the podium and looked up. Though I could see nothing beyond the blinding stage lights, I knew they would see my face, my eyes, and it would lend credit to the words I would deliver. "I stand before you humbled, begging for your forgiveness and pleading with you to hear what I have to say. For though not an excuse for the damage I have done, perhaps you will find my story will offer a clear picture of the enemy, and it is my hope that once you have seen the duplicity of the rebellion, we will be able to stand once again united as a nation transformed."

All rustling in the room settled, and a raw hush coated the room. Perhaps the country, as I knew the cameras behind the bright lights were broadcasting live on the central broadcasting network. Every American near a screen was watching me right now, as they had when Hannah convinced me to broadcast the video that had torn apart our nation. Now they waited for my confession and to see what my revelation would bring about.

Peace, I hoped. Mother hoped for so much more. A more solid unity, greater faith in the Party. In Kasen, and by extension, her. Perhaps me as well. Total loyalty. Perhaps absolute power.

A shiver zipped down my spine. My resolve cracked. I glanced at Mother. Her face, her eyes...unmoving. An unexplainable and fiery pain flooded my mouth, as if something strong and sharp was ripping into my palate and pressing against my jaw.

I turned back to the bright space where the people waited, and my resolve firmed. The pressure in my mouth eased, and I spoke again.

"Two weeks ago, I acted as one who was blind." I swallowed, an emotion I wasn't prepared for surging to my voice. Would it be damaging to let them see how much Hannah's lies had hurt? Perhaps not. Perhaps it would cast me in a more sympathetic light. Clearing my throat, I blinked. "The video that was shown has been proven unequivocally false, the source of which has shown herself to be a treacherous liar. I was mistaken to trust one who had set her face against the pure and honorable intentions of the Party, and we have all suffered the consequences. But now I can tell you with clarity there is nothing whatsoever true about the claims of the rebellion. Those images were nothing more than a cruel concoction of false accusations, cinematic trickery, and damaging slander. Nothing in the video was or has ever been true. And the Party has gladly supplied evidence for you to see the honesty of our claims."

I paused, as instructed, so that the network could switch the images being broadcasted to the videos I had seen while in recovery. The Reformation Camps, just as claimed before. People safe and well cared for at a resort-like location on a tropical beach.

"As you can see"—I added voice over to what I knew would continue to roll on the screen—"the ugly lies I'd been shown were nothing but fearful propaganda birthed by a people who feast on hate and selfishness. They have not changed. These are the same people who fueled the Bloody Faith Conflict we have worked so vigilantly to put behind us. People who refuse to embrace the progressive notion of the common good, of global stability and unity, who would rather serve self than others, and who would have you believe that evil lay at the heart of the Party's honorable intentions."

I drew a breath, let it shake as I exhaled, and finished the required words given me. "People who fooled even me. For that, I am deeply regretful. It is my hope that by standing in honesty before you, I can undo the harm I have done, that if you have doubted the Party's purity because of my actions, your faith in us will be restored. For it is by our hands we will move forward, will become what we always should have been. United. Complete. And unhindered by the ravages of war provoked by ideological bondage. Then, and only then, will we have true peace and prosperity."

Stepping back, I turned to face the corner of the stage where I knew the Party's flag stood beside the Stars and Stripes. With my right hand, I tapped the seal inked on my neck, followed by my heart, and then held my hand out toward the flag, knowing by the rustling in the room that every person within, and likely without, did the same.

"Power to the Party."

The chant, spoken as if one voice, saturated the air around me.

Though my lips moved, I didn't say the words.

***

Braxton

The speech was devastating. Not because we wanted civil war, but because Quinn had just negated the injustice Eliza and the others had lived through. He'd publicly denied our claim, making us sound like horrible people in the process.

He'd caved.

"That's not him," Hannah whispered while her eyes stayed glued to the screen we watched in Jude's lab.

"Hannah." I stepped toward her, my hand clasping her shoulder. "Sometimes we don't want to see what's right in front of—"

"No." She spun around to face me, eyes blazing. "I know Quinn. Something happened. They did something, tricked him. Something. That is not the boy I know."

My chest sagged as air seeped from my lungs. No one would feel the cut of Quinn's retraction more than Hannah. It wasn't worth trying to reason with her. She'd have to blunder through her disappointment on her own terms.

"Braxton," she hissed, demanding my attention. "This doesn't change anything. We still have to go back for him."

It changed everything. Mostly, because he clearly didn't want us to go back for him. He wanted life to be the way it had been as Charlotte Sanger's son—couldn't handle what it would mean for him to be one of the resistance. Jude wouldn't risk my life, or Hannah's, or anyone else's to put together a retraction team now.

But saying that to her in the middle of that dark room with a group of others watching our hopes fizzle away with every one of Quinn's eloquent words wasn't a good call. I shifted my attention back to the screen.

"Then, and only then, will we have true peace and prosperity." Quinn finished his address and turned to the flags at his right. The Party salute, fingers to his neck, then his heart, then outstretched to the flag, signaled the crowd.

"Power to the Party."

My heart shriveled as I remembered being entrenched in the crowd at the state center rally. The roar of the many calling out as one. I imagined the same sensationalism there in the room on Capitol Hill, where Quinn had successfully cleared himself of treason.

"Look," Hannah whispered, nudging my arm. "He isn't saying it."

I studied the man who, for a moment, I had thought would turn the raging tide that threatened all of the people I stood with now. Two weeks under the secret ministrations of the Party and all traces of his budding conviction against the Party had died like early blossoms in a late-spring frost. He looked like a Party loyal. And his mouth moved around those words.

No. Only around the word *power.* Hannah was right. He didn't say the rest.

"See, I'm right. Something happened. They did something—"

I frowned, looking down at her. "Something

did happen, Hannah. He's a sellout. Trust me. I know what it looks like."

True enough, and we both knew it. Her expression fell helpless before it flipped to anger.

"We don't know what happened."

"True." I held her pleading look, tempted to offer her sympathy. But I knew Hannah well enough to be sure that she'd take that sympathy and run with it. "We don't know what happened. But he's apparently made his choice. Which means it's no longer up to us."

"How can you say that?"

I scowled, because I didn't like playing the hypocrite. Again. "Look. I get it, kid. Really, I do. But look around. These people...they're broken. Defenseless. Aside from the fact that Jude has this Refuge that the Party can't track, they've got nothing going for them. We can't risk their safety for a guy who's apparently turned."

Her eyes now stormy, her face hardened. "That's not good enough, Braxton Luther."

Arguing with Hannah, though tempting, was a surefire dead end. With a long, controlled release of breath, I looked away—back at the screen hanging in front of the dirt-packed wall.

"It's not my call, kid," I said, not able to keep the hint of frustration out of my voice. "Take it up with Jude."

I felt her stare burn against my face but didn't give in to her silent demand for attention.

"Don't think I won't."

Didn't doubt it for a moment. But I prayed that Jude's calm ways, quirky wisdom, and gift of leadership would stand her down on this one.

It'd be a first.

six

Eliza

"She's going to make it."

A low rumble of murmuring softly touched the emptiness of existence. I mentally tried to push it away, not wanting to leave the comfortable slate of silence.

No dreams. No memories replaying, scathing my heart, making my soul heavy. Just the bliss of soft black nothing.

"The scabs have fallen off. The fever is gone. She's not contagious."

Warmth cocooned my hand, and the brush of skin grazed my forehead. I puzzled at the sensation, couldn't remember the last time I'd felt it. It drew me further away from the comfortable swaddling of emptiness.

I fought against the pull.

"Liza..."

That voice... My heart, though weak and sludgy, rose a tiny bit and skipped, and I moved a little more away from the nothing.

"Keep talking to her, Braxton. She's coming out of it." The deeper voice came from a distance.

I was. I could feel reality crowding in on me. My body ached—though my skin no longer shrieked with pain as if it were on fire. I could feel the dull thud of my pulse throbbing through my head. Hear the heaviness of my breath, each intake a fight, each exhale a moment to give up.

"I'm right here, Liza. Right here waiting..." A warm and tender sensation grazed first one eyebrow, then the other.

My heart did that thing again, and my breath stumbled.

I hovered somewhere in between that black comfort and Braxton's voice—his beckon for me to come back. For a moment, I retreated. What was left of me? Marred with scars, inside and out, I was too broken. Braxton would understand...

There's more to be done.

The voiceless words drifted softly through my mind. It was tempting to argue—who am I and what could I do? I had nothing to offer. No health. No strength. Not even my dignity anymore.

I've chosen you. Will you choose me?

A gentle challenge I was familiar with. I'd heard it in the depths of my heart ever since I was a small girl. Put into that kind of simplicity, my decisions usually became simple. *Yes, I choose you.*

But now...

It's too hard.

"I know it is, Liza." Braxton's voice hummed in my ear. "But we need you."

He answered me—not the silent voice in my spirit. Had I spoken out loud?

"You're almost there."

I felt the feathery wisp of his breath, soft and comforting, warm the spot near my ear. "I know it's not fair." His voice cracked. "I know it hurts. If there was another way..."

Way for what?

Almost against my will, my eyelids fluttered. A soft glow of light seeped into my reality, so unfamiliar it seemed to be a low burn behind my eyes.

A hand, large and rough but kind, cupped the side of my face. "There you are."

I could hear a sad smile in his quiet voice.

"Is she awake?"

I focused on the face hovering over me, its blurring edges wobbling slowly into focus. The last time I'd looked into those eyes, they'd been pleading. Intense. Loving.

I'd held on to that look. During the months at the camp, when it seemed like nothing good had ever existed on this earth, I summoned that memory. That look.

Those eyes.

He looked at me now with the same intensity. But something had changed. The pleading had turned to...regret? And the love?

There was still a tenderness in those dark pools that studied me. But...

Something else.

I imagined what he saw as I lay on that stiff bed. A thin skeleton of a girl, her hair spiky from having been shaved, horrible pox littering almost every part of her skin.

So ugly.

His eyes squeezed shut, and he leaned toward me until his forehead pressed against mine. A gathering of some kind of cloth at his neck brushed my chin.

"She's awake."

He breathed the words. They trembled. His hand slid over my cheek and cupped my stubbled skull. I cringed, hating what I must look like to him.

He pulled away, his hand retracting as concern flickered in his glazed eyes. "I'm sorry, Liza. Did I hurt you?"

My skin felt cold where his warm hand had just left. Hurt? Everything hurt. But nothing quite as much as imagining myself through his eyes.

"No." My voice rasped the word, and I looked back to the ceiling.

His warm touch covered my hand again, and I shut my eyes against the burn of tears his kindness provoked.

Braxton was fiercely loyal to me. Always had been. Even if his feelings had changed, if he found my scarred face repulsive, he would never let me do this alone. I grabbed on to that small comfort, fighting against the sting his sense of obligation brought to my worn-out heart.

"Eliza Knight."

I opened my eyes again as a man stepped behind Braxton. His face came into focus, and confusion jarred my brain.

"You are a straight-up miracle," he said, his strong voice oh-so familiar.

I was seeing things. I stared at him, not understanding. "You died." I'd seen him pressed in the middle of town. Cruelly executed as an example—a warning.

Braxton ran a thumb along my chin. "My

brother, Annyon, Liza." Sadness weighed his expression.

He knew what I'd thought.

Patrick Luther was dead. The nightmare I'd survived had been real. As real as the smallpox that had nearly killed me.

None of it made sense.

***

Braxton

I tossed the mask I'd worn into the sick room to the corner of Annyon's makeshift office and glared at my brother's back. "You can wait at least twenty-four hours before you go poking her with sharp objects."

"The virus is still out there, and it's only a matter of time..." His voice trailed off in muffled guilt. Then he cleared his throat.

"What does that mean—the virus is still out there?"

"I don't have control over it, Braxton. That's not how my research worked. And the reality is we could still be at risk here in the Refuge. It can take weeks to incubate, to show symptoms. Anyone of the team who were sent in to rescue the sick could have been exposed. We don't know for sure. We need to vaccinate everyone in the village as soon as possible."

His all-business, scientist-on-a-mission tone ripped at my self-control. With a hand at his elbow, I jerked him around to face me. "She just woke up."

"Which means she won." He met my glare, and for a moment I felt like I was in a standoff with my father. "And now I have the chance to find the antibodies I need. If I can identify and isolate them, I can create an vaccine, and this thing doesn't have to turn into the modern plague."

Those standoffs with my dad never went well, and I didn't want to repeat all the ugliness between my father and me with my brother.

I took a step back, not willing to have him draw Eliza's blood when she still looked like a skeletal ghost. "Look. Just give her a little more time. Please? She doesn't even really know what's happening."

Annyon's expression softened, became more human and less mad scientist, and he swallowed. "I know it's hard to see her this way—"

He had no idea what seeing Eliza's body ravaged by the pox—by the Party—did to me. But he wasn't going to understand it, because he didn't know the whole story.

"But you already understood all of this. I need you to tell her what's going on. If she knew that there was a chance her blood could save hundreds, thousands, would she do it?"

In less than half a heartbeat. But I didn't want to see her used as a lab rat. Poked and bled and studied. As if she hadn't been dehumanized enough already.

"Talk to her." Annyon tipped his head toward the room we'd just left. "Tell her that she's survived a genetically mutated strain of smallpox. Explain what that means and that because she survived, her blood will have the antibodies I need to—"

"She's sick, but she's not stupid, Annyon." I scowled at him, resenting that he thought so little of a girl I knew to be so much more. "And my guess is she knew what she had when it was trying to kill her."

One eyebrow on Annyon's face tilted, but he didn't dive back into an argument. "Then let it be her choice."

Didn't want to. Because I knew Eliza. I knew what she'd choose. And though this time it wasn't really life or death, I didn't want her sacrificing anything more. Not when she'd already given so much.

***

Quinn

I studied the bank of screens in the recon

room. Mother had left it to me now, knowing I understood how important it was that I find Hannah. She was the key to crushing the rebellion. If I could silence her lies, the unrest would die off.

Something in that theory needled me as overly simplistic. One girl could change the fate of a nation?

Not likely. But I had a purpose, and for the first time in my life, I finally felt like I was doing something more than posing as Mother's Party-perfect poster boy.

The images on the screens remained uninteresting. The officers flew the drones by remote over every part of the Vacant Plains, weaving a pattern of north to south, east to west. Nothing but empty land with an occasional artery of tree-lined streams or a wide field of wind turbines appeared on any camera.

"She really erased another town?" whispered one officer to another.

"Just like that," responded the woman. "Gone."

"Paranoid?"

The woman shrugged.

In the back of my mind, voices replayed a conversation I wasn't sure was actually real. *It is necessary... The girl could be our undoing. If they put her on display as proof...*

Hannah? What more could she do? And why

would the rebellion be hiding on the Vacant Plains?

Mother wasn't making any sense on this one. Why would anyone attempt to hide there? There was nowhere *to* hide. Thus the name Vacant Plains.

My memory flickered back to the week before, to the little ghost town she'd erased. That needling sense of injustice pricked inside my gut again, and I tried to dust it away. No one was there anyway. I didn't need to feel unsettled about it. If anything, her determination should fuel mine. Finding the rebellious Uncloaked was the key to moving our people into the future my mother had envisioned. A hope that was for all of humankind.

The needle jabbed again.

Hannah's influence had clearly gone deeper than I'd thought. I pulled up the image of her leaving with the other boy. Expected pain singed my chest. I pushed past it, waiting for the reaction I needed.

It lay there waiting, just beyond the pain.

I will find you, Hannah Knight. Anger shored up my purpose. *And then we will end this once and for all.*

seven

Braxton

I refused to leave the small house where the sick had been placed, hardly ever leaving Eliza's side.

She faded out and came to with sporadic consistency. Annyon said she was fighting off the effects of being starved and mistreated now more than she was the smallpox. That recovery couldn't be predicted.

Which had been another reason I didn't want Annyon drawing her blood for his lab work yet. But his challenge to let her choose had become a wall I could not scale. The gift of choice—right, wrong; compassion, resentment; forgiveness, hate—this seemed to me more clearly than ever the divine right of every person. A seal of the purest love was the freedom of choice.

A freedom granted by the Creator Himself.

After being imprisoned and abused, Eliza deserved that gift now. To know she was still valued, that I respected her, that I wanted her heart to heal along with her body.

"Liza." I leaned against her thin bed, taking her hand in a loose grip. "Do you know what you had in the Quarantine?"

She licked her lips, a sign that she was still battling dehydration. I moved to chip away a flake of ice from the block that Annyon had stored in an old Coleman cooler. Satisfied with a shaving about the size of my thumb, I sat back beside her and traced her mouth with the ice. Her eyes slid closed, cracked lips parted, and I ached at how this small act seemed to mean so much to her.

When the chip was nearly half melted, she looked back to me, closed her mouth, and swallowed. Enough for the moment.

"Smallpox." She answered my earlier question with a weak voice.

"You're right."

"Not the old kind though?"

I almost wished Annyon was there, hearing how smart my girl really was. "No. It was a genetically modified strain. How did you know?"

"They wouldn't have bothered taking blood

samples if it had been the old strain. They already have the vaccine and the antiviral for that."

Annyon, my genius brother, meet your intellectual match.

"How often did they take blood samples?" I hadn't been a part of that little project during my horrifying time as a guard.

"Daily. But not always from the same person."

"Did anyone in the Quarantine survive?" Everyone said no one had, but deception was a hallmark of the Party, so it was safer to ask someone who wasn't disposed to lie on command.

Eliza looked up to the ceiling. Her eyes sheened before they squeezed shut. "No. No one."

Leaning on one elbow, I cupped her shoulder and squeezed with careful pressure. "You're the only one who has."

One small dip of her chin acknowledged what I'd said.

I swallowed, wishing I didn't have to ask.

Let it be her choice.

I doubted Annyon understood how much power lay in his imperative. Because I'd seen the lack of choice, the freedom stripped. It was a weapon that went beyond the tearing of flesh, breaking of bones. It smothered spirits, stripped dignity, and left hollow people vacant of hope and purpose.

"My brother is a medical scientist. He's been studying this strain of smallpox."

Her eyes opened, but she focused on the ceiling rather than on me. Certainly putting the pieces together. His little Frankenstein virus had been used on her, on all of those people. And now...

She knew what was coming. I could tell by the tight clamp in her jaw, the wince that furrowed her pale brow.

"He didn't know what was being done with it." I felt compelled to come to his defense, though I resented his involvement with it too.

"There's no reason to mess with something like that." Her words came out harsh, taking me by surprise. "What good could possibly come from it?"

Silence settled painfully between us. I had no answer; I'd thought the same thing. But right now...

She licked her lips again, and I brought the remainder of the ice chip back up to her mouth. She refused it, turning her head to face the wall.

Damaged. Her heart was so painfully damaged. I shut my eyes against the sting of tears, lost in an empty sense of helplessness and guilt.

She was broken because of what I'd done.

"He needs my blood."

The softened tone of her voice drew me out of the emotional trench I'd fallen into. When I looked back at her, she was facing me again, the coldness of her expression a moment before now gone. Replaced by the generous heart of the girl I remembered. Loved.

I nodded, my throat still too tight to speak.

A beat of silence. Her eyes warmed, sending a vine of hope into my heart. Another beat. I leaned in, drawn by the familiar softness on her face.

"I give it," she whispered.

I swallowed. "It's your choice, Liza. I'm not demanding—"

A tear bulged from the corner of her eye, slipped over her cheek bone, and rolled toward her ear. I caught it with the knuckle of my index finger and traced its trail back to her eye.

She closed her eyes again, breathed in deep, and then gripped my hand that still hovered over her cheek.

"I choose life."

* * *

Eliza

I wondered if he could feel the battle within my heart. If he could hear the voices that warred in my head.

Let them die. The hiss of that thought had snarled through my head, repeating with maddening consistency while Braxton had worked up to his request.

I knew how viruses worked. I also knew what smallpox had been—a lethal killer that had taken more than a third of its victims. In the previous century, it'd been targeted for elimination for a reason, and its eradication had remained for nearly a century as a trophy of modern medical achievements. The disease, however, also had lingered as an unspoken danger. Weaponized smallpox—especially a genetically mutated strain—would be the supreme threat of any dark power. Little wonder the Party was messing with it.

Seemed, however, that mutating the strain was easier than controlling the monster they'd created. So the Uncloaked had become lab rats.

Annyon's lab rats.

Let them die.

The words had become louder in my mind. Demanding my compliance. I didn't have to give the key that would undo Annyon's irresponsible science nightmare. They'd infected me on purpose. Locked us up in a dark shed and let us die in agony one by one. I owed them nothing.

Is this the life you choose?

The voiceless words chilled the heat of resentment in my spirit, drowning the looping hiss of my bitterness.

To hate or to forgive. Those were the only options. One was easy, but I'd seen where it led people. To destruction. Death. One was incredibly hard. More than I'd ever imagined.

I squeezed my eyes shut, feeling the weight of this moment in every joint of my body.

Help me. It's too hard.

I've chosen you. Will you choose me?

I inhaled. Took the hand that rested lightly on my face, the hand that seemed in that moment to be God's supply of strength to my weakness.

Surrendered.

"I choose life."

My spirit shuddered within me, and though it hurt, a dark, snarled bit of my heart seemed to break away. *I choose you.*

***

Braxton

The blood draw seemed anticlimactic after the battle I knew Eliza had been through to submit to it.

She was without a doubt the most amazing person on the planet. I wondered if she knew that.

I had every intention of staying there, breaking ice chips when she was thirsty, savoring the draw of her breath as it increased in strength and consistency. But Tristan, in normal Tristan form, ripped my intentions and redirected my energy with one dark statement.

"Hannah's gone missing."

I looked over my shoulder at him, our glances connecting with solid understanding. No mystery there.

"How long?"

"Evan says he hasn't seen her in over twenty-four hours."

I stood, turning away from Eliza's bed to face him. "What does Jude say?"

Tristan's look flickered to Eliza and then came back to me. "We should go."

Eliza's long exhale drew my attention back to the bed, and a wrestling match began in my mind. I'd just gotten her back. She wasn't well yet, and more, her heart had become a battleground. I didn't want her to face that alone.

Hannah and her reckless impulses. The girl was going to get herself killed one day.

And that thought made my decision. Today wasn't going to be that day.

I nodded to Tristan, who looked again at Eliza. "I'll meet you in five. Then we're gone."

eight

Quinn

The vision had driven me from my bed. Different this time, and yet I knew I'd seen it before. A night terror from my childhood, but not the explosion.

The stallion that circled me was wild and fierce. The blaze of his eyes was like fire, the sound of his scream like the call of hell. He circled me, his heavy hooves pounding the ground as if to shake the foundations of the earth, and when he turned to face me dead on, my legs buckled in complete terror.

Paralyzed and on my knees, I trembled as fire streaked from his nostrils. He pawed the ground, let loose another withering scream, and then charged. Straight at me.

My shout for help woke me up. Rolled into a ball, on my knees in the middle of my bed with my arms clutched over my head, my heart felt near explosion, and sweat slathered my shaking body.

I fought to breathe, and when I could finally stand on my quivering legs, I tugged on the nearest clothes, left the heavy silence of my room, and slipped beyond the bunker where Mother insisted I was safe.

Wandering through the tunnels, I unwillingly deconstructed the nightmare. It was insane, really. And I shouldn't have been terrorized by it. But even as I tried to apply logic to the mysteries locked inside my head, fear twined through me again, making me shiver.

I felt the presence of another as I made my way through the labyrinth of the underground. Chills raised against my arms and neck, but I continued. When I came to the outer room, I paused. Turned. Waited.

"Show yourself," I demanded, searching the shadows of the dark hall. Stillness settled. Held. I was ready to turn and go back into the bunker, but then...

The silhouette that emerged was slim. Delicate. Familiarity poured through me, but I pushed it away. She wouldn't dare come here.

Not after what she'd done.

"Quinn."

My name on her breath slammed through me, twisting my insides with unmerciful cruelty. My eyes slid shut as I fought against an undeniable desire to see her. Fortifying against it, I remembered the scene that secreted bitterness through my veins.

"Quinn." Her voice was near, and her hand slid against my arm.

Tension snapped inside me, and I lunged, grabbing her arm and spinning until she was pinned against the wall that had been at my back the breath before. A muffled cry lifted from her mouth, and she looked up at me, a raw wildness dancing with terror in her brown eyes.

"How did you get in here?" I growled.

"Jude..." She moved a hand, an attempt to graze her fingers against my chest. I caught it and slammed her fist against the wall at her back.

"Jude what?"

"He has a map. I stole the information."

"Why?"

"To find you—"

"How dare you." I leaned down, seething my anger into her ear, letting the power of my anger surge into my grip until I could feel the ripple of her fear quivering through her arm. I shifted, pushing my bulk to her shoulder, trapping her small frame between myself and the wall.

Horror and confusion smeared across her expression, and for a moment, a soft ooze of guilt melted in me. She was small. I outweighed her nearly by double. She was a girl, seventeen maybe. I was a man...one who knew it was not okay to pin a young woman with brute strength.

No. She was a traitor. A deceiver. Nearly my undoing. "How dare you come back to me, you little viper." My mouth still hovering near her ear, I hissed, "After what you did to me, did you think I'd see your pretty little face and melt all over again?"

"What?" She angled her head, her face turning to mine until I could feel the warmth of her breath graze my cheek.

The boiling rage inside me took on a feral quality, and I moved again, this time gripping her neck with one hand, forcing her face away from mine. "Don't play me, Hannah," I roared.

"Quinn, I didn't—"

The grip I squeezed against her throat cut the words short. Her eyes, glazed and wide, bulged, and the arms I had pinned between her and me began to fight.

She was stronger than I would have guessed. I shifted, securing the arm I still held behind her back and pushing my full weight against her again.

"You're a liar, a siren! Do you know what they could have done?"

Her bottom lip trembled, and she fought to push a word past the vocal cords I was crushing. "Please..."

"Mercy? For you?" I blinked, the full rush of complicated emotions now crashing over me. Was I this man? A man who would murder out of vengeance? Who would take the life of a girl half my size out of anger?

Let the anger fuel you...to do what must be done...

Mother's voice snaked inside my head, dividing my resolve. This was what she would want. She wanted me to act strong. To do what was necessary.

To murder?

"Please..." Hannah's voice rasped against my ear again.

I had loosened my grip, allowing air back into her windpipe.

"Quinn, this isn't you. Please don't do this."

I slid my hand farther up her neck, forcing her chin upward at an unnatural angle. "Why shouldn't I?"

"This is her." She strained to speak, lifting on her tiptoes so that she could still breathe. "I know you, remember? I see the real you."

“No!” A quake gripped my chest as doubt and anger battled. “You left me to die, you little witch. You sold me out and left me to take the fall.”

Though caught in my grip, she shook her head. “I didn’t want to.”

I glowered over her, feeling fire pour from my stare into her agonized face. “Why did you do it then? I promised you everything, and you left me to die as a traitor.”

A tear slipped over her eyelid, and I felt her struggle to swallow beneath my hand. “You.” She choked on the word.

“Me?” I brought her forward and slammed her back again, feeling her teeth smash together when her head made impact with the wall. Her breath stalled, her eyes widened with full panic.

Am I this man?

“What do you mean *me*?” I seethed.

She shut her eyes, and a squeal eked from her trachea as she fought for another breath.

I’m not a murderer. But there I was, squeezing the life from her small body. Shaking, I loosened my grip, and she gulped in a rush of air.

“You told us to go. You told me to—” She choked again on the words, and I felt a sob shake her body.

“I did what?”

“I tripped—broke my leg.”

I looked down. She leaned on only one leg, but I didn't see a cast of any sort. Logic said she was lying again, but something in my head...

"You pushed me to Braxton and told him to get me to the chopper, and then you ran the other way. To them. For us—so that we could get away."

A faint image tried to surface in the back of my head. I squeezed my eyes shut, fighting to see the blurry and wispy scene buried there.

Only small shards came into focus. Blood on Hannah's leg. The shift of her weight from my arms to the other boy's.

Details not in the memories that replayed in my mind nearly every night.

"What did they do to you, Quinn?"

My grip had slipped, and Hannah leaned her head to my shoulder.

She's playing you again. You must be stronger than this.

Vengeance surged again, and I pushed her away, my hands gripping her shoulders this time. "Liar. That's all you do, isn't it Hannah? You lie. You manipulate to get what you want."

Another tear leaked from her eyes. "I'm not the one lying to you. Manipulating you. You have to remember—"

"I remember you leaving me. Alone. Pointing me out to the police while you ran with *him*."

She was convincing in her play—the agony in her eyes, the trembling of her jaw as she shook her head, still denying what I'd seen, what I remembered.

"Don't let them do this."

Rage took over again, and my grip returned to her throat. A small cry vibrated her vocal cords, pricking guilt in me again. I fought against it. This little pixie would not use me again, make me weak with her beautiful brown eyes.

"Let her go." A deep voice growled behind me.

Not loosening my grip, I slipped a glance over my shoulder. The boy. The one who had carried Hannah away now stood at my back, planted as if ready for attack, the gun in his steady hand aimed at my head.

And so it would go. I had been right. She betrayed me yet again. With hate throbbing through me, I looked back at her. She was scrambling against the wall, fighting for air.

"Brax...don't...please...don't..." Her words came broken, weak, and nearly believable.

"Quinn, I don't want to drop you, but you have to let her go."

Braxton, was it?

"Or what?"

"Just let her go."

"Don't think that because I'm not a Jackal I haven't been trained as you have."

"I don't doubt it, Quinn. But I have a gun, and you don't."

"I have your girl." Bitterness coated my tongue as the words crossed my lips. "And you don't know what I'm capable of."

"Hannah's not mine." He continued to speak with a steady tone, his words carefully measured. "But I will shoot you if that's what it takes."

"Brax..." Hannah squeaked again.

Begging for her life? Or mine?

Only a weak fool would believe her guise again. My grip strengthened, and her lips took on a blue hue.

Click.

A searing burn ripped through the right side of my waist, just below my ribs. With the next breath, pain exploded into my torso, through my limbs, and registered in my head. My body buckled against Hannah, and then I folded toward the floor.

"No!" she gasped. Now free from my hold, she gripped my arms and guided me to the floor. "No, no, no." Tears punctured her words. "Braxton, I told you not to—"

"Would you rather I let him kill you?" He came closer as he spoke. "It's not a mortal wound. I promise. It won't be much more than a scratch. He'll live."

The pain throbbing through me gave another testimony. I struggled to catch my breath, to think.

"Quinn, please believe me." Hannah shifted, rolling me to my back. "What you think you remember isn't the truth."

The lights dimmed, and the world spun as she moved me, and I couldn't grip reality. Jagged fragments of memories flashed past my vision. Hannah leaving me. Hannah bleeding. Hannah begging me not to go. Hannah pointing me out to the crowd. None were congruent. The pieces didn't make sense.

"I don't know what is true," I mumbled.

She hovered over me, one hand cradling my jaw, and then she sat back. My hand suddenly felt warm as her smaller one surrounded it, and then she lifted it, pressing my palm to the place where her heart pounded.

"This is true," she whispered.

She used you. Lied to you. Left you. Mother's voice echoed in the back of my mind. But then I was suddenly not there or back on the street where everything had gone wrong. I was on a hillside, lying on my back beneath a sky drooping with snow clouds. The sun fought to poke through, to give warmth to the stone beneath me. And the hand in mine was hers.

I see you, Quinn. Not your mother or the

Party. Just you. And you are good.

I had tucked those words away as if they were a promise. A hope for more than I thought possible. That I would be free to choose, to be who I wanted to be, no matter what my mother or the Party wanted. But after Hannah left me...

I'd forgotten them.

Because they are false. She is a liar.

Did I need further proof? I was lying at the entrance to our bunker, bleeding out from a gunshot wound. Because of her.

Forcing my eyes open, I speared her with a look and then turned to the boy behind her. He scowled, first at Hannah and then at me.

The sequence replayed rapid fire. His arms around her. Taking her away. The painful blow to my head...

"No!" Rage surged through my veins. I ripped my hand from Hannah's and locked both her arms in my fists. Muscles tight, pain sizzling, mind focusing on only the red-hot burn of hate, I picked her up and launched her away from me.

She flew over me toward the wall where I'd caged her before the boy had shot me. A sickening thud announced her collision with the concrete, accompanied by a distinctive snap.

"Hannah!" the boy darted over me, reaching her as she slumped at an unnatural angle against the floor. "Hannah, no." He lifted her chin.

Her body flopped to the floor.

"No. No."

My vision blurred and then became laser clear. Her eyes focused on me, not him, and she blinked. Life slipped from her gaze, still fixed on me.

What have I done?

The boy moved her so that she lay flat on her back. As her head rolled, still facing me, a trickle of blood stained her ear, running into her hair. Her eyelids fluttered, and again she looked at me.

"Don't..."

She gasped, and I felt a flood of tears burn my eyes.

"Don't let them tell you who you are."

Her chest caved. Eyes fell vacant. Mouth went slack.

She didn't move again.

The boy fell to his backside, his hands fisting his hair. "No. God, no!"

I looked from him to her and then back again.

"She loved you." He pierced me with a glare. "She came back for you, and you killed her!"

The pieces of my memories still wouldn't fit together. None of it made sense. But my heart splintered as I looked at her cold, lifeless face.

You are good. It was her voice, soft and warm and full of gentle hope now swirling through my mind.

But it wasn't true—she wasn't right. I was a murderer.

The girl I had loved lay dead at my side. By my hands.

I'd become what they'd wanted me to be.

* * *

Braxton

Drawing a breath became a fight. I stared at her limp body, the blood trickling from her ear, staining her neck. "You killed her," I mumbled again, my lips trembling. "She stole the information she needed and a vehicle we couldn't spare to get here. To you. For you!"

We had failed. Hadn't made it in time. Now Hannah was dead.

What would I tell Eliza? Was she to lose everything before this was over?

"Braxton, we have to go." Tristan came to my side. He gripped me by the arms and tugged.

I shrugged him away and leaned back over Hannah. "We're not leaving her here like this."

"Fine, but let's go."

I slid an arm under her shoulders and one under her legs and lifted. Her lifeless body rolled into my chest, and for a moment I saw Eliza instead of Hannah. Crushing pain clenched my heart.

Life was precious. Why did we treat it so carelessly?

A hand squeezed my elbow, and Tristan's voice came, less demanding this time, by my side. "Hold it together. You can lose it on the chopper."

I swallowed, the lump in my throat nearly choking me. With a nod, I stepped toward the hall we hoped was still clear.

The man on the floor pushed up to a sitting position, groaning as he moved. I had been careful with my aim. The bullet shouldn't have damaged anything vital. Even still, I might have missed.

He might die.

Not my problem.

"Wait," he moaned.

Instinct said to ignore him. Leave him to bleed. His people could handle it.

"Wait."

Tristan stopped in front of me. I lowered my shoulder, nudging him ahead. He ignored me and turned to face Quinn again.

His eyebrows low, face twisted in pain, Quinn looked back. "Take me with you."

"Not a chance." Darkness slathered my tone, and I didn't bother to look at Quinn, to see his reaction. "Let's go, Tristan."

Tristan squeezed my shoulder, a silent argument.

I glared at him. “You can’t be serious.”

He held my look with an even stare and then turned again to Quinn. “Why should we?”

“I need to know the truth.”

I spun around, clutching Hannah’s body as I moved. “No. You can stay here and rot with your people. You just murdered this girl. Do you think we’re stupid? Imagine we’d give you the opportunity to sell us out again? Not a chance, Sanger. Tristan, let’s go.”

Tristan didn’t move.

Clutching his side, his shirt wicked with the red stain of his blood, Quinn looked to me, to Tristan, and then to Hannah. His jaw jumped as he flinched. His eyes pinched closed, and he shook his head. Maybe Hannah had been right—they’d messed with his brain somehow. Even so, we couldn’t risk it. He wasn’t one of us, wouldn’t ever be one of us, and at that moment I felt a throb of anger so powerful it nearly pushed me to the threshold of murder.

“Tristan!”

“We were sellouts too.” One calm sentence, and Tristan had diffused the fire that had pushed me toward hate.

Yet I didn’t want this man anywhere near us. “He could give away the Refuge. Or the Party could claim that we'd kidnapped him. It would explode the conflict. More will die, and the people at the Refuge have nothing to defend themselves with."

Quinn's focus hadn't left Hannah's pale face. "I need to know. I need to see for myself."

"Hannah showed you. You still sold us out."

He looked at me with a sincere plea I wanted to ignore. "I don't know what to believe. There are memories I don't understand, and I need to know the truth." He paused, his gaze fell back to Hannah, and then he swallowed. "Please."

The air became as still as Hannah's lifeless body, the hum of silence between us so strong that it throbbed in my veins, pulsed in my head.

"You'll contact someone before we take off, tell them that you're on a mission so that your disappearance isn't pinned as a kidnapping. And then you will leave everything but the clothes on your back." Tristan waited until Quinn nodded, and then moved to help him to his feet. He paused, bent his hand on Quinn's arm, face inches from his. "If you try to harm anyone in the Refuge, I'll kill you myself."

The dead calm in Tristan's voice, backed by the powerful build of his large frame, rippled a chill down my spine. I had no doubt Quinn knew Tristan meant every word.

"If Hannah was telling the truth, you have

nothing to worry about."

"Nothing to worry about? Hannah was telling you the truth." Tristan pulled Quinn to his feet, his solid build dwarfing Quinn as he held him steady. "And if she was right about you, then you're about to find out what real worry is."

Quinn's eyebrows folded together.

"You want the truth?" I shook my head, still glaring at Quinn. "You have no idea what you're walking into."

nine

Eliza

The fog of unconsciousness refused to come to my aid anymore. I missed it.

Braxton hadn't come to see me either. Not for two days, at least. Weak and tender, and now feeling hollow without Braxton's voice encouraging my recovery, I submitted to Annyon's instructions. Turn every hour, allowing him to tend to the sores on my back and legs. The salve he applied stung, and lying on one side or the other made me stiff and achier. But I knew about bed sores, understood, though my body protested, that he was right.

And I agreed to more blood draws. Every time was a battle inside my heart and mind. That voice that hissed from the dark place that had been seeded into my heart, spewing against what I knew was right.

Let them die.

It was overwhelming, and I wanted to yield to it. To allow bitterness to determine my choice. But every time, those gentle, branded words in my mind called yet again.

Will you choose me?

Choose the light. To choose the light meant offering hope to people who had robbed me of mine. To give grace where I had been given humiliation.

To forgive.

I wasn't sure I could. How could I forgive such crimes? The memories plagued me in the small spaces of sleep that would claim my slow recovery. Images so strong I felt I was there again. I could feel the oppression. Smell the unwashed bodies slowly rotting even while they lived. Hear the murmurs of despair. Feel the hateful, inhumane hands that would handle us at their whims.

At the end of that line we'd first been herded into, where I'd helped the Purge girl stand because she hadn't the strength to do it alone, we were told to strip. Naked. In front of the Jackals who guarded the entry house.

They leered. My skin crawled, my stomach

filling with a sour burn. They took our clothes, made us stand in the chill of our exposure for more than an hour, refusing to let us huddle together to glean at least a bit of warmth from each other, and then finally they threw down a pile of what looked like scraps of feed bags and potato sacks. The pile stank like mildew, body odor, and rancid smoke.

Our new uniforms. Useless to fend off the cold. Scratchy. Ugly.

That was what they wanted for us. To feel ugly. Abandoned. Unhuman.

It worked.

We were not allowed to shiver into those scraps of cloth right away. Instead, we each took one, draped it over our arms, and then stood against the wall in a line while they took us one by one into the tagging room.

The tags were inserted into the spot just inside our shoulder blades, with nothing more than a bloody knife. The incision was an inch wide and at least two inches deep. I knew because I remembered removing Miranda's. They closed the gap of flesh with an unsterile upholstery needle and two long stitches sewn into an *X*. A quarter of our recruit, as we were called, suffered infection from the tags. They died within two weeks.

After we were tagged, we were moved to the

grooming room. Each woman's hair was gathered into a ponytail, pulled harshly away from her scalp, and then cut with a blade. After that, we were all shaved, men and women. I could finger the rough scars on my scalp from the nicks carelessly wrought from the dull razor. Finally, we were allowed to get dressed.

Bald, bloody heads atop bruised faces and bodies draped in cloth woven for grain did much to make us look frightening and unhuman. We had become the walking dead, delivered to hell on earth. Dignity stripped, we were pushed into the courtyard. One girl from our recruit was selected and at gunpoint told to run off toward the western horizon. Trembling and with tears carving trails down her dirty face, she silently refused with a slow shake of her head. The Jackal didn't flinch when he pulled the trigger, and he barely waited until her body dropped to the dust before he selected a different subject. A boy, fourteen maybe.

"Run," the Jackal demanded, the muzzle of his weapon pointing west again.

The boy took off on shaking legs, stumbling over the uneven dirt. He continued for three hundred yards until he jerked to a stop, his body yanked back by an invisible force. His voice lifted high and tortured through the air, his right hand reaching desperately for his left shoulder, where he'd been tagged. Still shouting in agony, he fell to the ground, writhing against the jolts of electricity pulsing into his body. Two Jackals strode casually toward him, stopped where he squirmed against the dirt, grabbed his arms, and dragged him back to the "safety" of our prison yard. They left him lying there, trembling, gasping, sobbing.

"Now you know your boundary," the first Jackal said. He looked us over with a smirk. "That will be the only time a Jackal will help any of you should you choose to cross it."

With that, they walked back to the entry house, leaving us to our hopelessness. I looked around for the Purge girl that I'd helped before the tagging.

She was gone.

The black spew of smoke just beyond the boundary of the courtyard stole my attention, and I knew what had been done. I hoped that she had died quickly.

Hoped that she'd found relief.

With these images I could not erase, forgiveness seemed too much to ask. And yet every time Annyon needed more sampling of my blood, to find the antibody that would save those who might have been exposed during our rescue, the Voice pressed again.

Will you choose me?

The choice, and the offer of dignity in it, lent me just enough strength to say yes for that moment. Even through my resentment.

* * *

Quinn

Flames seemed to lick the flesh at my side. The wound was clean. The bullet passed all the way through, and apparently the boy named Braxton had been right. It wasn't a mortal wound. The bullet had cut through the skin and muscle at my side but not into the cavity of my abdomen.

The bigger, dark boy called Tristan hovered near me while I made the call he'd insisted on as part of our deal. One wrong word and I was pretty sure the burly guy would snap my neck. He looked more than capable.

That idea didn't sink fear into me as much as it probably should. I glanced to the corner of the bunker where Hannah's limp body hung in Braxton's grip. Dead. I'd killed her, just as my mother wanted. Inky filth oozed into my conscience. I'd become a murderer. My mother had wanted me to murder.

Bile churned violently in my stomach, the burn surging up to my throat.

"Quinn, I'm in a meeting." Mother's clipped

voice jolted me back to the task.

"You need to listen." I rarely demanded anything from Mother. Her silence was likely from shock. "What you wanted has been done, and now I must see the rest through. I'll contact you when I can."

"What?"

"Hannah Knight is dead."

A mild hum drifted over the line. Her pleasure cloaked me with a strangling sense of evil. I swallowed, glancing at Braxton. His rage-contorted face made mine fill with heat. I sounded like the devil—if there was actually such a being.

"I need confirmation," Mother said.

This time I looked at Tristan, who stood close enough to hear both sides of the conversation. He dipped a small nod, and I understood.

"There will be a picture on my All-In-One. I'll leave it on the table."

"You will do no such thing."

"Mother, I have to go."

"Where?"

"I'm fine, so don't worry. Goodbye, Mother."

"Qui—"

I pulled the speaker away and tapped the End sign on the screen. *Goodbye, Mother* settled in my ears, sank into my chest. It felt final. I couldn't identify all the convoluted emotions that sensation provoked, and I was relieved not to have to examine it as Tristan snatched my All-In-One, turned me to the wall, and told me to brace my hands against it.

The criminal-esqe pat down darkened my mood significantly. Though he was careful around the gunshot wound that he'd quickly wrapped tight with a towel from my bunker, he was thorough, which was degrading.

"I already told you—I'm not armed," I growled.

"Like I'm gonna trust you."

Tristan had this placid way of speaking that commanded control. Maybe respect.

"And I'm not just worried about weapons."

I looked over my shoulder at him. "They won't be able to track me."

"Better not." He finished patting down my legs and stood to tug on my button-down shirt. "Take this off. I need to see your shoulders."

"What?"

From the corner where he still waited, a deep scowl embedded on his face, Braxton growled. "Just do it, or the deal's off."

Paranoia gone bizarre. I fumbled with the buttons at my shirt front, studying the boy I remembered from that day several weeks back. He was the same build, same looks, but something about him seemed off. Though clearly angry at me, his eyes didn't taunt me like they had in my dreams. He didn't seem to celebrate my pain.

I shrugged out of the body of my shirt, letting the bulk of my sleeves settle against my wrists. Tristan pushed my shoulders forward, causing the muscles of my back to round to his inspection. With firm pressure, his fingers prodded around the inside of first my left shoulder blade and then my right.

Again, I glanced over my shoulder at him. "What exactly are you looking for?"

His eyes flickered to mine. "A tag."

My eyebrows lifted. "A tag? What is that?"

Tristan backed away. "Button up. Let's go."

Something truly insane had gotten into their heads. But I didn't press for answers. They'd agreed to take me to whatever prepper shelter they'd been holed up in. Once I got there, I'd find my answers. Maybe I could help them overcome their crazy obsessions, even end this violent rebellion I'd incited.

My shirt back in place, I turned to follow them out of the bunker, stopping to leave my All-In-One on the table as promised. A message flashed as I set it against the rich cherrywood.

Hannah has a sister. She must share her fate. Don't fail me again.

A shiver overtook my body, and I couldn't

help looking at Hannah. Her dark, wavy hair hung in a fall from Braxton's hold, and I remembered its softness when I'd raked my fingers through it. She'd smelled of cucumbers and jasmine that day. Her eyes had grown wide and soft when I'd leaned down to taste her kiss for the first time. She'd trusted me, leaned into me. Kissed me back in what had seemed a shy but honest breath.

She had been my new hope, and I'd trusted her.

Now she lay as a stone. Life gone. Everything in me jumbled, and I felt blind and helpless.

Braxton turned, cutting off my view of the girl who mixed me up, shutting down the whirlwind of confusion blinding me at the moment. Tristan lifted my left arm, stretching the place where the bullet had entered and exited. A rocket of fiery pain shot from the wound into my shoulder, and I grunted against it. He settled my hand on his opposite shoulder, and I understood he meant to help me.

"We'll look at the wound once we're up in the air," he said, moving us both forward. "We have a doctor at the Refuge. You'll be fine."

Leaving the bunker unseen was easier than I'd imagined. I hadn't stopped to think about how Hannah had stolen into the underground and found me, but the two Jackal uniformed boys knew exactly where they were going, and the halls were clear.

How was that possible?

We ran through the tunnels, the bigger of the two boys leading while he kept an eye on his All-In-One like it was his GPS of the hidden pathways that supposedly didn't exist. He led us to an intersection. We stopped, backs pressed tight to the wall, while he checked for the military guard.

"We're clear." Tristan knelt, then pressed a hand to his ear as if to activate a com. "We're at the lower access." He paused. Waited.

And then the floor in front of him opened. It was like a cellar access, only in a place that was already deep underground, completely hidden.

Tristan turned to descend the fireman's ladder, looking at Braxton as he climbed down. "I'll go down first. Quinn can follow. You can lower Hannah to me once we're both down."

Trust wavered. His disregard for me felt like cuffs on my wrists, my will entirely ignored. But I wasn't a prisoner.

"Go, Quinn," Braxton demanded. "Now."

As I knelt near the access hole, I glanced over my shoulder, back toward the home I was leaving. This could all be so wrong. I'd seen what they'd done to the city. How many lives had they taken in that attack?

Had they done it? If so, did they have a reason to? A clip from the video Hannah had tricked me into airing emerged with blaring clarity in my mind. So many sick, dying in agony. The others...appalling.

Who would do that? Hannah said the Party, and at the time I had believed her. It didn't seem like she had a reason to lie, and there were other things in the system that I'd seen that definitely weren't right. The Den, the Commons. My mother's strange relationship with a boy most people called Hulk. But that place in the video? The camp? Had it been real?

I wanted to know the truth.

"Stay if you're going to stay." Braxton nudged my shoulder with his knee, his voice more impatient. "But either way, you're going to have to move."

One more glance at Hannah. Dead. Twice now she'd risked her life. Once for the video Mother said was a lie. The second time? Me? That didn't make sense. Not if she'd been lying before. Not if she'd been playing me.

I needed to know. Had I'd done what I should, or would I wear the stain of blood guilt for the rest of my life? My head was a Ferris wheel of questions and doubts.

Focus on the next move. Only on what's right in front of you.

A bolt of pain plunged through my body when I flipped to my stomach and then scrambled down the steps. A warm sensation gushed from my side as a fresh ooze of blood soaked the towel bandage Tristan had wrapped me with. The scene blurred as I stumbled to the ground, and Tristan steadied me to a wall. I leaned to catch my breath. They'd shot me. What was I doing, going with them?

What is your purpose? Think only on that. I focused on the instructions of my combat trainer.

Find the truth. That was my mission. I locked it in my head as the world around me straightened and became clear once again.

Tristan's size made transitioning Hannah's body easier, and when he had her, the tender part of my heart took over. I reached to trace a section of her hair. The thick silk between my fingers triggered a surge of ache.

Wake up. Don't be dead.

Her limp body didn't stir.

Braxton landed beside me, his boots a dull thump on the ground. He took Hannah back into his arms, and I wanted to push him aside, to cradle her myself.

He'd probably kill me.

Why hadn't he killed me already? Had this been reversed, would I have killed him?

We were moving again, the halls strangely abandoned. I had to employ every ounce of disciplined determination to keep up with them while the bullet wound throbbed, radiating pain into my hips, chest, and shoulders. Strength seemed like water, and I a sieve. I might die before we got to wherever we were going.

After we turned the third corner and still there was not a soldier in sight, suspicion pushed to the front of my mind, a ticking bomb ready to explode.

"Did you kill everyone?" I snapped.

To my right, Braxton's scowl drew deep. "We didn't kill anyone. That's not us." His voice was heavy with accusation, demanding me to look yet again at the girl he carried.

The bomb in my mind diffused.

"Where are we?"

I was ignored. We continued.

"Left here. The exit's just ahead." Tristan pointed and ran faster.

I fell behind, my breath more labored than it should have been. Weakness continued to assault me. The blood loss at my side continued. The temptation to quit and let them go became a thirst that I almost couldn't push aside. Just ahead was a solid rock wall, like all the other walls closing us in. But I hadn't known about the hole in the hallway above either. And I'd seen my mother pass through what looked like solid rock before.

They both slowed and then stopped, and I had no choice but to do the same, because I had no idea where we were. I didn't have an exit strategy, and at that point I was completely at their mercy.

Strange. In the deepest part of me, somehow I trusted their mercy more than my mother's Party. That blow to my head weeks before must have messed me up more than I'd thought.

***

Braxton

A thread of murderous desire still stirred around inside of me, looking for a weak spot to embed itself. Hannah lay on the floor between our seats, her body swaying to the jostling of the chopper as we made our way back to the Refuge. Her profile so strongly resembled Eliza's.

I agonized over how to tell her that her sister was dead. That left only her father, who hadn't been the same. Grief seemed to swallow Evan whole, to toss him around through the unpredictable whims of anger, sorrow, disbelief.

After Jayla's death, the solid rock of a man Eliza and I both had admired had become lost.

How would Eliza respond to all of it? She was

incredibly strong, her moral center like granite. But even rocks cracked.

"Did you love her?"

The peacock of a man across from me had opened his eyes and ground out the question with palpable resentment.

"Hannah?" I shifted my focus, pinning it on him, hoping he could feel the heat of my anger in my glare. "She was like a sister to me. So yeah."

Hot color splotched his jawline, more obvious because of his pale papery skin color. He had lost a lot of blood, and when we reached the chopper, he'd passed out. Guess he'd recovered. For the moment.

Quinn's attention shifted back to Hannah. His jaw jumped twice, and his Adam's apple bobbed hard. A wisp of soft compassion came out of nowhere and landed against the hard anger in my heart. Jude had said Hannah's theory was possible—that the Party had done something to Quinn's memories to twist the truth of what had happened. I didn't understand it—it sounded like science fiction to my simplistic brain—but if it was true, then Quinn was just as messed up as the rest of us in this nightmare.

"I told you"—my voice came lower than the minute before—"she loved you. She believed you were a good man."

Quinn flinched but didn't look away from Hannah. Beneath his hard mask, war raged in his eyes.

He had no idea whose side he was on. He likely didn't even really know who he was. Which made him particularly dangerous to everyone at the Refuge.

I glanced at Tristan, who sat toward the front and near the door. Posture straight, eyes focused, he was clearly ready to take an enemy down if needed. Which meant his thoughts mirrored mine.

It was very possible we were about to bring destruction into our village. We should have left Quinn behind.

ten

Eliza

My heart was regaining strength. I could tell by the surge of blood that throbbed through my body when I heard his voice near my ear.

Braxton was back.

I turned my chin toward the sound of his whisper, breathing in deeply. His smell—outdoors and mild sweat and something that I could only define as Braxton. For the first time since I'd regained consciousness, I felt my lips push upward.

The slightest touch grazed the corner of my mouth. I blinked my eyes open as he traced my bottom lip with the pad of his thumb.

"You can hear me," he said, the lightness in his

voice not reflecting in the seriousness of his eyes.

I lifted my hand, which shook a little because the muscles in my arms had become so weak, and covered his fingers. His eyes closed, mouth trembled.

"You left," I whispered, hand fully resting against his.

He lifted his head, studied the skin sagging from my arm. I followed the trail his eyes made, taking in the littering of scars left by the ravenous pox. They covered me. Little white specks of damaged tissue, deeply puckered and so many they ran together, sometimes so close that they created craters in my skin. I hadn't seen my face yet. My heart sank as I imagined my appearance. Horrific and ugly.

My nose burned, and I blinked against the liquid heat in my eyes. Braxton turned his hand, gripping mine, and lifted my palm to his mouth.

"I'm sorry I was gone." He held my hand, palm spread, against the roughness of his unshaved face.

The boyish Braxton was gone.

"Annyon says you're getting better." He leaned down, resting an arm against the bed at my side and tucking my hand against his chest. "Are you?"

I searched for misgivings in his stare. A sign of

his repulsion by my disfigured appearance. He only studied me with love.

Had I imagined the hesitancy I'd sensed before he'd gone?

"I'm getting better." I tried another smile. "At least, would be if your brother would stop stealing my blood."

His serious gaze grew darker, more direct. "You don't have to give it, Liza."

That look. He'd been that intense when he'd demanded I take the citizen seal over two years before. It was how I'd known he was trying to protect me, even if he was wrong. How could a girl not love that?

But he was wrong again. He didn't seem to understand the voiceless challenge in my head. Possibly because I'd never told him about it. It was there even then, asking me with such a tender hope that I could not deny it. *Will you choose me? Will you do this for me?*

"Yes, I do."

I expected him to argue. The old Braxton would have, and that had made me feel divided. I would sometimes waver in his passion, wanting to give in to his instinct to preserve self.

He didn't. Instead, his expression softened, the depth of his gaze warming even more. With his free hand, he brushed the place on my head where my hairline was trying to regrow, his fingertips gentle. "You amaze me, Eliza Knight."

I didn't mean to. If he knew the battles I kept hidden, he might be shocked. Disappointed. I wasn't the superhuman good girl he always thought I'd been. But in that moment, his admiration lifted my heart. I selfishly kept that warm coddle and tucked it away so that I could soak in it later.

The sensation of his lips against my forehead brought me back to the moment, and I realized I'd closed my eyes. When I opened them, I found his expression had changed, and a tear rolled in the crease between his nose and cheek.

"Braxton?" I lifted my other hand and traced the moisture with my finger.

"It's Hannah."

Yes. They'd left because of my sister. A small push of resentment weighed in my chest. "Did you find her?"

He nodded. His mouth formed a pressed line.

"Is she hurt?"

His eyes squeezed shut. Jealousy found a frail spot in my heart and began to dig a hole. What had happened between Braxton and my sister while I was at the camp?

"She's dead, Liza." His voice cut on my name, and then his shoulders shook. "I'm so sorry. I couldn't stop it. I'm so sorry..."

Dead?

My breath caught on the word. My sister was dead. Just like most of the others I'd loved. With the others, though, there wasn't this complicated swirl of mixed emotions. There'd only been sadness.

Hannah, though...

With her there was guilt and sadness and, though I didn't want to admit it, a side helping of bitterness. Because the boy I'd always loved sat at my side broken up over my sister. I was too confused to know what to do with that.

The hole that had poked into my heart widened a little bit more.

***

Braxton

A tear slowly grew in the corner of her shut eye. When the moisture overflowed capacity, it trickled down the side of her face, catching on the fuzz of hair covering her skull.

One tear.

I knew she had more in her heart. My chest hurt to see in plain sight how the cruelty of the Party had forced Eliza to shelter her true self. Walls fortified against the pain.

I leaned down, touching my temple to hers to whisper near her ear. "I'm sorry, Liza." I could think of nothing else to say. Hannah had been my unspoken responsibility. Had I been watching her more closely—

Regret had a million what-ifs but only one real outcome. Nothing could change what had been. My choices. Her choices. They all led us to this moment, and now Hannah was gone.

I tried to imagine life beyond all of this. Someday this nightmare would end. It might have to get worse, but eventually, it would cease. It had to. Then what? I sat up a bit, examined my girl silently, stoically grieving not only the loss of her sister but of everything. She was riddled with scars, on the surface, but more concerning, in her beautiful heart. What would the damage bring? What would she be when she faced the world beyond this recovery room?

Please be the Eliza I know.

She sniffed, her gaze finding mine. "Have you buried her?"

The deadpan of her voice made my heart throb.

I nodded. "We couldn't wait." I hated that too.

Her attention trailed away, drifting to the ceiling. "What happened?"

A story I wasn't ready to tell, even though I'd known she would ask. The explanation would be too long, and I wasn't sure Eliza's heart could handle all that had happened over the previous year.

"She went back to DC for a friend. He turned

on her."

She didn't look back at me. "DC?"

"Yes."

"Who did she know in DC?"

My hands shook as I leaned back. "Quinn Sanger."

Slowly, her head turned toward me, a delicate eyebrow lifting a small bit. "As in Charlotte Sanger?"

"Yes." I swallowed. Looked at my feet while heat crawled over my arms and neck.

She waited for an explanation. I couldn't tell her though. It'd be too much, and I didn't want her to battle bitterness even more. Not against me, and especially not against her sister. How much crushing disappointment could one small girl take?

After a long draw of breath and an equally extended exhale, I settled my attention back on her, pleading in the silence for her to be patient, to try to understand. "I'll tell you the whole story, but not now." With my index finger, I traced the now-dry line of that single tear. "There is a time to grieve," I whispered.

Eliza turned away. I sat in silence, praying that I'd see more evidence of her tender heart.

When she shut her eyes, they were dry, and not another drop of moisture rolled. I waited, hoping, until her breath rose and fell in deep, even draws. I wondered if sleep had become her refuge.

If so, was that good or bad?

Again, I tried to picture a future beyond all of this darkness. I couldn't. The shadows were too thick.

***

Quinn

The walls between our rooms were thin. Doubted Braxton realized that.

Now I knew who was in the room right beside mine. Mother had been right. Hannah had a sister, and the girl's name was Eliza.

As promised, Tristan had helped me to their "hospital" when we landed at the Refuge. My glimpse at their village wasn't much, but what I had seen didn't at all line up with what I'd imagined. I'd pictured a military base, overtaken and swarming with serious soldiers who would glare hate into the center of my being. The reality of the village couldn't have been further from that image.

Thin-bodied people swathed in little more than rags wandered, moved, worked, heads down, backs bent over the ground as if to coax the budding life cautiously sprouting from the earth back into their anemic souls. Tents covered the lower valley. A few scattered buildings rose up among the crude dwellings, one of which was a farmhouse looking to be at least a century old.

The hospital.

Peeling wallpaper, a faded black-and-white print of trees and birds, welcomed me into the gloom as I struggled down the hall to the room they'd assigned to me. Brown circles stained the sagging ceiling, and an undertone of musk oozed past the strong smell of bleach and rubbing alcohol. The room Tristan delivered me to was tiny, six by ten at best. Half of its original size, judging by the wall patched together by what looked like pallet boards and scraps of Styrofoam. The bed he lowered me to was nothing more than a worn-out cot—probably army surplus. It squeaked and groaned, protesting my weight, and I wondered if I'd be better off on the blistered wood planks of the floor.

Clearly they spared no expense. Or they were scavengers.

The second seemed more likely, by the looks of the Great Depression Hoover-style village and the dilapidated house. That collided with the information Mother had woven through my head. The rebels were supposed to be well-armed selfish holdouts who wanted nothing but to demolish the Party because of greed and ambition. The vision around me leaked a whisper of *liar, liar* about my mother's claim—a whisper I'd heard before.

But this whole scenario could be a pretense. They could have another location.

The suspicion threaded through my mind as I'd drifted off, another black gulf taking me into its depths. Blood loss, likely. I didn't have the strength to fight the fade.

Hannah and Braxton met me in the darkness again. Her cold, betraying glare. His cocky smirk. The medieval blow to my head. It all stirred up the hate inside me, as well as a fresh confidence in the Party and my mother. Before I left the gray mist of that nightmare memory, my emotions dark and dangerous, Mother's voice, low and honey smooth, spoke into the heat of my anger.

Hannah has a sister.

I'd blinked against the yellowed flickering light, a grunt snapping me out of the memory. Mine. A white-hot burn singed along my side, and I jerked away from the pain. Two firm hands kept my shoulders down, and another bolt of lightning slashed through my waist.

"Breathe, Sanger," rumbled a deep, quiet voice, which was vaguely familiar, and yet I didn't know, beside me. "I'm just making sure it's clean."

More pain bolted through me, and I recognized the smell of antiseptic.

"You're lucky Braxton's a good shot. One inch lower and your liver would have been damaged." Pressure provoked a new throbbing pain as two large hands covered the entry and exit wounds from the bullet.

I grunted again. "Lucky, huh?"

The pressure increased. I squirmed against the cot, and the hands that held me down squeezed tighter. I glanced up, the instinct to fight against the captor above me rising strong.

Tristan, with his emotionless stare, looked back down at me.

"Lucky." Tristan repeated, the word a firm proclamation that would entertain no argument. "Not like Hannah."

I stopped struggling. The man who had sat at my side bandaging my waist moved away. He looked at me, his face also tight and grim, before he reached for a scrap of a towel, soaked it with antiseptic, and began rubbing his hands and arms. He flicked the cloth over his shoulder and met my gaze again.

"You'll live," he said.

His looks. I knew him. I'd seen him before in DC. A scowl pinched my forehead, accentuating the dull headache that had been birthed somewhere during that interlude. I continued to study him. "Who are you?" I growled.

"Dr. Luther." He didn't offer anything more. Stood. Moved for the door, as did Tristan. "Don't wander around."

I pushed up against an elbow. "So I'm a prisoner?" I spat.

Dr. Luther's stone face didn't change. "More blood loss could change your luck. And we have smallpox in the village. Only one girl has survived. You want to risk that, I guess go ahead. Likely, you deserve it."

Tristan didn't look back as he exited my tiny room, and Dr. Luther followed him out. The light dimmed. The door clicked. Only my thoughts continued to swirl. Dr. Luther...he'd been at the research hospital near the capitol. I knew I'd seen him there. Hadn't known his name.

Couldn't be coincidence that it was the same as Braxton's last name. Which meant that they were both related to the famous pastor I'd once secretly admired.

Eliza Knight and the Luther brothers. The heart of the rebellion, just beyond my miserable cot. I knew exactly what Mother would want done.

A fresh throb of pain exploded in my head and crawled down my neck. Hannah's dying face floated into my mind, her labored whisper a sound I couldn't shut out.

Don't let them tell you who you are.

I squeezed my eyes shut, summoning the other memory. The one that would fuel my resolve.

It waited just beyond the darkness of my shut eyes. As if it had been planted there on purpose.

eleven

Braxton

Relief and anxiety played a match of Ping-Pong while I waited for Eliza to change. Annyon said that fresh air would do her good, and I'd seen the sores on her back from lying so long. But she still looked ghostly pale, and her body was a frame with scar-speckled skin draped loosely over the top.

She wasn't anywhere near out of danger, and it really didn't help that we had only marginally more food to give her than what she'd received from the malevolent hands at the camps.

But she'd asked for a walk—to go see where her mother and sister had been buried. Hope and compassion couldn't deny her request. True grieving would perhaps usher back the heart of the girl I'd once known. Gravesides where known to trigger that. Or so I'd heard.

The door to her room slipped open, and my brother, arm around her body as support, walked beside an upright Eliza. She paused at the doorframe, squeezing her eyes shut, and I rushed the three steps from the wall opposite to her open side.

"Dizzy?"

She licked her lips. "A bit."

"That's expected." Annyon guided her one more step forward and then transferred her minimal weight to me. "Just go easy."

I'd only held her in my arms a few times before the camp, but this wisp of a girl felt foreign to those memories. So light and fragile it made me want to weep. Her head tipped into my shoulder and rested there.

"Eliza, are you—"

"Yes." She nearly wheezed the word, and then drew a fortifying breath. "I'm sure. I want out of this room, this house. I want to breathe air that doesn't smell like death and cleaning supplies."

She forged forward, and I matched her slow steps. We reached the front door, and she had to rest again, her head tucked close to my heart.

The sun poked through the scattered clouds as if on cue, sending a ray of warmth and light to drench her deprived body. Her head moved against my chest, chin tilting up. The shift drew my attention to her. Eyelids shut but relaxed, her face angled to make the most of the shaft of sunlight. The small frame beneath my hand expanded as she inhaled, and her lips smoothed.

I inhaled with her, imagining it was my first draw of fresh air in who knew how many months. The coolness filled my nostrils, then my lungs. "Tell me what you smell."

"Earth. Sky. The buds on the trees. Grass, new and determined to live." She moved again, her face burying into me. "And Braxton."

"Yes?"

"I smell you."

The weight I carried in my chest lifted a smidge. "Yikes. Face the sun again."

Her forehead pressed into me harder. Her body expanded with breath again.

Lighter still. There she was. My Eliza. The girl who could make a hero out of a cockroach. I'd do just about anything to see that she had been right about me, even if it hadn't been anywhere close to true back then.

With one hand, I covered the pokey fuzz of hair regrowing on her head and pressed my lips to her temple. For a moment, she held, like she'd found home and never wanted to move. Then she covered my hand and lifted it away from her head. The action didn't register meaning to me until she pulled away enough to lift the hood of the oversized sweatshirt we'd salvaged for her outing.

The thick fabric swallowed her, shadowing her face. I couldn't see her expression, and I wanted to tug the barrier away. She moved forward before I could. Again, I matched her abbreviated steps.

Silence escorted us down the path to the checkerboard of graves that lay past a stand of five cottonwood trees. She stopped twice, her breath labored. I wanted to take her back inside, but bit my tongue and held my impulses. Most of our relationship had been characterized by me making decisions, her warning me that I was wrong, me doing what I thought best anyway, and her helping me figure a way out of the mess that resulted.

It was time for her to lead for a change.

She was determined. A sign the old Eliza still remained.

Hannah had been buried next to their mother. The dirt of their graves had been churned only six months apart, and the mounds still hilled clean and stark. We stopped in between the two, and Eliza pulled away from me, using her feeble strength to stand on her own.

"Was it pneumonia?"

I followed the direction of her hood, tracing her line of sight to Jayla's carved wooden marker. "Yes. She'd get better, and then it'd hit again. The cold, sparse winter proved too much."

The hood moved. A nod. Another move, a shift toward Hannah's name.

I waited for the questions. Assembled an explanation. She should know what had happened before Hannah had gone back to get Quinn. That it was Hannah and Quinn who had torn the veil. Set her and the others free. Though Hannah's last act had been a bad plan from the start, it hadn't been completely selfish. Her sister hadn't died a sellout.

Eliza turned, and I caught a glimpse of her face as, for a moment, the sunlight broke through the hood's shadow. Stony and dry. My heart cracked. The weight in my chest pressed down again. The shadow replaced the moment of light upon her face, and she moved back toward the house.

Swallowing, I glanced back at Hannah's grave. "Eliza—"

"I'm tired, Braxton."

The earth seemed to draw me lower, a stormy ache stirring within. "Okay, Liza." I stepped beside her, my arm sliding around her tiny frame. For a moment she stayed stiff, keeping a barrier of invisible distance, but then she allowed me to take her full weight.

It didn't take much to slide my other arm around her legs, and lifting her seemed heavier on my heart than my arms.

I hoped she understood the intention was more than physical.

* * *

Eliza

His disappointment throbbed into me as I turned from Hannah's grave.

I sank into it. Felt the pulse of distress. Let it surround me. Who was I to judge my sister?

Really, it wasn't judgment that had turned me away. I hadn't wanted to see his reaction to her grave, to hear her story from his trembling lips. It shot a spark through my chest—not the good kind. Imagining their closeness, sharing the sort of life and mission they had for the past year, ate into the raw, dark spot that continued to burrow into my heart. He hadn't planned it—I understood. But there it was. Something he shared with my sister that I couldn't comprehend.

Braxton had always been mine. The one thing in life I wasn't willing to share with Hannah. She'd found a way.

An ugly burn singed through me.

The warmth of his presence drifted first to my side, then draped over me, surrounded me. He'd become so much stronger than I'd remembered him—not just physically. But yes, physically, because he lifted me as if I were a sack of fallen leaves. Light, detached, and easily crushed.

Not far from the truth.

Braxton's smooth, confident stride took me away from the graveyard but not back to the house. He moved toward a small cluster of trees near the lip of the rise that sheltered us to the north. The green haze of not-yet-opened buds contrasted with the hard, brown angles of the arcing branches. I heard the trunks cry for the glory of their coverings to hide their winter nakedness. Or maybe that was just my own.

I wiggled to catch my hood as it slipped from my nearly naked head.

"Are you cold?" He cradled me tighter, as if the question didn't require an answer.

"No." Not with his heart beating so near to mine and the tingling sensation of the warm sunlight soaking into my skin. I didn't realize the intent of his question until his chin nudged the drape of my hood away from my eyes.

We'd reached the edge of the trees. His momentum stopped. "Then you're hiding."

Gently, he lowered my feet to the ground. The strong probe of his searching gaze penetrated beyond the screen of fabric. This was too much. I felt the grief he carried for my sister and the obligation he felt for me. I wanted neither. They both stung too much. But I had nowhere to go, and even if I had, no strength to escape.

I angled my chin away, my gaze locking on the ground near my slip-on shoes. His fingertips traced the rounded outline of my hood and then sought to brush my chin. I pushed them away.

"Not from me, Eliza." His low voice cracked.

I held the intruding hand away, stepped back.

He followed. "I won't let you hide from me."

My palm met his chest, and he stopped. My heart stalled, and beneath my hand, I felt his do the same. I wondered if it hurt him as much as mine did me.

"Liza, please." Torment edged his whisper, and I blinked against the heat of tears.

I shook my head. "It's too humiliating." The memories, the reality, the scars. Where we were now. They all pulsed pain into the moment. How could anything ever be the same? "You look at me, and I see it in your eyes."

"What?" He moved. His hand lifted toward my covered face again and then paused. Fell, shaking.

"Pity." I swallowed, drew a breath, clawed for strength, and then lifted my chin so that our gazes would connect.

The storm between us surged. Hot and aching and full of longing.

"Horror." Like a shot, the word left my tongue.

Braxton winced, and then his eyes focused, a dark gush of anger. "No."

"They made us into monsters." I thrust my arm out, tugging the sleeve up to expose the loose, pocked skin for his examination. "Pitted and scarred and barely human." Bitterness coated my voice, making it foreign to me.

It didn't seem to strike a blow on him. He leaned in, the intensity of his stare now fierce. "I don't see a monster. I see you."

"I am ruined." I spat the truth as if it were an arrow that could strike him dead.

His head tilted. Eyes squeezed closed. The poison had found its mark. His lips rolled together, and a tick leapt from his jaw, but as quickly as the intensity had come, it left, and when he opened his eyes, the expression was soft.

The storm eased.

"Are you?" The question had barely left his lips when he closed the space between us. His nose brushed mine, then traced a soft line over my cheek.

In even puffs, his breath spread over my face, fanned down my neck, moist and warm. My mouth tingled. A small twist of my head, and his kiss would fall against it. He waited. I agonized.

I wanted his love. But there was something between us. A secret buried. I had seen it—even if it wasn't horror. He was holding something away from me. My heart told me it had to do with my sister, and the black seed of resentment grew.

The strong surge of his pulse beneath my palm calmed. He moved to hold me, one hand cupping the back of my head, hood still in place, and tucking me against his shoulder. The intimacy of his breath so near my mouth evaporated, and the storm between us passed.

Calm settled. Nothing washed.

I kept my hood in place when he walked me back to the hospital. We would both continue to hide.

* * *

Quinn

"Who's under the hoodie?"

I knew, but my best cover was to ask. Tristan's needlepoint focus remained on the pair down by the stand of trees. His expression remained impenetrable, and I wondered what investment he had in the scene that had just played out.

Whatever brewed between Braxton and Hannah's sister was serious. And complicated. I'd wished I'd heard what had been spoken.

"Tristan?"

He folded his arms across his chest. "Eliza."

"Eliza..." *Say it. Let this charade play out.*

His startling green eyes turned toward me. "Knight." The tone of his voice held warning and meaning, as if he suspected this news could detonate my world. I let it play.

"Knight? As in Hannah Knight?" I turned to square with him, my hand covering the sore spot where the hole in my gut was still healing.

"She told you?"

"I knew her last name, yes." And also that Hannah had a sister. She'd shared that with me too. I wondered, for a moment, how Mother had known that detail. She hadn't gained the information from me.

"Did your mother?"

Not until after I'd come to from the blow to my head. After Hannah had betrayed me. But he didn't need to know any of that. "Why? Does that worry you?"

His unreadable expression didn't crack. "I stood up for you. Don't mistake that for trust."

"Should I mistake your threats as valid?"

His eyebrow lifted. The muscle in his arm jumped. "Your mistakes are your prerogative. But if you touch Eliza, no one will stand between you and Braxton."

"And that should worry me?"

"More than you can comprehend." He glanced to the wound I still covered with my hand and began to move off the crumbling porch.

I let him go. The info was scant, but it would work for the moment. Braxton was dangerous. Eliza was in fact Hannah's sister. And Tristan's loyalties wouldn't waver.

Tristan's long strides came to a sudden halt five feet off the porch. His head tipped, ear toward the sky, and he seemed to hold his breath. I moved to gain a view of something other than the decaying boards shading the porch and caught the hum rattling the air as I reached the edge of the planks.

My breathing paused too. Along with, it seemed, every bit of life in the village. The air hovered with tension. Braxton and Eliza stopped their slow wander back to the house. He pulled her close, dipped his mouth toward her ear. I wondered what secret he'd just shared.

A white drone broke into sight, a foreign spot of terror on the canvas of deep-blue and puffy-white sky. I pictured the control room back in the bunker and couldn't rationalize to myself why I secretly begged the pilot to somehow miss the obvious camp below.

The scene in that bunker replayed against my wishes, my mother's demanding voice crisp in the memory.

Erase it.

She would.

I moved my attention from the trail of the drone to the couple tangled in each other's arms fifty yards away. They were dangerous. Rebels. A threat to progress and all that we should be as the human race.

He held her. She curled under his protection. They looked like the hunted, not the predator.

Confusion pushed into my conviction.

Please don't see us. Don't see them.

Thoughts unbidden and irrational. Yet I didn't take them back.

I wanted the truth. Somehow, I knew that I wouldn't find it if they were erased.

twelve

Braxton

"There were more attacks." The mechanical scratches of Jude's explanation greeted us as we crossed the threshold into his lab.

My heart, already pulsing faster than normal, stuttered. The flyover had buzzed high alert through all of us. If it was connected to an attack blamed on us again, we weren't clear. Not that we ever were, really.

I glanced at Tristan and then Miranda. His face remained steel. Hers paled under her pixie-styled auburn hair.

"What do you mean?" Skye stepped forward, her to-the-point personality taking charge of the situation.

Jude turned his chair, his head already angled to meet our confusion as his face came around. "Whoever attacked DC before Hannah went for Quinn has hit again. One strike, north of the White House."

"What does this mean?" Tristan, ever calculating, asked in his even, dark tone.

"It means that we're in trouble," Skye answered for Jude.

Silence cut the conversation, letting our nerves unravel in the space.

"Is that true, Jude?" Miranda's timid voice made me want to squeeze Quinn's neck, just on principle, because he was the only Party official I could get ahold of at the moment.

Jude drew in a lungful of air. "They're blaming us, yes."

"Is that why the drones are out again?" I asked.

"They're *always* searching," Tristan reminded us.

"And they're getting way too close." Skye's slim but toned frame took on a fight stance. She'd face them bare handed, and she'd probably inflict some notable damage before they'd put her down. I often wondered why. What had driven her from the squishy *we'll take care of you in exchange for your undying love* security of the Party. She would never say. When asked, she'd give the curious imposer her death glare and then walk away.

I hoped Eliza wouldn't bury herself like that. Layers of resentment and mistrust, baked solid and held together with a solid spread of bitterness. Not that I didn't like Skye. She actually scared me a little bit, and I admired her. But she was nothing like the Eliza I remembered, nothing like what I hoped to see her become as she healed.

"The Umbrella will hold," Jude said, his assurance meant to refocus.

"Unless they start searching from the ground," Skye argued. "We can't hide forever, and we have other problems. The refugees are growing in numbers—and many of them are Cloaked. It makes the Uncloaked nervous."

I fidgeted, glancing to Tristan. The ink on my neck seemed to catch fire.

Tristan held a steady look on Skye. "What would you suggest?" The dry challenge in his voice spoke the message his words didn't. *Hypocrite.*

Skye didn't shrink from his implication. "There has to be a limit."

Tristan tipped his head and fingered the brand we'd all taken. "And the cutoff is what? Me? Luther? You?"

"We've proven our loyalties, even with the seal. Jude knows he can trust us."

"So what? The rest get left to the whim and mercy of the Party?" He stepped forward, his towering frame making her look even smaller than her five-four stature.

She didn't shrink, proving why she'd earned the position in the Pride she'd held. "We have others to think about. To protect." Her dark eyes sparked at him and then moved to settle on Miranda. "What do you think?"

As if beckoned by a magnetic force, my attention moved to Miranda's creamy neck. Clean, unbranded. I wondered, while we waited for Miranda's response, what Eliza would say to this conversation.

I knew what I wanted her to say. But I'd felt the war in her heart, and now I wasn't so sure I knew her answer.

Miranda studied the floor, then searched Jude. Silence returned to the room. The stillness became as a held breath.

The crackle of Jude's voice stirred not only the stalled air but the hairs on my neck and the depth of my soul. "Whom would you show mercy, child?"

Would you love at all costs?

That was the real question on the table here.

The pulse of tension beat a wordless and defining moment. Miranda's expression softened. "Any who would come."

She formed the words on a breathy conviction. It gave strength and voice to my own.

"We welcome the refugees." My voice sounded like a memory—like my father's—rather than my typical sarcastic snap. There was something both commanding and final about it, and I finished with a definitive look to each of my companions. "Cloaked or Uncloaked. They will find a safe place with us."

Tristan, though his expression didn't really change, seemed to agree. Approve. Miranda seemed to cling to my announcement as if she'd draw more strength from it. Skye's mouth tightened, her gaze casting away toward the opposite wall. Jude's probing study landed on me. A whisper threaded through my heart, unheard but felt.

Well done, son.

Though the voice wasn't his, approval echoed from Jude's expression.

A sense of evolution surged through me. As if I was moving forward, becoming the man I was intended to be. Equal parts freedom and burden. A feeling, I was sure, my father knew well.

***

Quinn

They were not as unified as we had supposed.

Like a note on a pad, the thought scrawled through my brain, adding to the list of quirks this Refuge had unveiled. This revelation was, perhaps, the most surprising. And one that worked like a battering ram to push me back toward my mother and her Party.

A group of new refugees gathered near the stand of trees. If the hesitant glances and the few outright glares of the villagers indicated anything, the group of seven huddled together near the burial ground were not brought here with open arms and a round of "Kum Ba Yah."

One careful examination of their necks proved why. They were Cloaked.

Hypocrites, both groups. The Cloaked and the villagers. Just as Mother had warned of the religious masses. They welcomed whom they determined worthy. Kept outcast those who fell outside their rigid standard, and only made exceptions for those who would be beneficial. Mercenaries. Like Braxton Luther.

A commotion broke out from the building across from the hospital house, where I still remained, though it wasn't necessary. Four villagers stepped out, two of whom were Braxton and Tristan, and a small crowd gathered around them.

Tristan didn't stop, his face set in mission

mode. He pushed through the gathering, his stride strong and purposeful. Directed toward the new Cloaked refugees. Braxton looked to the girls who'd come out of the dugout building. One girl, the smaller of the two, who reminded me of a little ninja warrior, scowled up at him but kept her mouth firmly closed. The other, a tall girl with very short brown-red hair, let her attention wander past the gathering until it settled on the refugees at the trees.

The tribal council had met, it seemed. Who put them in charge?

At the moment, that wasn't relevant. I wanted to hear the two-faced poison drip from the Luther boy's forked tongue. It would cement my view of him, of his people, and make Mother's demands easier to carry out. She'd been right all along.

Though determination filled me, a burn smoldered in my stomach.

I swallowed back the taste of stomach acid and strode through the doorway of my room. No sooner had I stepped into the hall, than a small, hooded figure darkened the spot across from me.

Eliza Knight. In the flesh. Or what there was left of her. Frail seemed the best adjective for this wisp of a young woman swallowed by the hooded sweatshirt she wore. In the dimness of the hallway, I search for the definitions of her face, wondering how much she looked like Hannah, and then hating that I let the little viper-witch possess my thoughts yet again.

Cutting the argument in my head to an annoying prattle that I could mostly ignore, I searched the shadows swallowing her face only to find that she kept herself well hidden. We would have to move beyond the confines of this house if I was to make out her features.

"Were you going somewhere?" I waved my hand through the air, as if we'd run into each other at the White House and not in a dilapidated house that ought to have been flattened years ago.

She refused to look up. "There's something going on outside."

"I saw." I waited.

She said nothing.

I swept the space between us again. "Should we go see?"

Her head tipped a tiny bit. But not enough to scatter the shadows in which she hid. "Only if we keep to the edge."

So. She was shrouding herself on purpose.

Perhaps she knew she was wanted by the Party. Perhaps Braxton had kept her identity hidden from the others.

Perhaps I would not have to do Mother's dirty

work after all. If she was an outcast here, exposure was all that it would take. Both of the Knight sisters would have been their own undoing.

A feeling I could only describe as upside down tugged my mind. I was just not cut out to be dark.

I nodded once, offering my hand. "To the edges. I promise." I would keep it. For today.

thirteen

Eliza

The man slipped his hand under my elbow, and with a small nudge, he walked with me through the hall and out the house.

I didn't know him. But he seemed kind.

Height was the only similarity he possessed with Braxton. This man's hair and skin were fair, and the flash of his eyes had been blue. His voice was smooth and practiced, as if he'd spent his educational years training to be an orator or something.

I wondered why he was in the hospital.

"Are you a doctor, like Annyon?"

We stepped off the porch, and I immediately searched the gathering for Braxton. He stood in the middle of the crowd, glancing from Tristan to Miranda before he held up both palms.

"No." The man beside me answered. "A patient."

Keeping my hood's shadow secure over my face, I glanced at him, searching for injury.

"What damage have you?"

"I am healed. Your doctor is quite proficient."

Proficient? Only the most educated Career Trackers talked like that. Where had this man come from?

"We are not mobsters." Braxton's voice carried over the now-hushed gathering.

"We're not doormats either," a man tossed back.

"Nobody is walking on you, sir."

"It isn't safe, and you know it," a woman said.

"The pursuit of safety landed us here," Braxton countered. "Would you treat others as you have suffered?"

"We would take care of our own!"

The stranger and I neared the fringes of the gathering, and I stopped. He halted too, and when I shrank behind him, he stood as if to shield me.

I liked him, whoever he was.

"They have come to us for help." Braxton spoke again.

"Funny, no one was around when we needed

help. Where were they then?"

I watched the boy in the middle fight for words. I wanted to stand by him, to give him encouragement. At the same time, the black part of my heart burned against him.

The Cloaked had turned us out. Hid their faces to our suffering. Accepting them here was...

The dark ink of the tattoo on Braxton's neck peeked out at me, and a breath later, his wandering gaze landed on the man who stood half in front of me. His face hardened, eyes darkened. And then his look slid just enough to find me.

I cannot say how long we stood, caught in a silent confrontation extending over the crowd. Emotions that had lodged deep inside boiled upward, and I couldn't fight them back down to the safety of the darkness.

They didn't know suffering, these double-minded Cloaked refugees. They had no idea of it. Nor did Braxton, really. What a debt I had paid, and they had escaped...

"Forgiveness isn't optional." Braxton's voice somehow carried over the crowd, though he spoke low.

Conviction gathered with deep humility in his tone, and for a moment I thought I was listening to his father.

"It is imperative. Hate will not be confined. It

is viral and deadly. But still, you get to choose."

His eyes didn't leave my face, though I knew mine were well hidden. He spoke to the crowd and to my soul. I felt the softening of both.

"What will you do with what you believe?" His gaze left me and widened to meet the gathered crowd. The challenge settled. The people hushed.

Will you choose me?

The answer kept getting harder.

Braxton's question fell upon the crowd like an electrical charge, subduing their anger and redirecting their energy.

What would we do with what we believed? What would I do? Whom would I choose?

Braxton's focus came back to me, and I felt exposed even though I was still hiding underneath the hoodie and in the stranger's shadow. Even as the crowd parted, the gathering breaking into smaller clumps of two or three people as they dispersed, Braxton's attention remained on me. I wondered if the disapproval I read in his posture and gait was because I had left the hospital again, this time without him, or if it had more to do with the man I stood behind. I began to believe it was the latter, because when Braxton's glance slid to him, his scowl deepened.

"I see you found your way out of the hospital." Braxton's hard glare met the man beside me.

"I did," the stranger answered smoothly. "I'm not a prisoner, right?"

A prisoner? I watched Braxton's response. The muscle on his jaw ticked.

"No. You are not." He swallowed. Held another moment of wordless confrontation. Then looked down to me. "Are you feeling better, Eliza?" His voice softened, though his expression still seemed strained.

"I am. I feel stronger." I swayed away from the shadow of this man Braxton clearly didn't like and, like a mouse, took a tiny step into the light. "I saw the crowd, and I wanted to know what was going on."

"A question of who will be shown compassion." Braxton's face moved away, toward the small group by the trees across from the graveyard, and his shoulders seemed drawn down. When he looked back up, however, the sternness in his voice had returned. "I think you better get back to the hospital. My brother will be wondering where you are."

The man beside me arched an eyebrow, challenge crossing his face, though he did not argue. He turned with a hand still on my elbow and began striding back for the hospital. Braxton came to my other side. His possessiveness made me feel secure and a little curious as to what was going on between them.

When we reached the hospital, the man who had walked me out turned to me and smiled. “I wish you well, Eliza Knight.”

A thread of discomfort wove through me. How did he know my name? I looked to Braxton. His stern face gave away nothing.

Braxton held my elbow, keeping me by his side while the other man walked back into the house and through the halls.

When he was gone from our sight, I turned to Braxton. “Who was that?”

“He didn’t bother to introduce himself?” Braxton’s voice was dark and accusing.

“No, but I didn’t ask either. I only asked if he was a doctor. He said no. So who is he?”

“None other than Quinn Sanger.” Braxton’s eyes matched his dark voice, the implication dropping hard on my heart.

Quinn Sanger. I swallowed, anger turning hot inside my chest. “He’s the reason my sister is dead?”

I watched as Braxton wrestled with emotion, battling something inside that I didn’t understand. He swallowed, ran a hand down his face, looked across to the graveyard, and then his eyes came back to me. Distance spread between us again, and so did the resentment I felt toward Hannah.

How had she gained so much of his heart? I

turned away, moving to step inside the house, but his hands stayed on my elbow.

"Are you strong enough for another walk?" The emotion in his voice surprised me, and I wondered if it had more to do with me or with Hannah. Or perhaps it had to do with Quinn.

"I am strong enough."

A tender spot of warmth grew on my arm as he closed his hand more securely on my elbow and guided me back down the porch steps. We walked, this time away from the graveyard, away from the house, and away from the village. We were to be alone this time. Truly. Perhaps he would share with me what really had happened. Why every time Hannah crossed his mind, regret and despair passed through his expression.

I wasn't sure I wanted to know.

I looked to Braxton. His face gave away nothing.

A breeze stirred the air. Chills crept over my skin beneath the sweatshirt, but I inhaled long and deep. Spring seeped into my lungs, the smells of damp earth and budding trees. The ground beneath my thin shoes seemed almost like foam, the tender green shoots giving comfortably beneath my steps. So different from the hard, dry cracked earth I'd known only months before.

Braxton's hand slid down my arm until our palms met. His fingers wove between mine and locked. How often had I longed for him to hold my hand back when we were in school? When life was simpler? I had wondered what it would feel like and if our friendship would survive that kind of shift.

My hand in his felt like security. But our friendship felt shadowed. Not because he held my hand. Because he held something back, and suspicion made me edgy.

The level ground began to rise. The hills guarding our village surprised me. Not what I expected on the Vacant Plains. Even the prairie has its secrets.

I slowed my steps, and Braxton halted. His thumb ran a gentle trail over my knuckles while his intense study searched for my eyes beneath the cover of my hoodie.

I tipped my chin up, allowing the sunlight to graze my face. "Will you tell me what happened?"

"There were Cloaked in the recent group of refugees. Many of the camp survivors in the village didn't want them here."

I nodded, glancing at the ink on his neck. He'd taken an awkward position—very un-Braxtonish. But very Luther. He had grown into his name.

I took a ghost of a step toward him. "That wasn't what I meant."

His other hand gripped mine. "Oh."

"What happened with my sister?"

The hold on my hands tightened. "I told you what happened. She went back for Quinn, and it got her killed."

"He's here."

Strain edged his face. "I didn't invite him."

"But you brought him."

Braxton looked past me, his jaw working against emotion. "It's a complicated story."

"The one I'm asking you to tell me."

That intense look fell back on me, and he rolled his lips between his teeth. Weighing his answer.

"Don't hide from me," I whispered.

He blinked, a sheen glazing his eyes. His hands lifted from mine, leaving them cold, my heart confused, and when he pinched the edges of my hood, he hesitated.

"You're hiding from me," he answered.

I looked to my feet, squeezed my eyes shut, and then covered his hands. My arms shook, though reason said it was dumb. He'd seen my scars. Sat beside me while I sparred with death.

But what if he looked at me now and wished...

The security of darkness pulled away from my face. Sunlight sank into the skin of my forehead, ears, head.

Nearly bald head.

He settled the hood against my neck and cupped the back of my head. His hand felt both warm and strange against the stubble of my regrowing hair. I couldn't look at him as a fleck of a tear ran over the ridge of my nose.

"Eliza." He closed the space between us until my breath stirred the shirt against his chest.

Still, I could not raise my gaze.

His head hovered ever closer until his gentle kiss pressed against my head. "I see strength and beauty, Eliza Knight." Another kiss, this time near my ear. "You. The same girl I have loved since forever."

Trembling, the tears now rolling one after another, I gripped the sleeves of his shirt. "I am not the same."

The weight of his head lay against mine as he tucked me closer, wrapping me against him with his free arm. Words vanished. What could we say? I had spoken truth, and neither of us knew what to do with it.

We only knew tears. Mine soaked his shirt. His splashed against the top of my head. How could life recover? The promised spring I'd inhaled only minutes before seemed a mocking taunt in the ache of that moment.

***

Braxton

She needed to know the truth. All of it. Not just about Hannah, but about the mill, the Persuasion.

But I couldn't. Not in that moment. And not because she'd hate me.

Because it would destroy her. She wasn't ready—and if I told her in that horrible moment, she would crumble under the weight of darkness.

Or my Braxtonian-centered logic had made an uninvited reappearance. In my head, I tried to converse the issue out with the Eliza I'd known back in Glennbrooke. The conversation went something like:

ME: I can't tell you the truth. It'll hurt too much.

ELIZA: Who will it hurt?

ME: You.

ELIZA: Only me?

ME: Mostly you.

Long, contemplative pause in which I feel saturated with incompetency and insecurity.

ELIZA: Do what you know to be right.

That trip down friendship history didn't help much. I knew being honest with Eliza was right. I also knew that she carried more than she could handle right then. One more sandbag of ugly might break her.

This wasn't about me. Honest.

Is it, God?

Eliza lifted her head from my chest, and though her fists remained tight on my shirt, she shifted to look into my eyes. "You can't tell me now, can you?"

I swallowed, searching her eyes for help. I'd always depended on her moral compass, even when I didn't take her advice. I knew she always pointed true. She held my gaze with an openness that I hadn't seen since she'd been rescued from the Quarantine. A bittersweet taste coated my tongue.

She nodded, accepting my silence as an answer. "When you're ready then." Disappointment draped her expression, but then it changed, as if on command. I swear I could read her thoughts.

I choose to trust you.

Not, *I trust you. I choose to trust you.*

Sometime in the not-so-far-off future, she'd find out exactly how unworthy I was. That her hero really had been a cockroach and everything she struggled with now had been my fault.

But not yet.

fourteen

Quinn

They accepted the sealed refugees. Some with more enthusiasm than others, but the village sheltered them. Offered a share of their meager food supplies. And invited them to work alongside them. An expanding garden was being plotted, tilled, and prepared for planting. The cool-weather garden was being tended and harvested, supplying leafy greens, sugar peas, and baby beets. Hunting troops left daily, usually returning with a few rabbits or prairie chickens, sometimes both. Scavengers, as they called them, would leave the village one morning a week and return in the early evening with whatever supplies they could find.

The scavengers were usually the same team of people. Tristan, Braxton, and two girls. I wondered why. Were they more skilled at hiding? Because they'd been trained by the Party? Or was it because they were disposable, given the traitorous tattoo branding them as outcasts?

The last option didn't follow logic. Not when I saw how this group operated. Jude, the strange man in the dugout whom I'd never seen but heard about, was the unquestioned leader of this rebel population. Under him the four who were scavengers also seemed to hold a place of leadership, Braxton near the top of that hierarchy, as evidenced by the grudging acceptance of the most recent branded refugees.

His leadership seemed a contradiction. He didn't seem to want it. He deferred to Jude or to Tristan more often than not. But then there was that gathering, his decision, and the passion with which he spoke to the group.

He'd sounded like Pastor Luther. Whether he'd intended to or not.

Their scavenging trips made me think of the town that Mother had erased. I knew now what the pilot had seen on her screen that day. Which begged the question: How had the drones that had passed over us last week not seen the refugee village?

Life in the village didn't answer my questions. I couldn't sift through the contradictions of what I'd known in DC and what I saw at the Refuge. If this was a facade, a distraction or manipulation to make me sympathetic to the rebel cry, they were good at it. No one ever broke character. But every time I allowed the possibility that this was real, the dark, malicious look on Hannah's face when she'd betrayed me would etch with perfect clarity in my mind. The nightmare would steal my rest, the constant reminder that she was a liar. In the mornings after, the temptation to buy their sincerity would vanish.

This was all an act. It proved nothing.

Eliza Knight continued to come and go from the hospital. I never saw her face, as she kept the hoodie drawn. Curiosity would compel me to the halls or porch when she was up and around. One glimpse would tell me if she and Hannah shared similar appearances. I wasn't sure why I wanted them to. Why would I want to see that face again?

Because I had loved her. At least, I'd loved the version of her I'd invented. Letting go of that was impossible. The only way to survive it was with hate. So I fed it.

Seeing Hannah in her sister would be fodder to the rage.

"I get the impression you're stalking her."

Braxton Luther climbed the two steps to the porch where I stood. Eliza, covered by her oversized hoodie, wandered toward the graveyard to the northeast.

I slid a look of indifference at him. "Jealous?"

His heavy footsteps stopped right beside me, and he waited to answer until I moved my full attention from her to him. "If you so much as give her a paper cut, I'll—"

"Kill me?" I shook my head. "No you won't. You've got too much of your father in you."

"You have no idea what you're talking about."

I snorted a small laugh. "Your father? I didn't hear about him from the Party." Again, I passed a look over him. "I used to listen to Patrick Luther."

"And your mother..."

"Didn't know."

"Ah. A closet rebel. Very brave. Almost as brave as killing a girl half your size. The one who'd come back to save you."

A burn raced down my chest and exploded in my gut. "I didn't mean to—"

Braxton turned away. He didn't care. I shouldn't either. If I didn't think about it, replay Hannah's last breath or the pain in her eyes, I could pretend I didn't care.

That wasn't working. "I didn't need saving," I said to his back.

He stopped. Shook his head. "You have no idea." He started walking away again, flinging his final jab over his shoulder. "Maybe we should have just left you there."

Propelled by anger, I stomped down the steps and across the thin grass until he was within arm's reach. Hand to his shoulder, I ripped him around to face me.

With one fluid move, he had my hand squeezed, my thumb and pinkie drawn inward so tight the knuckles nearly touched. Hot pain shot through my wrist and up my arm as he bent my wrist backward, using momentum to push me toward the ground. With his foot, he tangled my balance, and I landed on my back before I realized what he'd done. Air launched from my chest, and before I could draw another breath, his knee sank into the tender bullet wound.

"Ahh..." I arched against the earth at my back, struggling to wriggle free.

"Sometimes reality bites, doesn't it?" He hovered over me and then threw my hand to the ground. He stood, the removal of his knee relieving the fiery pain in my side. "The Party trains their mercenaries well. Don't try to take me by the back again. And don't underestimate me when I tell you not to mess with Eliza. You won't touch her. Got it?"

I struggled to my elbows, the wound he'd just aggravated throbbing as I moved. Braxton glared at me, his breath coming deep and hard as if he were wrestling back a fit of rage. With a last huff, he stepped to my side again, this time holding his hand toward me.

A hand up? I scowled.

"I'm not Hulk," he muttered.

That had meaning to him. The Hulk I associated with my mother? I didn't get it. But I accepted the offer.

He pulled me to my feet. "Jude asked to see you."

"Me?"

"You're the only Quinn Sanger I know. Thankfully." He turned his back on me again.

Ignoring the throb that still knifed in my side, I jogged the three strides it took to catch up and then matched his pace as we walked toward the metal dugout thing where this Jude person hid.

The queen bee of the hive. Without him this whole operation would fail. He was my real target, not Eliza Knight. Mother would grin. I shivered picturing it—the sly, satisfied expression that would tip her lips, light her eyes with a determinative glint.

Evil.

I recoiled at the word and seriously considered the possibility that I had developed a split personality. Whose side was I on?

Mother's. The Party's. Unless...

I stamped out the debate as the light went from bright and airy in the afternoon sun to dark and ominous within the dugout. The narrow hall we'd entered didn't allow for the breadth of both Braxton's shoulders and mine side by side, so I stalled a step and then followed his lead.

"What does this Jude person want with me?"

Braxton employed that emotionless, indecipherable tone. "Didn't ask."

Did that mean he didn't care? Not likely. Didn't approve of this meeting? Possible. He didn't like me, trust me. And he shouldn't.

I didn't trust me either. The double-minded struggle going on in my head had me self-diagnosing mental issues. I hadn't always been unstable, had I?

Braxton led me to the end of the long passage and paused at a door. We waited, a buzz vibrating in my ears, and then he pushed the heavy metal door open. The dugout reminded me of the bunker in DC, only on a smaller scale.

"Mr. Sanger."

My name was spoken from an inhuman voice, startling me. I looked around for some kind of droid or a character from the old *Star Wars* movies, prepared for a masked storm trooper or a tall guy in a black helmet. I blinked when I found a man possessing only a torso and one shriveled arm below his lolling head. His long face was tipped up to me, as his head rested against an angled brace anchored to his mechanized chair. Narrow lips and a long, pointed nose made his face look something like a bird's. But his eyes, focused on me, blazed with intelligence and something else that was unfamiliar.

"I am Quinn Sanger." I balled my fists at my side, not sure what I should do with my hands. Or anything else for that matter. Was I to stand? Move to shake his single, marred hand?

"Yes, I know. I've known you for quite some time."

"That's very strange. I have never heard of you until I was brought here."

His thin mouth quirked, as if to form a sad little smile, but they wouldn't quite cooperate. "You knew me once. As a small child." He held eye contact. "But that is a story for another time."

"Then why am I here?"

"You asked to come. You are seeking the truth." He paused, glanced at Braxton, and then looked back to me. "Have you found it?"

We were getting straight to it. All the better. "Unless you keep it hidden in your so-called hospital, no. I see nothing here that would make me believe Hannah was anything but a liar."

"Why would you think that?"

"You used me. You all used me and then left me to hang as the Party traitor. You had me do your dirty work and then left me for dead."

Braxton stepped forward. "You keep saying that—but it isn't so. You've been tricked."

"My memories are very clear." I crossed my arms and masked a scowl to guard my growing doubt. "Hannah manipulated me and left me for dead."

"No." Braxton let that one-word spike sink in before he drilled it down solid with the next accusation. "Your mother is manipulating you. She messed with your mind."

"Why would I believe that?" *Aside from the fact that the pain in my gut said that it was true...*

Jude's computer voice regained the conversation. "Braxton is right. Your memory of that day has been altered. Somewhere buried under all the false layers you have been subjected to, you have the original. If you search for it, you will find the truth."

"The original? What are you talking about?"

He pulled in a lungful of air, the sound making a static noise against whatever he used to speak. "It's called memory manipulation. It's very much like what you would do with an image or a photo when you change the scene or the background or the details until the original becomes what it wasn't. It becomes what you want it to be rather than what really was true."

I stared at him, the space above my nose pinched. "You do know you sound crazy, right?"

"A name I've been called many times over my lifetime. But crazy doesn't mean that something isn't true."

The sequence of that day replayed in my head, the details clear. And then...not. No. Jude was nuts, and *he* was the one messing with my head.

"Why would I want to change the memory of Hannah into something I hate if it wasn't the truth?"

"I didn't say you did this."

"My mother?" Again the details of the memory blipped through my mind. In a few places, the sequence scattered—the details fuzzed. I shook my head. "My mother is into politics and social reform, not experimental brain control."

"Aren't they the same thing?"

Braxton's deadpan question struck me as almost funny.

This whole thing was almost funny. Especially since Jude seemed completely serious about his wild and ridiculous story.

"My mother has no access to that kind of crazy operation. You're seriously certifiable, old man. Maybe you should lay off the sci-fi flicks."

Jude stared at me, his unwavering gaze unaffected by my disbelief. "Charlotte not only has access to the technology for memory manipulation, she controls it."

"Really?" My fist balled. I crossed my arms and bent toward him. "And how exactly have you gained this secret knowledge, living all the way out here—illegally—like a rat in a dirt-packed hole?"

His dark eyes squinted, which made his expression seem like a hawk's. Intelligent. Fierce. Predator. He studied me, then looked past me as if into something else entirely. A different place. A different life. Regret washed over his damaged face as he refocused on me. His voice, though that of a computer, sounded sad.

"I know"—he paused, looked into the past again—"because I created it."

fifteen

Braxton

My arms fell to my side, and I felt my chin drop. "You what?"

Agony sifted through Jude's eyes. "I invented it. Or, we invented it."

"We who?"

"Kasen and me."

Kasen Asend and Jude had worked together? In what life? And how were they both connected to Charlotte?

"We worked together in an experimental lab. Kasen and I were fellows in the experimental psychology department at MIT. Memory manipulation was supposed to be a healing process—a way for victims of trauma to be rid of the memories that haunted them. Particularly for the men and women who had been damaged during the Bloody Faith Conflict, as a way to circumvent PTSD. But it didn't work as well on adults as it did children. Their memories were too concrete, less likely to remain altered, and when the original events started pushing forward, our patients began displaying signs similar to multiple personality disorder. We hadn't helped them—because the wounds in their hearts and spirits needed healed, not smothered. When we tried to cover them over or erase them, the wounds only split wider. Our efforts made it worse."

He sighed. Took another long breath. "But with the children..."

"You manipulated memories on kids?" My voice took on a feral rage. How could he do something that awful? That invasive?

Pain continued to spill from Jude's expression, something I'd never seen from the man who was always composed. "Trauma victims." His voice broke off, and then his mouth quivered. "I honestly thought what we were doing would be good. I never saw this."

"This? What?" I asked.

"Kasen met Charlotte as we were concluding the experimentation with the war department—they defunded our research, with good reason.

Kasen and Charlotte...their relationship is...complex. She came on board, and he convinced me to allow it, because her financial backing was seductive. I didn't know what she was capable of. Didn't have any idea how she would use the monster I'd created. Didn't understand the dormant monster she was herself."

His fists doubled at his side, Quinn stepped forward and leaned over Jude. "Monster?"

Jude didn't cower; his expression took on more pain. "There's so much you don't know. And this latest—tell me. Do the dreams still replay? Do they confuse you? Does it feel like something's off, but you can't identify what?" He raised his eyebrows, though the expression he held on Quinn remained compassionate. "And the explosion? Do you still see that?"

Quinn's jaw locked. His body trembled. Anger? No, fear. Shock. Jude was right. How could he have let this happen? And Hannah. She'd walked into—

I stepped closer, the muscles in my body coiling tight. "You knew what had been done to Quinn, and you didn't tell Hannah?"

Jude's attention remained on Quinn. "I knew, yes. I didn't tell her because I feared it would convince her all the more to go to him. Obviously, I miscalculated her determination."

"Miscalculated!" I grabbed Quinn's shoulders and shoved him to the side and then took his place hovering over the man that up until this moment, I had only respected. "Hannah. Is. Dead! That's not a miscalculation."

Jude's eyes slid closed, and his chin dropped toward his chest. The unmasked regret tethered my fury. Who was I? A Jackal. A sellout. I had plenty of my own *miscalculations.* One very large one that I still hadn't owned up to before the girl I needed to beg forgiveness from most. I was still being the coward.

Jude was laying his sins out.

My coiled shoulders relaxed, and I straightened, taking a backward step.

"I never intended any of this." The inflection in Jude's mechanized voice felt heavy. "I know the responsibility I carry. That is why I created the Umbrella, why this Refuge exists. Once I learned what Charlotte was capable of, what her goals were, I knew how unsafe our world was about to become."

"The explosion?" Quinn's question ground from his throat, hard and heated.

"Yes." Jude looked back to him. "It was real."

"How do you know about that?"

"I was there." Jude snorted a scornful laugh. "So were you. And your brother."

"I don't have a brother."

"Indeed, you do. You were close. Both very intelligent—genetically designed to be so. But while one boy showed all the markers of leadership—persuasiveness, strength, compassion, and that intelligence that was engineered before your birth, the other possessed a personality glitch. He was easily provoked. Rage simmered beneath his groomed personality, and as he grew into early childhood, it surfaced more easily and often."

Though it seemed impossible, understanding lit through my mind. "Hulk."

Lips pressed tight, Jude nodded. "One boy was ideal for public appearance. The other for public compliance."

"I don't know a *Hulk*." Quinn scowled, his voice growing hot again. He looked to the ground at his left, and paused. Then, after a pull of an angry breath, he said, "I've never had a sibling."

Quinn was lying. He knew...something. Somewhere in his damaged brain, he knew.

"You were the crown of her experimentation. Genetically engineered perfection. Garrison was the convenient flaw in her design. If it is a comfort, know that she did feel for you both, but needed you in different capacities. She allowed the cruelness of a world mostly unconcerned with abandoned children to mold and inflame

Garrison's childhood. With you, she poured out both nurture and manipulation—a similar tactic she used with Kasen. But she was never quite able to detach herself completely from Garrison, which was why you ended up meeting Hannah in the first place."

"He was the reason Charlotte was in Glennbrooke." The mysteries were sliding into place. "And she was the reason he was given so much power."

"This is all a fantastic tale, old man. But you have no proof, and I have no reason to believe you."

"I am your proof," Jude said. "And your dreams give you plenty of reason to believe me. The explosion was our lab, and I was in it. It was meant to destroy all evidence of our work—including me—without destroying the product. You weren't supposed to be there, but you had a tendency to wander. Kasen got you out of the building, but not before you saw the flames and heard your birth mother's screams."

"Birth mother?"

"Some of our experimental programs were as perverse as they were secret. Your birth mother volunteered as a surrogate to the Aristos Project—an unholy attempt to create the best possible human. She carried you and your brother and nursed you until you were three, though Charlotte was designated as 'mother' to you both. When my moral compass awakened, and your birth mother began to protest her subservient status, Charlotte found she had a situation to deal with."

Jude swallowed, and his one functional hand shook. "Your birth mother died, as I was supposed to. The years I spent healing—this is what I was left with." His head dipped, indicating his damaged body. "Kasen had fallen entirely into Charlotte's grip. There was no one left to protect you or your brother anymore."

Jude's story died, and we stood in the wake of it, silence weaving the conclusion for us. Quinn and Hulk were brothers. Bred for Charlotte's intentions, whatever they were. Power, to be sure. I didn't know what to do with it, but that didn't seem nearly as important as whatever Quinn was going to do with it. Jude clearly hoped for something near impossible—that Quinn would prove to be the one who would stop her.

"The kids." Understanding cleared. The house fires. Eliminating oppositional parents while reaping the younger children. "The Party is using memory manipulation on them, aren't they?"

Jude didn't lift his eyes. "It's possible."

"We are doing no such thing." Quinn's heated

voice singed the quiet room. "You're insane. You're both insane." Pain and fury alternated with disbelief several times over on his face. Though the tight muscles of his arms and shoulders caused his hands to shake, it was the darkness of his scowl that was most telling.

Charlotte had woven her lies deep. Even if deep down inside he had an inkling of truth, he wasn't willing to accept it. He wasn't going to believe Jude.

All hope might be lost.

sixteen

Quinn

"They're all crazy."

Slamming the splintering wood door behind me, I muttered to the empty space that was my tiny room. It wasn't possible—any of it. Was it?

Maybe *I* was going crazy, being confined to this cramped space, stuck among the villagers, who all seemed to have lost their grip on reality.

Why would they live like this? All they had to do was cooperate with the Party, and boom. Life would be normal. This subsistence living—and barely that—it was insane. More proof they weren't stable.

Jude. He was clinical. His claims—

What if? How did he know about my

nightmares, about the explosion and the screaming woman? And Hulk... I'd known about Hulk. Had never understood Mother's connection to the sour, burly boy.

An abyss expanded in my being, a sense of something lost that I must find, as if my existence depended on plunging into that gap to discover what lay in the darkness.

Emotions. That was all this was. Jude had expertly tugged on the raw places I wanted smothered. I growled and fisted my hair as I took another turn around the room before I slumped onto the sagging canvas of the cot I'd been given. Maybe I was crazy.

I'd never trusted Mother. Maybe there was, in all this time, a real reason.

She took your heart and ripped it in two.

Mother's voice. Her claims. About Hannah.

Don't let her play you for a fool again.

Why was Mother always in my head?

Breathe in the anger. Feel it as it fuels your strength.

I bowed forward, my fists still rolled in my hair. I pressed my forearms tight against my ears, willing the voice in my head to be still. Squeezing my eyes shut, I focused all of my energy on drowning out the clatter.

The stallion met me behind my shut eyelids. Eyes blazing. Nostrils flaring.

My heart raced, and I rolled back against the bed, curling into a ball like a small boy. The steady throb in my brain became a cruel pounding. Harder. Harder. The color behind my eyelids flashed red and orange and yellow, burning the back of my eyes and stinging all the way to the base of my skull.

Give in to it, son.

Sweat seeped from my body, bleeding moisture onto my shirt. My core trembled, and I awaited what was next. I knew what was coming...

How do I know this?

The high-pitched squeal came hard and fast, penetrating my ears until that was the only sound I could process. The colors flashing before my eyes blurred as they came faster, more vibrant, creating a violent spool of light and darkness.

Stop. Please stop.

I was locked. Trapped. Breathing hurt, my body demanding more air as panic took me hostage. Reality whirled, the piercing colors jabbing my brain and setting off vertigo. Nausea wrenched my stomach.

"Stop!"

I couldn't hold it in. I made it to the edge of the bed before the force of vomit wracked my body and emptied my stomach onto the floor.

The blaze of colors stopped, replaced by images I was familiar with. The material of my secret terror.

"Quinn!" Her voice...the one I couldn't name. "No! Quinn is here!" The woman's panicked scream turned into a cry.

The ground shook, and the sound of thunder beneath my feet rumbled so violently I dropped to the floor.

"Jude! My son! Save my son!"

The roaring gave birth to flames. Heat slathered my skin. In the next moment...

Darkness. It swallowed me.

Darkness. Sheltered me.

Darkness. Terrified me.

Shaking, I lowered my hands and clutched my shoulders, rolling to my back. My eyes refused to open as I desperately gulped in stale air. *Breathe. Just breathe.*

"Quinn." The harsh whisper didn't come from inside my head, and the voice was also not one I was sure about. Different from the nightmare—memory?—and also not my mother's.

"Quinn." A small, cool hand brushed over mine. "Wake up, Quinn. You're sick."

I was sick? Smallpox. I froze, fear slithering through me. Braxton said they'd had smallpox in the village.

"You just threw up."

Something cool and damp grazed over my forehead and then one cheek.

"Could be our water. You're not used to well water yet." Her voice was kind, and she sounded similar to Hannah.

My heart squeezed. Hannah...she said she saw me. Not my mother or the Party. Me, and goodness in me. I'd wanted it to be true. Because that dream...

"There now." Her palm rested against my chest, in the small space between my folded arms. "Your heart rate is coming down. You're okay now."

I unclenched my crossed arms, the rigid muscles in my shoulders screaming a spasm as I tried to relax. It took work to convince my eyes to open, but when I did, I found the girl I'd escorted to the gathering now sitting on the edge of my bed, leaning over me.

Compassion filled her eyes and her soft expression. "A night terror?"

She and Hannah had the same color, shape, and quality in their eyes. I waited for resentment to rise. Almost craved it. But also dreaded it. While the burn lingered somewhere in the background of my consciousness, it didn't flow. Perhaps there wasn't enough strength behind it.

I remained heavy against the pillow and shook my head. "I wasn't asleep. I just got back."

Her nod was the tiniest movement of her head, and a shadow fell over her face. "I've had those too. Is there a name for it, do you think?"

"You've had what too?"

"Moments when the darkness takes me under, replays the worst of my memories. It's paralyzing and awful."

Memories...

What if?

"Tell me what happened," I said, not understanding myself at all. "How did you get sick?"

Eliza sighed but didn't jump into an answer. Instead her weight sagged against the cot, tipping me just enough to jostle the tiny balance I'd been able to grasp. I struggled through the wave of dizziness that followed and was glad that she didn't begin her story for several more breaths.

"I'm not sure what you want to know..."

"Smallpox." I pushed through the bouncing light behind my eyes, past the waves of nausea. "No one is supposed to get smallpox anymore. How—"

"They found a way to put it in aerosol form. Bioweaponry? It's happened, and I guess we were the test run. The first wave hit after a group was shut in what became the Quarantine for reasons we were never told. Once the virus took hold... Well. You know the rest."

I felt my brain sear down the middle, as if it was tearing in two. One side listened to her story and allowed sickened pity to settle heavy within. The other side took the tale and slapped it down hard with a firm dose of cynicism. The divide shifted my center, making me feel loose and unstable.

What if she's right? They're right?

That was what triggered this. I was playing crazy with the lunatics. "It wasn't a memory." I growled out my protest even as something turned inside of me, saying in that hollow abyss, *yes, it was.* Pushing away her hand, I rolled until I could prop up on one elbow. For a moment, I studied Hannah's sister, disguising my scrutiny with a glare. This was the first I'd seen of her without the covering of her hoodie.

Pocked scars mottled her face, the blotches particularly severe near her right eye. Her head was nearly bald. What was with the women in the village and this shaved-head hairstyle?

"I know." Her fingers traced the rises and valleys of her skin, as if reading braille. Then her opposite hand covered her head, and she looked away, to the ground. "Not very pretty."

"You look like your sister."

She bobbed another small nod. "We look like our mother. But beyond that, we are—were—

really nothing alike."

Pain snarled in my chest and squeezed. I pushed it away, searching for the smoldering burn of resentment that lay in wait. "Do you say that as a means of protection?"

Her gaze lifted, searching me again. "From what?"

"Me."

She swallowed. "So it's true. You killed her."

Weakness won again, and I looked away. Where was the fuel of anger? "Yes." I ground out the word, hating the emotion that rattled my voice. "She died because of me."

"By your hands?" Words carefully chosen, spoken on a whisper both harsh and broken.

This isn't who you are...

I closed myself off from the memory of Hannah's words and gripped suspicion. "Why do you hide here?"

She studied me, her expression deep and yet unreadable.

I probed harder. "You chose misery. You have become an enemy of the state. Why?"

The silence that dripped between us cooled the sputtering heat I had tried to ignite. How did this girl disarm me without a word?

Her answer finally came, gentle, and yet solid. "I know who I am."

I searched for meaning in that and came up

with nothing. Her elusiveness flared the fire again.

"Do you? Do you know that you are hunted?"

"By you?"

I clamped my jaw.

"I don't know the whole story, but Braxton tells me that Hannah believed you are good. She died believing that you are more than the Party's pawn." Again, she studied me, her eyes probing for answers I didn't have for myself. "Was she wrong?"

"I am not evil."

"You are lost though."

"Only because your people will not tell me where I am."

She breathed a tiny laugh through her nose, shaking her head. "You don't know who you are. Knowing your location is not going to change that." Rising, she pushed the cool cloth she'd brought with her into my palm. She then turned and took the three steps that brought her to my door.

"Eliza Knight."

She paused, turning her head to look at me over her shoulder.

"You don't know me."

A nod.

"Why do you trust me?"

"I've seen monsters before. You cannot even

imagine."

I waited, a sense of desperation billowing in the space of her pause. "And me? How do you know I'm not one?"

"My sister was a lot of things, and we didn't always see life the same. But she knew good when she saw it. If she was willing to die for the good she saw in you, then I am willing to look beyond your name and seal."

My brain split around that. Again. One side gripped it with hope. The other side took a knife and pierced it dead center. The dichotomy tossed me into a stormy sea of instability.

She slipped through the door, the soft yellow light in the hallway making her silhouette blend into Hannah's form. The need to warn her pushed words past my unwilling lips.

"Do not trust me, Hannah. I can hardly trust myself."

"I'm Eliza. Hannah is dead."

I fisted the blankets beneath me. "Exactly. I'm not your ally, Eliza Knight."

***

Eliza

Tremors coursed through my body as I scuffled back to my own room.

What had come over me? Going to Quinn

Sanger? He'd killed my sister. Why had I gone to pull him out of a black nightmare?

Because you are mine.

The silent impression of words calmed my spirit, and I sank into the comfort. The man next door battled a darkness he didn't comprehend. His spirit warred for freedom, and his mind tore against the reality he'd been told and the truth that demanded to be known.

"What are you doing?" Braxton's scowl matched his harsh whisper, meeting me as I crossed into my room.

I stopped, painfully aware that I hadn't slipped on my hoodie. He held me with a stern glare, his eyes level on mine as he stalked forward, closing the empty space between us.

"Quinn had a—"

"Quinn's a big boy. He can take care of himself."

I eyed him. I was a grown woman. I could take care of myself too.

"He's not safe." Braxton coaxed reason from me.

I arched an eyebrow. "Apparently, that's not his fault."

He balled two fists at his side, clearly putting my implication together.

"You were listening?"

"I was." I lifted my chin. "I've had enough of

the secrets swirling around here. I am well enough to function, and I've survived the camps. I can handle more than you think."

With one tight nod, he acknowledged me. "Fair enough, but I don't want you near him, Liza."

I felt my face twist into a scowl that certainly mirrored his. "You don't get to choose for me, Braxton. I may be ruined on the outside, but my mind still works just fine."

He flinched. The heat in his eyes cooled and then softened as he took in my complete portrait.

Panic fluttered through me as a sense of exposure sank into my gut. I stepped back, tucking my chin near my shoulder as a desperate wish for the shelter of my hoodie throbbed through me.

His fingers brushed my chin, and then his palm cupped my jawline. With gentle but insistent pressure, he turned my face up, back to his. "You are *not* ruined."

My eyes slid closed as I melted under that warm tone and his tender touch. Cool moisture gathered beneath my lids, coating my lashes. "I feel ruined."

His thumb grazed my cheekbone, but the uncertainty between us played out in silence. His hesitancy pricked doubt and rejection against my already raw heart.

"I can't stand you lying to me, Braxton. Don't tell me things you don't feel."

"I feel more than I can say, Liza."

I blinked until the blur of my tears cleared. "Then why?"

"Why what?"

"This gap. You're keeping a space between us, and you think I can't tell. But I know it's there."

There. I saw it again—the pulling away in his expression. The shadow falling over what had once been beautiful between us.

"Eliza...there are things...but..." He stumbled on the words, pushing more distance between us with every pause.

"Then tell me."

Pain twisted his expression, and his gaze fell away. "I can't."

"Was it my sister? Did something happen between—"

"No."

Pulsing silence drove the wedge deeper. He was lying to me. I stepped away, toward the bed I'd spent the past six weeks bound to. His hand turned around my arm and pulled. "Liza, there was nothing between me and Hannah except that I failed to keep her safe." His voice, low and hot near my ear, broke again. "I failed you, Liza. Over and over again. In ways you don't understand, and I can't bring myself to tell you."

I moved back to stand before him. This tall young man who had once been the reckless boy I'd claimed as my best friend. Always, in the quiet corner of my heart, I knew I'd love him. He was my opposite—impulsive and outgoing—and our strengths complemented the other's weaknesses. He would speak when I couldn't find my voice. I would stand when his knees would buckle. Our paths had seemed destined to weave together since we were children.

And I did love him. But here we were, reunited but fraying.

I lifted my gaze to his, one palm sliding against the roughness of his jawline. "You take on too much."

This time he did not shy away from me, but the penetrating look he settled on me was sad, not hopeful. He shook his head. "No. If you knew—"

"Just tell me."

His mouth trembled.

"Please. I'd rather know the truth than have secrets pushing between us."

Tears bulged in the corners of his eyes. Face crumpled, he squeezed his eyes shut.

"Brax—"

"It's my fault." His voice cut hard.

"Hannah did what she wanted."

"Not Hannah." Torture seemed to pulse through him. "You."

"Me?" I exhaled, relieved that really, it wasn't my sister tying up his heart. "Braxton, I understand why you took the seal."

The shake of his head was slow and defeated. "No." Finally he looked back at me. "Remember the day Hulk found you?"

I stared back at him, hating that he asked me to replay that horrible moment.

"Where did Hulk find you?" he asked, though clearly he knew the answer.

"In the woods."

"By the mill?"

"Yes."

"Did you know he was there?"

I allowed the replay of that day to unfold, though I'd worked to push it to the shadows of my mind. Yes. I'd known, but—

"Why didn't you run, Eliza?"

That feeling returned. The terrifying sense of being unable to function, to see, but not really comprehend, and feeling paralyzed. I trembled as that cold sense of helplessness washed over me again. "I couldn't."

"I know. It was my fault."

"You're not making any sense."

"You went back to the mill and you found my backpack, didn't you?"

I nodded. "I remember that you'd left it, and I didn't want them to find it there—they'd be able to trace it back to you, and they'd put you together with Miranda's disappearance."

The muscle in his jaw ticked. "And the water bottle?"

Dread sank through me. "I...I was thirsty..."

His face pinched again, and then his shoulders quaked. "It's called Persuasion."

Though I knew it wasn't, I felt as if the ground beneath me was crumbling, and suddenly I stood precariously at the edge of a cliff. "Why was it in your pack?"

Shame darkened his skin, and I felt him tense even through the space I'd unknowingly put between us.

"I found out what they did—what the camps were, and what happened to some of the girls. I didn't want—"

"You brought it for me?"

Both of his hands pushed into his hair and fisted. He nodded and then curled his head into his chest. "I was going to take you to be sealed."

I was falling. Pushed over the drop by the boy I'd thought I'd loved. My lungs refused to pull in air, and my stomach burned. "How could—"

"I changed my mind as soon as I saw you again. I knew I couldn't do it—that it was like murdering your soul, and I couldn't. But then

Miranda showed up, and everything happened so fast...” He stopped, the words stolen by the gasp of his regret.

I couldn’t move. My look, fastened on him, had to have been pure horror. I couldn’t mask it.

Braxton lifted a trembling hand and traced the constellations of my scarred face. “This is my fault.”

My chest felt hard, and a chill sank through me. I moved away from his touch.

“I’m so sorry, Eliza.”

Truly he was. I could hear it in every breathy syllable he’d choked out.

But I kept falling. He’d been right.

I wished I didn’t know.

seventeen

Braxton

Now she knew.

I tipped my head against the wall, slumping as my weight shifted down toward the floor. Now she knew, and we were all the worse for it.

I wondered if she crawled against her bed and rolled herself into a ball. If there were tears flowing from her eyes. It was easy to picture. And it made my heart ache.

All of this I had done.

Scuffling from across the hall drew my attention away from my misery. I looked up, finding Quinn leaning against the doorframe to his room, his attention stuck on me with questions on his face. “Is she all right?”

I studied him, as if he were a puzzle. Because he was. But he was becoming clearer, easier to understand.

One moment rage would ooze from him, reminding me very much of Garrison, who was apparently his brother. I wondered if he'd met Hulk, had a feeling that he had, even though he'd claimed to never hear of him. How he felt about having such a brother. But another moment I saw the man Hannah described. Intelligent, strong, compassionate. Perhaps because he was bred that way.

The Aristos program. Charlotte's attempt to create the perfect man. Ideal genetic programming, controlled, manufactured, and birthed in a lab. The new way of humankind. The Party's new aristocrats. What would a society like that look like?

Could we selectively breed ourselves a utopia? I wouldn't make the cut.

Clearly the attempt had gone wrong, though Quinn was a success. Perhaps Charlotte had miscalculated. They all had. You couldn't breed for personality. You couldn't predict spirit. This was the failure and the result of Garrison, whose rage defined him so much that before he'd turned fourteen he'd been permanently tagged as Hulk. Rage that I could see blooming in Quinn.

That was terrifying. Two Hulks wielding the power of the Party. God help us all.

"Braxton. Eliza Knight? Is she okay?"

Hannah's version of the man was the one who looked at me now. Intelligent. Compassionate. One who listened, who was not defined by the Party or all that Charlotte had designed him to be.

"That's a complicated question." I flicked a clump of dirt that had fallen to the floor. It hit the wall opposite me and shattered into dust.

"Her scars. Where did they come from?"

I tipped my head to look up at him again. "Smallpox. I told you that."

He dipped his head.

"You didn't believe me."

He shrugged. "I don't know what to think."

"Seek the truth. You'll find it."

Quinn snorted, shifting against the wall and folding his arms. "The camp. I need to see it."

I anchored my feet against the floor and pushed up to stand across from him. "You've seen it. On the video. What Hannah showed you was the truth. It was your mother—"

"I don't want to talk about my mother." Anger gathered in his brow again. "Jude's stories are too crazy for me to just swallow. Don't think because I'm asking you questions that I suddenly believe everything else."

"Fair enough. Eliza got the smallpox from the Reformation Camp. She was exposed intentionally, although I don't know how. Maybe she would be willing to tell you the story."

Quinn scowled at me again. "I need to see the camp. Where is it?"

"About two hours' drive south."

"Can you show me?"

His focused stare felt like a challenge. Like this was a make-or-break moment. But I didn't have what he needed to see. "I can show you the scar of the earth. But that's all."

His frown deepened. "What do you mean, 'the scar of the earth'?"

"When you and Hannah aired that video, Jude had two purposes. One, to reveal the truth to a population who had spent the past two years covering their ears and closing their eyes—and it *was* the truth, Quinn. And two, it was the distraction he needed to break through the camp's electric boundaries to free the captives kept there."

"Boundaries, captives..." Quinn's voice mocked the words. "You act as if we're at war."

I raised my eyebrows.

He shook his head. "The Party didn't start this conflict."

"Tell that to Eliza, or to any of the other camp survivors. They're easy to identify. Just look for the buzzed haircuts and thin bodies."

Belief didn't register on his face, but neither did his contempt remain. "That still doesn't tell me why you can't show me the camp. Give me proof, Braxton, not just more wild stories."

"It took less than twenty-four hours for the Party to figure out what was going on out here. Once they realized the electric fence was down, that survivors were escaping, and more, that people would begin searching for the place you'd shown on the national network, they erased the evidence."

"Erased?" The hesitancy in his voice hinted that he already knew what I meant.

"Bombed. They destroyed what was there. All you'll see now is the charred scar of the earth."

His gaze wavered. He believed...for a moment at least. But then hardness drained it away. "Then at least show me that."

Likely, it wouldn't help. He'd choose to believe what he wanted, and it was easier to believe the web of lies his mother had wrapped him with. But I nodded anyway. "I'll clear it with Jude."

I took two steps down the hall, away from him, when his voice stopped me with one more demand.

"Eliza Knight comes too."

My back stiffened. "Not a chance." The last

thing she needed was more reminders to feed her nightmares. And resentment.

"I'll go." Her voice, though soft, drove in that resolution that had always defined her before everything had gone dark.

I turned my face toward her door, finding her challenge set dead on me. In the tense silence charging between us, she shook her head.

"You don't choose for me," she whispered, the fierceness in her voice giving the words double meaning.

Shame crawled over my skin with a scalding burn. I swallowed against the bulge in my throat and nodded.

She looked away as pain continued to dance between us. "I'll go, Quinn."

His eyes traveled over her, scrutinizing the scars she'd not hidden beneath her hoodie. The expression he masked became hard and unreadable, and when he spoke, the low chill of his voice set off all sorts of warnings in my head.

"I'm still not your ally, Ms. Knight."

She held his look, and for a moment I saw her as I did in years past. Times when she stood up to Hulk. Despite his size and his threat, he'd been no match for her resolve. Neither, apparently, was his brother.

"Neither am I your enemy, Quinn."

***

Eliza

Braxton sat near me in the back of the van. Near. Not as near as he would have a week before. His fists lay rolled near his sides. Closed but available.

I summoned the sensation of his fingers closed over my hand. That was how this two-hour ride would have been spent if it weren't for the fact that I kept my hands clutched together in the protective pouch of my hoodie's kangaroo pocket.

I missed the feel of his calloused palms.

He'd betrayed me though. Well, nearly. I hated that he'd even thought of poisoning me with Persuasion, taking me to the Party officials to have me sealed. He *knew* how I felt about that.

He didn't do it.

But he'd thought it...planned it to the point of near execution. And I went to Reformation Camp because of it.

Sour heat rolled inside my chest. I swallowed, my jaw a little shaky, and blinked.

"You okay?" His low voice seemed like a touch of cotton against that broken wound.

I tilted my head just enough to send my whispered answer to him around the black hood I'd tugged over my head. "Fine."

His fist opened, fingers wiggled. "You don't

have to do this, Liza."

"Quinn wants to know the truth."

"You don't have to go back to the camp. We can tell him what we saw. It would be enough. And even if it isn't, his choices don't rest on you."

But yours fell on me. I didn't say it, but he seemed to sense my resentment anyway. His fist closed again, and he wrapped his arm around his knees, which were drawn up close to his chest.

The hum of the tires against the road beneath us, and Tristan and Skye's conversation up front, filled the prickly space between us.

I was piercing him with the ever-silent throb of my bitterness. His pain brushed against me, begging me to unclench my anger. I wanted to. Didn't like the feel of expanding blackness coating my insides. But...

Sometimes we must force ourselves to yield, because knowing what was right and being able to do it weren't the same. At that moment, I didn't seem to have the strength for it though.

So the sharp jabs of silence remained between us. He respected my hurt, didn't demand that I stitch it up and move on. But the dangling expanse separating his heart from mine was becoming more like a canyon.

Quinn, who had tipped his head back and shut his eyes five minutes into the ride, now dropped his chin and bounced a look from Braxton to me and then back again. "Lover's quarrel?"

That would have been easier.

I tucked my feet closer and wrapped my arms tight around my knees to press them close to my chest. My hoodie sagged over me as I tipped my head against my arms, enclosing me in darkness—away from Quinn's snarky jab and Braxton's tense glare.

"I keep waiting for the compassionate guy Hannah thought was worth risking her life for to show up," Braxton said.

"Seems you're wasting your time."

"Seems so."

Quinn was a completely different version of the man I'd pitied the night before—the pity had been why I'd gone into his room to pull him out of his night terror. Even when he'd warned me that I could not trust him in the clipped tone that he'd used, he hadn't seemed inhuman. This ice cube of a man nearer the front and across from us now—he was Party material. The man I'd witnessed last night...wasn't.

Did he see his own duplicity?

Jude had said the adults they'd treated with memory manipulation had shown signs of split personality. Quinn didn't need to look at the remains of the camp for proof of the Party's black secrets. He'd needed only to check a mirror.

Then again, he got to choose what he would believe. We all did.

The momentum of the van slowed, physics pressing me into Braxton's side. One of his large hands reached over to steady me at my kneecap. I winced and yearned for his touch at once.

He only kept his hand there until the van parked. As soon as the engine cut off, he stood. Waiting, he looked down at me but didn't offer to help me to my feet. His dark gaze swirled hurt and regret, and I couldn't take it right then. Not when I knew the landscape of my nightmares lay just outside the vehicle's doors. Shoulders tucked, Braxton ducked through the small passage of space to the exit and then pushed open the door.

Light blazed into the windowless space, chasing the darkness until it could no longer be found. As the warmth penetrated the material of my hoodie, I let my eyes slide closed and lingered in that moment. The Whisper pressed again.

Embrace the light. Chase the darkness.

Would I? The old Eliza would have embraced the hope. But the seed of black inside of me gripped harder, rooted deeper. Bitterness held on with breathtaking strength.

But the light. The warmth. It encased me. The

invitation remained...

"Can you do this?" The boy at my arm wasn't Braxton, and though his voice was Quinn's, it wasn't the version that had been with us three minutes before.

"I can." I would. I quivered. I swallowed. I straightened. I moved forward.

Into the light and the scene of my nightmares. All in one place. But the scene was not the same.

The blackened earth was startling. The dried grass, though brown and dingy, had at least hinted toward life and hope. Now it was gone. Only charred dirt remained, along with piles of sooty ashes where the barracks and the Quarantine had been.

"Wait here." Tristan spoke to the group, but more to Miranda really.

She frowned at him, but the anxiety in her posture said that she wasn't going to argue. I wondered what the camps had been like when she'd been here. What kind of memories this scalded canvas held for her.

Tristan moved with almost predatory purpose past the mounds of what had once been buildings. Beyond the boundaries of our pathetic existence, the horizon stretched long and clear and empty.

Except for the stack. I'd never seen the actual stack before; it'd always been shrouded with dark-gray smoke as it had billowed angrily into the clear blue sky. But this day, no smoke fisted upward, and the stack looked harmless. Not at all as if it were the final curse of the Purge.

I cast my gaze downward as faces passed through my mind. The prisoners who'd tried to end their misery by running into the powered boundary line. They'd only make it far enough to lay tortured and unable to move. Sometimes the Jackals in the tower must have felt nearly human, because occasionally one of them mercifully fired a shot, ending the agonizing death. The girl who'd been in my railcar when I'd been sent to the camp. In my mind, I called her Hopeless, for that was the quality of her eyes. Wherever she'd been sent before she was finally dragged to the Purge had scraped her soul barren, leaving her vacant expression very much like the blackened prairie that sprawled before me now.

It reflected, precisely, the damage that had been charred into so many souls. The damage I felt smoldering in mine.

I inhaled, the sharp breath pulling in an unfiltered taste of burnt sulfur and dusty ash. The acrid flavor coated my nostrils, tongue, and lungs, making my mouth like dust and my chest like a furnace.

I'd hoped the sight of the camp's destruction

would bring me resolution and loosen the footing of bitterness burrowing deep inside. It brought neither.

Instead, I saw the skeletal ghosts of my fellow prisoners—not literally, but in my mind—scraping with their hands in the blackened dirt, a soft, mournful chorus pressed into the dry, foul air.

Revive us. Deliver us from the darkness. Cover us with compassion. Breathe on us new life. Revive us... Revive us...

Revive me.

The prayer lifted from my heart unexpectedly. I clutched my chest as pain suddenly punctured my heart.

"Eliza!" Braxton's hand came around my waist, catching me as my knees buckled. "That's enough," he said, but not to me. "You're asking too much, Sanger. You want the truth, watch the video. Eliza doesn't need to be here."

Quinn ignored Braxton, stepping in my line of vision. "What do you see?"

Panic pressed down on me.

"I said that's enough!" Braxton's grip around me snugged tighter, and he began to turn me away.

Quinn persisted. "What is the chimney over on the horizon?"

I pushed against the solid chest of the boy

trying to shield me. He quit moving but didn't let me go.

"The Purge."

"Isn't real," Quinn argued.

"Go look and see."

The wind stirred the sooty ground. Nothing else moved.

I looked up at Quinn, his face slowly coming into focus as I regained steadiness. He didn't move, not even to turn back to face the stack he'd questioned.

"Go look," I said again.

His lips paled as he pressed them into a firm line. "What will I find?"

"What do you suppose?"

Trouble brewed in his expression and posture. He scowled as he looked at the scene around us.

"You know the truth, Sanger." Braxton, still behind me, let his fingers loosen into the lightest hold. "You knew before we even came. You knew exactly what I meant when I said that this had been erased, which means that you've seen it done before. You know what your mother is capable—"

Quinn slashed the air with his hand. "Enough!" He jammed the same fist through his hair and gripped until strands stood on end. "I've had enough. No more of this."

In the distance, Tristan made his way back to

us with long, purposeful strides. His face was set hard, his jaw locked as if to keep all emotion in firm control. But his eyes...

Tears sheened those green eyes. The anger radiating from his rigid frame dared anyone to make note of them.

He stepped to Quinn, glared for two breaths, and then held out one flattened palm between them. Quinn hesitated before he plucked the object from Tristan's hand, his movement forced and his expression horrified. They exchanged nothing more, and Tristan marched a straight line back to the van.

Quinn stared at the object Tristan had retrieved, and I squinted to make it out too.

A charred chain. Like a necklace. Holding two small rings. The fulfillment of a vow—*until death do we part*—lay in Quinn Sanger's palm.

How much more proof did he need?

eighteen

Quinn

Fire. Black smoke. Desperate cries. Explosions. Black-scarred earth.

The scenes blended together, and I couldn't separate them. I squeezed my eyes shut, willing the reel of images flashing through my brain to stop. They haunted me in my dreams, and now I had a fresh, poignant landscape to add to them, complete with the curdled smell of explosives, burned grass, and the undertones of death.

Not to mention the wedding set on a chain now pressing heavy in my palm.

"I've seen enough! Let's go," I repeated. The group hadn't moved. Their stares glued on me, each one wore a different expression. Anger.

Sorrow. Bitterness.

Eliza's though... She wore them all, but in the complexity of the emotions playing on her face there was understanding. Maybe sympathy?

I shut it out. All of it. The strength that I had was in the fiery place of anger that I'd stored up toward Hannah, so I retreated there. In the heat of that rage, I could drown confusion and focus on my mission.

Take down the rebellion. Starting with their symbol of resilient hope and strength. Starting with Eliza Knight.

The thought soured, even in the place of my bitterness, and I marched away from the group, striding toward the van. Even still, I could feel that soft, penetrating gaze of hers brushing against my back.

A new picture surfaced in my mind, one I'd loved, one that I had stared at as a boy and a young man. I used to stop in the hallway of our loft, my fingers brushing the frame, as I committed the words to memory.

By our hands others know compassion.

Mother had hung that, one Party slogan among several. But though Mother had been the one to read the words to me when I couldn't read them for myself, the voice I heard speaking wasn't hers. Or mine.

Hannah's. I glanced back to the group. No.

Eliza's.

Her brand of compassion didn't make sense. She sought nothing from me. I'd snarled at her the night before—warning in a deadly tone that I was not her ally. She'd accepted my position without judgment. Even now, as her gaze was still hooked on me, I felt her quiet acceptance.

She'd demand nothing from me in exchange for her empathy. Nothing whatsoever. That was a whole different level of compassion—one I'd never seen from my mother or from the Party.

Why? Where did it come from?

I couldn't help but picture her scarred face and hands. If what she'd claimed had been true, she had every reason to hate me. In fact, even without the camp and smallpox, I'd killed her sister. She should hate me.

She could be our undoing... Hannah? Or Eliza? How...

Enough. Ripping open the side door to the van, I stomped into the cavern and slumped my way onto the floor in the back. I couldn't stand the division of my mind and heart. It was driving me crazy. I was crazy to feel bad for this girl who had apparently incited, or at least approved of, the attack on DC and thousands of innocent citizens there. She couldn't be that compassionate—that saintly—if she'd given consent to that, could she?

"What makes you angry?" The slim girl whom I'd nicknamed as the Little Ninja stalked into the vehicle behind me. No compassion there. She was as sharp as she was muscle toned and ready for battle. "Like you really didn't know what went on out here."

"Stop playing this game, Little Ninja. I'm not buying the lies."

"You're not looking at the truth." Her face puckered into a glare that said both *I hate you* and *You're worse than a fool.*

"Why should I believe a ragtag group of traitors?" I looked at the seal on her neck, putting heat into my stare until she brushed the ink with her fingertips as if my gaze had caused the tatt to burn. "You took the seal. Took the advantages and protection of the Party. Even became a high-ranking member of the Pride. You're the traitor—the liar. Not me. Not the Party. Nothing you say is going to erase that from my mind."

"Yeah, I took the seal. Right alongside my mother. Because we believed in you—in your uncle. You know what happened? Mother was placed as the commander of a Pride on the other side of the country, and I was moved to Glennbrooke. Safety? Prosperity? You ripped my family apart, and we had no choice. Don't think for a minute that after that I bought the whole *we're for your good* charade. And now that we know what your mother has been up to all these years—mind control, genetically modified biowarfare, human genetic engineering, power-lust—it makes all the more sense. When you remove choice and human connection, you control everything."

Her voice changed, dropping lower, slathered with determination. "But not me. She's not going to control me. You—" the Little Ninja stopped, let her look fall over me from head to foot and back again, as if she were taking a measurement, but not of my physical body. "You can choose for yourself. Submit to her, let her take your mind and determine your future. Or stand. We've done what we can."

My face contorted as my head throbbed with a mighty pain. Dividing again. I couldn't look at her anymore. But I couldn't bow to her either. "You are senseless. Even if your passion is impressive, your logic is ridiculous."

"Really?" Sarcasm laced her tone.

"Power-lust?" I shook my head. The split there scored deeper. A high-pitched ringing played in my ears. The beginning of the terror. I stiffened, fighting it away even as I tried to convince her of her foolishness. Or perhaps, convince myself. "Mother was never after power. If she was, why would my uncle have the presidency? That doesn't make any sense at all, does it?"

I sensed the Little Ninja's movement as she dropped to the floor across from me. "Depends on what you view as power." She snorted a laugh. "Public image? Some crave it, and to a degree, your mother claimed that too, didn't she? The most sought-after public stateswoman? The charisma behind the Party's platform? She has that. But..." Her voice dipped low, as if the secret she was about to share would unlock all of my confusion. "Control. That's where the real power lies. If you have that, you really don't need the public's eye, do you? You get what you want, and you don't have to risk public disapproval. She's the force behind it all, and someday Kasen will take the fall. Won't cost her a thing."

The ringing stopped. Though I could feel the others climbing into the van, the jostling of the vehicle as they settled into their places, and the rumble of the engine when Tristan started it, a narrow sense of isolation and stillness overcame me.

Power. Control. Lies.

Mother.

A flash of pain seared through my head again, and then...

Numbness.

"She pulls the strings." Little Ninja's voice

hissed, swirling through the vacuum of my vacant reality. "Kasen is just a slick-bellied puppet. You're just an image she wants to project. But your mother..."

Is the cause.

***

Braxton

Madness looked terrifying. At least it did on Quinn. He was losing it, more and more every day. By the minute, actually.

Crikey. He was dangerous. Couldn't he see the brain damage Charlotte's messed-up power-play mind warping had caused?

Jude was going to hear about this. We couldn't keep the enemy in our camp for much longer. Quinn was ready to explode at any moment, and the way his attention kept finding Eliza kept my protective-guy alarms on constant frantic buzz.

I couldn't understand his fascination with her. Though always beautiful and near perfect in my eyes, Eliza really hadn't commanded much attention from others. Ever. Now scarred and determined to remain hidden under her stupid black hoodie, she was more of a shadow than a girl who would mesmerize an uber-popular, highly sought out, and, let's just be real, ego-inflated guy like Quinn Sanger.

Instinct said it had something to do with Hannah, which made me even edgier.

I sat between Eliza and him on the trip back. Remained the meat in the middle when we got to the Refuge village and they both took a direction toward the hospital house.

One of them needed moved out of that house. I didn't like them sleeping under the same roof. I was lining up an argument for a rearrangement to present to Jude as we approached the dilapidated porch. The creak of the front-door hinges drew my attention away from the dirt-packed trail and my silent argument.

Annyon stepped onto the outdoor floorboards, wearing three defined creases on his forehead. A flashback of my father, in the flesh. "You're back." His frown lined his face even deeper. "Something's happened. We're meeting Jude right now."

My brother spoke in a tone that had typified Dad. The *no-discussion, get-on-it* tone. It rankled me, even now as a twenty-year-old man who wished intensely he could have some do-overs with his parents. The sound shouldn't have irked me, but that Luther concoction of stubbornness and self-assertion still mingled strong in my veins.

"We just got back, and Eliza is—" I stopped, weighing my words.

Father had said I was most like him. He also proved that he had mastered self-control. I still was working on mine, because in the thick of the darkness I'd bound myself to, I'd made a life-altering decision.

Though he'd failed in a lot of ways, my father had been worthy of my respect. I wanted to be like him.

Annyon's steady gaze measured me, and I thought I detected the tiniest nod. "It's important. There's news out of DC, and it's big. You all should hear it—from Jude."

A quick glance at Sanger told me what I'd already guessed. He'd watched Eliza's reaction.

Jerk. Yep. Still very much myself there.

I slid my attention to the girl at my side, my fingers twitching to weave with hers. She'd kept her hands in her hoodie's pocket though. A clear sign.

She couldn't forgive me. The raw spot in my chest sagged painfully. But I couldn't expect much else. For all her goodness, she was human, and I'd really, really screwed up.

Quinn stepped toward her. My back coiled tight. He cast me a sidelong scowl, then motioned a hand before Eliza and me both. "Shall we see what new lies your leader has spun?"

"Been a big day, pretty boy. Maybe you

should stay here." I lifted my eyebrows as I deadpanned my thoughts. "You look like you have a headache."

I nearly jumped when Eliza's arm snaked around mine and tugged. At that point, a feather could have pulled me down the path toward Jude's bunker. Eliza's wish was my command. Now. Forever.

If she told me she never wanted to see me again, I'd turn around and walk away. If she said we should run away, leave the complications of all of this behind and try life out on our own in the big wide somewhere else, I'd find a way.

Let her be. Fight for her. Marry her.

Whatever Eliza wanted from me, I'd do it. And at the moment, it was to leave Sanger to himself.

Annyon set a pace that felt more like a jog than a walk, which was telling. Annyon was a critical thinker, not a knee-jerk reactor. If this news triggered a sense of urgency, then it was big.

Jude waited for us to gather. We created a semicircle around him, the unofficial leaders of the Refuge village, and waited for the voice we'd grown accustomed to and now simply accepted as Jude's rather than a computerized vocal adaptor.

He waited only until the foot shuffling

stopped. "The rebellion has focused its aim."

"I thought we were the rebellion." Skye's heated comment draped a stifling sense of confusion.

"We are the resistance." Jude moved his head until his awkward position allowed him to make eye contact with her. "There's a difference."

Quinn, standing behind Eliza and me, snorted. I started to turn my head, but Eliza gripped my hand and squeezed. I looked for her eyes beneath the cover of her hood. She didn't show them, and her hand slipped from mine in the next breath.

Annyon, in his ever-on-point logic, refocused the meeting. "Tell them what you mean by focused its aim."

Jude drew a breath and moved his chair back to give the majority of us a clear view of the center screen on his monitor bank, and then motioned to Annyon. "Show us where your lab is."

Annyon nodded, stepping forward. With a reverse pinching motion, he focused the image of the Capitol Hill area on a spot past the damaged White House. I knew before he spoke where we were going...

"My research was contained here."

"What research?" Quinn interrupted.

Annyon shifted his gaze and focused it into a

glare. "Don't pretend you don't know."

"I'm not a good actor."

"We all know that's not true," I muttered.

"Humor me with an answer." Quinn volleyed back to Annyon without acknowledging my jab, which was frankly more irritating than if he'd sparred.

"Smallpox." The word lifted from Annyon's lips with a sense of horror and regret. "Genetically modified smallpox, a project commissioned by the Party several years ago."

A chill settled in the room. I felt Eliza shiver by my side, and I risked an arm around her shoulders. She didn't stiffen, so I pulled her into my side.

Quinn responded with a clipped and cavalier voice. "I know nothing of it."

"Well, you're about to know all about it, because the rebellion has targeted the research lab where the virus was kept."

"You kept a lethal virus in a VA hospital?" Quinn mocked with a voice coated in speculation.

"No." Annyon's scowl darkened. "It was kept in the bunker below the hospital." He turned back to the screen and pointed to a black crater blasted into the city landscape. "Here."

Tristan stepped forward, studying the image of smoking rubble. "What does this mean?"

Even the air seemed to pause. We all knew what it meant.

"It's out." Eliza breathed quietly. In the stillness of the room, every ear heard her whispered fear. "Everyone's in danger."

"Yes," Jude confirmed. "There are already confirmed cases."

Skye stepped forward, her fierce glare pinned on the screen. "What goes around..."

We all thought it. Well, I did at least. Play with fire, mess with the lion, all of those clichés.

Annyon cleared his throat, glancing to Jude. "I'm going in, and I need a team."

"In?" I barked. "In where?"

Silence. Because, hey, captain obvious, what were we talking about here?

"DC?" I growled the unspoken answer. "For what?"

"Liza's given me the viral antibodies, but I don't have the equipment here to reproduce it on a large scale. And we have the vaccination. It may be too late for those who've been exposed, but we can at least begin a larger production if I can get it to the lab. But I have to get it there, and I'll need proof that—"

The pieces slid into place. Central to the puzzle was Eliza Knight. His proof that his research finally found success. Ignore that it only cost hundreds of other lives and most of

Eliza's dignity.

Instinct jumped to the front, and I grabbed Eliza's arm, pulling her behind me. "Not a chance. Not one freaking chance on this damaged planet or anywhere else, and you should know better than to ask."

"It's not your choice, little brother."

Though silent behind me, I felt Eliza's stare boring into my back and remembered what she'd seethed at me the other day about her involvement with Quinn.

It wasn't my place to choose for her.

Unwillingly, I relaxed my grip on her arm and stepped to the side, allowing the focus to fall on Eliza.

Not a soul questioned what she would do. Not even me. But there was no way I was going to let her go alone.

nineteen

Eliza

I wanted to slip behind Braxton again. He *would* choose now to decide to *not* be his normal, overbearing, overprotective self.

Jude finally severed the concentrated silence. "Will you go, Eliza?"

I felt as if even the earthen walls had eyes and they were all zeroed in on me. Waiting, their heavy gaze pushing hard on my shoulders. Assuming my choice before I tried to use my thick tongue. Because the old Eliza—the one who didn't have nightly terrors tormenting her dreams, or an unwilling buzz cut to testify to what had only been a few months ago an involuntarily shaved head, or her face so punctured with scars that she felt her only option was to hide it—that girl wouldn't have thought twice.

But I was thinking more than twice. DC? The viper's pit? Hate swirled at the base of my gut, beneath the black spot of bitterness that hadn't yet been removed. Perhaps the unleashing of their mutated and deadly virus was God's retribution.

"Eliza, you must. I need you, to show the department head—"

"Annyon." Jude interrupted Braxton's brother, silencing his argument, and then focused pure compassion on me. "This is not a mandate, Eliza."

My lips quivered. It was a mandate, but not from Annyon or Jude. I knew what was right. But the will of the heart wasn't as easily told.

"I will not rob you of your God-given right to choose." His voice seemed to reach inside me, sweeping past the sour burn of resentment and into that festering blackness. "It is one of His greatest gifts, you know. The gift of choice—it's one of the surest signs of His purest love. And in this, Eliza Knight, you have a choice. No one else will make it for you or take that dignity away from you."

I blinked against the liquid burn in my eyes, hearing Jude's words press against the silent question that had impressed upon me my whole life.

Will you choose me?

I wanted to. Desperately. But this mark on my soul—the scarring was thick and felt impossible to break through.

God, help me.

"I think the rest of you should go," Jude spoke again into my hard silence. "Let Eliza and I talk."

Footfalls shuffled. I didn't watch as the others filed out of the bunker. Braxton's presence remained behind me, though the warmth of his touch didn't brush against any of my skin.

Because he knew I hadn't forgiven him. And he was honoring my choice.

My emotions twisted further, and suddenly anger surged upward, taking the place that had been broken only a moment before.

The heat from his body draped near as he leaned toward my ear, still without contact. "Do you want me here?"

My vocal cords tightened. "No." I regretted the harshness of my answer before I felt him withdraw and walk away.

I was losing everything all over again. Only this time, it wasn't by the Party's hands. I was letting them take it. Letting it all go. Holding instead to an anger and a hate I really didn't want.

The room emptied of all but Jude, who still wore compassion like a beacon of inspiration. I didn't want his inspiration. I wanted the burn of anger. It felt like power, and after months and months of feeling humiliated and powerless, I wanted to feel that strength.

"You're afraid," Jude said.

"Shouldn't I be?"

Silence.

"I'm safe here." It was only part of the reason I didn't want to go. Something in me knew Jude saw that. I turned away and walked toward the door, letting that hot surge wash through my veins.

"You are safe here. And you can stay, if that is what you want. Huddled under the safety of the Umbrella, bound to the Refuge. But you need to understand..." He paused, waiting, I was sure, for me to turn and face him.

I did not. Nor did I really want to hear what was coming.

"You won't push back the darkness with fear, Eliza. Nor will this hate you're carrying bring you healing."

I did not save you so that you would spend your life hiding under a hoodie. Living safely when you were made for so much more.

Jude's unspoken thoughts? Or God's? I didn't look back over my shoulder. I didn't want to face either, though I was sure the words were from both.

"I know you hear me, Eliza." His voice lowered. "And you know I am well acquainted with the fight you are in right now."

I glared at the packed dirt wall in front of me. "How would I know that?"

"I wasn't always bound to this chair, half a man and dependent on a computer to voice my thoughts. I was quite the opposite, in fact, and my future was very promising. I misused my gifts though. And now here we are. Would you do the same?"

Charlotte had taken his brilliance and perverted it. She'd tried to take his existence and erase it. And what did Jude do with what he'd been left with?

He'd saved us. But—

Why hadn't he ever gone after the devil woman? I rolled my fists together and turned to face him.

"How do you know we can't push back the darkness by fighting? By keeping away all that destroyed us? Maybe we shouldn't just be the resistance. Maybe we *should* be part of the rebellion."

"Our reason for doing so would be vengeance." He gazed at me steadily, as if he could see the part of me that already knew the answer and was gently drawing it forward again. "And that's not what I see in God."

My clenched hands trembled, fingernails biting into my palms. **Listen**, the Spirit whispered. I wanted to cover my ears. This would be too hard...

"What do you mean?" My voice cracked, lips quivered.

"God has the power to create and the power to destroy. He has the power to give life and the power to take it away. He, above all, deserves our fear. But He didn't leave us that way, with only fear. He reached us with Jesus, with love. We deserved death but received compassion. That changes everything, does it not?"

I swallowed. I didn't want to forgive Charlotte. Or Hulk. Didn't want to forgive the Party. They took my life, my dignity. My hope and my future, and I didn't want to forgive them. I wanted to destroy them. I didn't want to break their bondage to darkness.

And Braxton...

No. I *wanted* to forgive Braxton. It just wasn't coming.

"Liza. This is your moment—the one where you determine what you will do with what you believe. You have feared God rightly, and because of Christ, you have loved Him faithfully. Now, complete the circle. Go, and love others fearlessly. Even those who do not deserve it."

I fought against the tears, but they rolled anyway. I wasn't that brave. Or good.

"Begin with this, Eliza." Jude said. "It will not be easy, but when you do, the love that was broken will begin to heal. *You* will begin to heal."

The rest he left unspoken, but I knew the remainder of his thoughts. It was my choice. I was the only one who could make it.

***

Quinn

Sweat beaded down my spine and across my forehead. My stomach ached, and the smell of fresh vomit offended my nostrils.

The terrors that plagued me weren't letting up. Instead, they were twisting. In one sitting, I'd see the explosion, hear the woman screaming my name, and then suddenly the context would change and I'd be on the Vacant Plains, dust blowing around me with the cries of suffering strangers swirling through the air. I'd see them lined up like near corpses, skin grotesque with the pox. The putrid smell of death mixing with the flaky ashes that fell from the sky.

And then...Hannah. Always the terrors would go back to her. I'd see her eyes, warm and filled with trust—as she'd looked when I'd taken her to the park the day I'd skipped classes to be with her. Then that warm moment would freeze. Her face would morph into taunting, her eyes cold. She would point at me. "That's Quinn Sanger." Before the sharp black pain would shoot through my skull, I'd watch her turn away, held in Braxton's arms.

The visions should have ended there. I would come to reality, a burn in my body strengthening my resolve.

But they didn't. Not anymore. I would open my eyes against the dark pain throbbing in my head and see her again. That warm expression in her eyes. Blood trickling from her ear, her final breaths used to speak to me.

This is not who you are.

The scenes would reset and then spin through my mind, blending. Confusing me. Making me sick and terrified and angry and sad all at once.

"Who am I?"

My own booming voice woke me. I was on my hands and knees on the floor beside the cot. My heart thundered, head whirled, stomach emptied again. A surge of quakes shook my limbs, and I crumbled to my side on the floor, unable to summon the strength to lift myself back onto the bed.

"Who am I?" I whispered to the night.

The semidarkness did not whisper back. I squeezed my eyes shut, my mind resonating the question again and again.

"My delight and hope." Mother's voice cracked through the silence, sounding more evil than maternal, manipulative than hopeful.

"An experiment." The digital voice was Jude's.

"The enemy." Braxton.

They mingled, those voices and answers. I covered my ears, clenching my head in between my arms.

"Quinn."

My body, already tight, recoiled at the brush of fingers against my shoulder.

Real?

"Fight through it, Quinn."

"I can't."

"Yes, you can."

"I don't know who I am. I don't know what is real."

She didn't respond right away, but her hand squeezed the spot she still touched.

Please be Hannah.

No. Hannah was dead. By my hands.

"You are who you choose to be."

You are good... Don't let them tell you who you are.

That was Hannah. She'd said that. I reached to cover the hand that warmed my arm. Small, like hers.

Hers?

"Hannah?"

No answer. Because she was dead. And my mind was broken—getting more so every day.

Hannah was dead. Because of me. I was too weak to push down the sob that tore through my body. "I killed you. I'm sorry..." I curled tighter. "I'm sorry..."

Her touch remained, though she said nothing. I fought through the dense fog of my damaged brain, forcing my eyes open and rolling to look at her.

Not Hannah. Her sister.

Small and scarred, Eliza kept a steady gaze on me. Tears flowed down her pocked face. For Hannah, for herself. And for me.

I knew because she lifted that hand from my shoulder and in the next breath, her fingertips traced the streams on my face.

My mind quieted. Dreamless sleep claimed me. And when I woke up, I was alone in my room.

The darkness didn't feel as black.

* * *

Braxton

"We have a problem." Tristan spoke from

behind me.

I shoved my only extra pair of pants into the Jackal-issued duffel I'd been packing, glancing over my shoulder at Tristan as he came into our tent.

"That one's old. Give me some new news."

"Okay, try this," Tristan deadpanned. "Quinn's gone."

I froze, my fingers pinched on the duffel's zipper, ready to tug the bag shut. "Gone? Where?"

"And now you're catching up to the problem."

Tristan hadn't moved from the entry flap of our tent, and when I turned to look at him, I found he stood with that crossed-arm, *we're in deep* look that usually triggered dread through me. The adrenaline spike flooding white hot through my veins was something in the neighborhood of terror, and only one thought surfaced in my head.

"Eliza—"

"Is safe. She's still here."

I swallowed, feeling like the banging of my heart was in my throat, not my chest. Knowing the panic that I'd just embraced wasn't helpful, I gripped it tight and locked it in a secure back closet of my mind so I could focus on the real problem.

Quinn gone could mean a whole lot of things.

Most of them would end in disaster for the Refuge village. If he could get out of the Refuge, make it back to DC from the Vacant Plains, that meant he could give us away. It'd take less than a day for the Party to send a bomb to erase us once Quinn made it back to DC.

"How did he leave?"

"One of the vans is missing. Our best guess is that he retraced the road back to the camp and continued south from there."

"Could he make it to the rail station?"

"Yes, with a little bit of luck in his favor. If there's not a flyover. There was enough fuel, and the old highway would get him there, if he stayed on it long enough."

"How long—"

Tristan cut me off. "Don't know. Long enough. Eliza went to check on him this morning, and he was gone."

The unstable, split-minded, angry Quinn—Hulk's long-lost brother—loose in the big wide somewhere and headed back to DC. We were in so much trouble.

twenty

Quinn

Instinct had me traveling south. Well, instinct and a little bit of educated speculation. I had a mental map of the LightRail system, and it only cut through the Vacant Plains in two places. One track was way north, and the lack of snow in early April, even in the shadows near buildings and under trees, pretty much ruled that out for me.

The other vein cut just south of the center of the country. So south it was.

After two hours of road travel in a van that smelled of oil, fossil fuel, and aged plastic, I passed a road that curved west. The scar of the camp lay at the end of that short artery, a huge black carving into the otherwise greening plain. A shudder rippled over my shoulders, and I glanced at the sooty chain and charred rings I'd placed on the dashboard.

Tristan's stoic face, interrupted only by the emotion sheening his eyes, implanted itself in my mind. What more proof did I need?

I wasn't sure. My mind felt scrambled, and my grip on what was real—true—had slipped. But Eliza's haunted face, her scarred body, helter-skelter haircut, all of which she tried desperately to keep hidden under a dark hooded sweatshirt—it all demanded an answer. And I didn't like the one that incessantly whispered in the back of my mind.

Confronting Mother seemed like a futile course. I could hear her answer before the question even formed into words.

Don't be fooled again, son. They are rebels, and I asked you to take them out. Starting with Eliza. Did you do it?

Then what would I say? This mostly crazy plan I hadn't completely figured out wasn't going to solve anything.

But it was all I knew to do.

And the Refuge? What would I do with that knowledge? From what I saw, they were simply trying to piece a life together. Nothing there hinted at the rebellion waging war against the

White House right now. The attacks that had happened while I was there...no one had gone missing during that time. Braxton, Tristan, Little Ninja girl—all key players within their group, and really the only ones with any sort of combat training at all—they were all there when the latest attack had happened.

They weren't a part of it.

Which left the question spinning in my head as I approached the only sign of life I'd seen in the little more than three hours since I'd snuck out of the Refuge. What would I do with Jude's location?

If I gave it away, the people I'd seen in the village would be gone before the day was out. Erased by executive order—an order fed to Uncle Kasen—who I suspected was not actually my uncle at all—by the vindictive and power-lusting commands of my mother.

If I had full command of my mind, I wouldn't feel so uneasy about any of that. But I didn't. And deep in my gut, I knew who did.

Still. I needed answers. I'd literally go crazy without the truth. And the people who held those answers also held my life in their hands.

Maybe not just mine.

***

Eliza

"Eliza, this changes things..." Braxton's expression was torture as he shoved his hand through his thick hair, reminding me of the way his father would pace when he was working in his office. Deep thinkers, both of them.

I wondered if Braxton had realized how much he really was like his father. And if he did, if it bothered him.

"Quinn is out there, and I know I can't make your decisions for you, but—" He stopped moving, dropped his hand from his head, and set a pleading look on me.

The hard spot in my heart wobbled a little, letting a tender warmth sprout in between the cold cracks. I felt so much for him, and not all of it was anger. The collision of emotions hurt, and I pushed them away so that I could think.

Quinn was gone. I'd found his room empty, and Tristan had discovered a van missing. Wasn't hard to put together. He was heading back to DC, and when he got there, we'd be fish in a barrel.

"The smallpox will spread quickly," I said quietly, almost more to myself than to Braxton. Because, really, I needed to convince the darker version of who I'd become to do what I already knew was right. Fear had long since become a close companion. But I hadn't buckled under it. Not when Hulk had shoved me onto a railcar, nor when I'd entered life at the Reformation Camp.

My knees felt wobbly though. Nearly ready to buckle.

Braxton stepped closer, hand held out. And then stopped short, letting that hand fall. "Liza..."

I swallowed, looking away. "Quinn knew we were planning to go to DC, and he snuck away to leave ahead of us. That doesn't add up." Safely in the realm of logic rather than emotion again, I looked back to him. "If he wanted to expose us when we got there, it would have been easier and more cunning to go with us. He could have betrayed us with less effort by slipping in with the group and waiting until we all got there. And doing that wouldn't have set the whole village on alarm. If he was going to give us away, it just doesn't make sense for him to do it like this."

"But if he wasn't going to turn us in, then why did he leave at all?"

Braxton had a good point.

"What if he wanted to get ahead of us—make it to DC before we even left the Refuge—and give away our location?" he continued. "They'd eliminate us without much more than a lift of a finger and a push of a button once they knew where we were hiding."

True... "But if he'd wanted to do that, he should have figured out a way to leave earlier, because even with the speed of the LightRail, it'll take him a full day to reach DC, which gives us enough warning to evacuate. And he knows we have the chopper. It's possible that we can still beat him there."

Braxton listened, nodding. A new addition to his personality, this employing the listening skill before he laid out an argument—one that made him resemble his dad even more. Probably Braxton didn't realize that, because it wasn't something that his dad used much with him.

Those memories still sagged against my core, and I felt the pain for him. Did those moments from the past still blister his heart?

Not a matter for this conversation. I refocused, again, on the Quinn issue.

"He's up to something, but I don't think he's planning to give us away. Especially now that he knows the smallpox claim is real and it's out there. Annyon has the only viable vaccination and, maybe more importantly, the only antibodies taken from my blood platelets that would help the sick to survive."

Still listening, Braxton's mouth flattened into a tight line. "You're right, but Quinn's not thinking straight. We don't know what he's doing, because he's irrational. They've messed with his memories too much, and he can't find his way out. We can't trust him."

He held me with a look that said so many things. That he was sorry. And *please, don't do this*...but he would respect what I decided, even if it might kill him. When I didn't turn away or tug my hood farther over my face to hide deeper in the shadow it cast, he moved closer. Enough to take a gentle hold on my arm.

"You've always been better at this than me," he whispered.

I did look away then, focusing on the floor because I was folding under the bulk of his emotion.

"So I'm asking you," he continued, "and I'm listening, really. What should we do?"

My eyes closed as a dull ache pulsed in my head. He'd never been like this—so humble. Trusting me to do the right thing. It thrilled me and killed me at the same time. He didn't understand how weak I really was—always had been. That so many times I wanted to hide rather than stand. He'd always been there, had my back, and I'd stolen that strength and claimed it for my own. He didn't know how much I'd leaned on him—every bit as much as he was leaning on me now.

But I wasn't the girl he remembered. And that was partly his fault. I stepped away, and his fingers drifted back to his side.

"Liza..."

I shook my head. He didn't finish. We couldn't do this now. Not when everything was closing in.

Drawing a breath, I focused on the problem of Quinn. Oddly, it seemed easier to deal with than the problem of us—of Braxton and me.

"We're their only hope for survival right now. Quinn wouldn't take us out."

Distance fell over Braxton's face, though his eyes still beckoned with depth. He nodded as he stepped back. "Okay. We'll go."

He turned away and strode through the door, leaving me alone in my room. With the fear.

The thing was, Quinn's mind was ripping, and he wasn't stable. Braxton was right—we couldn't trust him. And that was what had my knees wavering. His unpredictability meant anything could happen.

Anything could be permanent. Which meant that everything unsaid and unresolved between Braxton and me could stay that way. Forever. Not what I wanted, but I couldn't find the courage or strength to change it.

I really wasn't the perfect girl he had in his head. Truthfully, I never was.

***

Braxton

Annyon sat next to me on the chopper, his hand covering the mic to our group com so whatever he was about to say stayed between us. "You surprise me, little brother."

"Good to know. What have I done this time?"

"You didn't stop this."

He nodded toward Eliza, sitting toward the back and opposite us. Opposite me. Keeping the distance she'd reinserted between us when I went to talk to her this morning.

"You said you needed her."

"I do. But I thought—"

"Eliza's always been better at using good judgment than me. Her body might bear the marks of damage, but her heart and mind both work just fine. She's more than able to make her own choices." I snapped the last part, resenting that my brother would meddle in the mess between Eliza and me. He had to know I didn't like her going to DC. Also had to see that things between Liza and me weren't exactly peachy.

I didn't need this.

Annyon studied me with that professor-ish *I will figure you out* quality that he'd apparently mimicked from our dad and perfected as a fellow at the hospital. The same one that had made me furious when Dad had employed it on me. It still lit an angry fire in me.

"Save your scrutiny for the virus," I mumbled,

trying only slightly to smother the heat.

"It's going to be fine, Brax. You'll see. I'm pretty respected in my field, and when—"

I cocked an eyebrow. Apparently, he didn't get the *shut up* code. "Look. We're going, aren't we?" I glared at him. "You still don't know half of anything when it comes to what really happened to the Uncloaked, and you know zilch about Eliza and me. Clearly you haven't been paying attention to anything beyond your lab—even in the village. You're completely ignorant if you think that the medical research center is going to whip out the streamers and confetti to celebrate your return."

"The academic world will not be as closed."

"Really? So they're going to see you have a big brain and rejoice in their good fortune. Is that how you see this playing out?"

"I'm just saying I have a position there..."

"Yeah, so does Quinn. Look how well he's turned out."

"Look. Try to take this as an opportunity."

"What?" My harsh whisper had a dark quality to it. My brother was acting like the real mad scientist.

"We can go in on something of a mercy mission, and the Party can see that we're not a threat."

I stared at him for three full beats and then

snorted a disgusted laugh. "Annyon, are you serious? We're going to go in there with a vaccine and save their sick people from dying of the death virus you helped them make, and then we're all going to what? Gather around a fire and sing unity songs?"

He blinked. Twice.

Crikey. He was serious.

I shook my head. "How is it possible that you still don't get this?"

"I get diplomacy."

"There's *no* diplomacy in the Party. It's comply or die. Why do you think they had the Reformation Camp? Why do you think Quinn's brain is as broken as Humpty Dumpty? Why do you think Jude created the Umbrella so that we could hide a Refuge village under it?"

"But the academic world—"

"Is under Charlotte's control." I growled at him. "Everything is under Charlotte's control. Including her son. And quite possibly the president. You're going to have to see things for what they are, or you're going to get us all killed."

Annyon scowled at me and then sat back against his seat, focusing his glare on the metal body of the chopper.

Great. The Quinn problem gained an exponent. Annyon had just become a possible liability too. One who was leading this whole insane mission.

twenty-one

Quinn

"I gave you a specific task." Mother's mouth thinned, her eyes burning. "How can I trust you to lead when you cannot effectively follow?"

"I had no bearings. Nothing to give me any clue where I was. The Vacant Plains have been called such for a reason."

Her eyebrows quirked as her stare hardened. "You are a brilliant young man, Quinn. That is a subpar excuse."

"I was shot, Mother."

"Another foolish move of your own doing. You have had the training necessary to avoid those kinds of problems."

"So what did you want me to be when I grew

up? A politician or a soldier?"

"You need to be both to become what you are destined to be."

Her riddles were infuriating, and they summoned Jude's claims to the front of my mind, giving that story leverage. If I was genetically engineered...

"I was unarmed, Mother. And outnumbered. The next time you're in that situation, we'll see how you do. Until then—"

"It's not an accident that I've never been in that situation, Quinn. Which is exactly the point. Stop acting stupid."

My lips met as my jaw hardened. Mother continued to glare.

"We need that location," she said, her voice quieter, more controlled, and yet no less demanding.

"I can't help you."

"It's in that complex brain of yours somewhere. Figure it out." She moved as if to leave but stopped short at the door. Over her shoulder she tossed one more question at me as if it were an afterthought. "Hannah's sister...did you find her?"

I pressed my tongue against the roof of my mouth and refused to turn to meet her question with respect, as I had always been taught.

"That compassion of yours, Quinn." Mother's

voice changed, softened. Became...believable. "They're pulling it like the strings of a marionette."

Remaining silent became more difficult.

"The attacks on the hospital?" she continued, her footfalls soft and whispering nearer and nearer. "They came with a message. Did you hear about that?" She chuckled softly. "No, of course not. Whoever was feeding you whatever they were telling wouldn't have given you that."

With a slow turn of my head, my gaze fell on her. She looked at me with pity.

"We received a transmission right before the bomb hit. *An eye for an eye.*" The pause she laid down was full of intention. Allowing me to connect the dots. Understand.

That wasn't Jude's way. Was it? Eliza? Would she sanction an attack that would result in the release of the deadliest bioweapon known in history?

"Did we release it on them?" I asked.

"The virus? No. We were studying it because of foreign threats. Do they have it?"

"Some were sick."

"Ah. And so the message makes sense, doesn't it?"

"Why do they think the Party released the virus on them first?"

"Anger and reason do not work well together,

son."

My heart throbbed in the space of silence. *An eye for an eye...*

Jude was clever, there was no question of that. Would he attack a place he knew was housing bioweapons, just so he could send in his team of rebel saviors?

The moments right before the butt of a gun had met my head zipped through my mind again...

Hannah, selling me out after she'd used me to tear apart this country.

Yes. They were clever enough. Conniving. And I'd nearly been taken again.

"Quinn, my hope and delight, do you know where they are?"

I stared at a spot on the floor across the room while heat swirled through my mind. "Somewhere north of the southern LightRail. North of a town that has been erased."

Her hand slid against my arm, the gentle touch encouraging as her fingers squeezed. "And Eliza Knight?"

"She's with them." I turned and met her expectant gaze. "And they're on their way here."

The corners of Mother's mouth tipped up the slightest bit, and she nodded. "Thank you, son." She moved to walk away, but I caught her arm before she left.

“Why is Eliza important?”

Mother glanced to her left hand, flicking her nails as if dirt had dared to settle there. “She will never bend to our ways. Her family, their connection to the stubborn Pastor Luther and his son. Her stubbornness is dangerous, and we can’t allow her to continue to influence the rebellion.”

“Did you know about her before? Did you know Hannah—”

“I figured Hannah’s connection to her shortly after you brought Hannah home. But they weren’t the same, those sisters. The fact that Hannah wanted the seal was proof enough of that.”

“But Eliza? How do you know—”

“Eliza has been on our watch list for much longer than our social reform. That is all you need to know.” Mother moved her hand to squeeze mine and then floated toward the door again. The whoosh of the automatic exit sounded, and she took two steps beyond our bunker and then stopped, turning back to me.

“I’m proud of you, son.” She smiled. It looked...mechanical. “I know you won’t let us down.”

She disappeared, and the door slid shut. I reached into my pocket and fingered the chain and ring set lying at the bottom. The small round metal seemed hot. Burning hot.

She could be our undoing...

A bolt of pain knifed through my head, and blinding white covered my eyes. The terror was coming again...

The explosion, the blaze, Hannah's glassy, dead expression. Then Eliza's pocked face and arms. They all blended through my dizzying nightmare, making me ache as if I felt the scorch of pox on my skin, the infection on my face. The death blow to my head.

But then the swirl of faces and scenes melted into one. A horse, big and black, strong and wild. He circled me, his nostrils flaring and something like glowing embers in his eyes. He watched as he loped around me, his hooves pounding a maddening rhythm punctuated by throaty snorts. When he finally stopped, he faced me dead on, and his head bobbed to the ground as if to point. I looked at the spot near my feet. A bridle lay there, gleaming metal that seemed too small for such a great beast, and appeared oddly sharp where the metal should have been round and blunt. The stallion snorted again, his red eyes burning into my chest.

I stood frozen, not understanding. He let a chilling scream rent the air between us and then lowered his head. Within two seconds his long, powerful strides began eating the ground in between us.

He charged me. I couldn't move. The thunder of his hooves shook the ground. Still, I was stuck. Closer, closer, closer...

When I found consciousness again, I was on the floor, a putrid mess near my head, my clothes soaked with sweat. A sense of darkness pressed my trembling body into the ground.

I wished Eliza was there. When she had sat with me, I wasn't afraid of the dark.

* * *

Eliza

Braxton had been to DC before, but I hadn't. I'd seen pictures though. The National Mall, the White House, the Smithsonian, and the cherry blossoms.

We missed cherry blossom season. And everything else lovely about DC.

Capitol Hill had become a war zone. Blackened rubble of historic monuments lay scattered over punctured earth. Their split corpses stood jagged and ruined against the bright-green grass, set off with an ironic glow from the rising eastern sun. The slow death of a legacy spotlighted by the continuation of time, as if the sunrise didn't care...

Our party moved in heavy silence, weaving

through what remained of concrete sidewalks, stepping over heaved landscapes and smashed statues, each of us likely wondering if these pocked scars would remain the new vision of our country. Our future.

Once there had been beauty here. I wondered if God felt this deep current of sorrow at the end of Eden. Maybe He felt it now, about this smoldering destruction. And about my heart.

Head tucked safely in my hoodie, I blinked against the tears. Left to our own, it seemed mankind would rip itself apart. What could stop the rage?

I didn't have an answer. I couldn't even dam the resentment in my own heart.

"When we get to the hospital, there's bound to be resistance," Annyon said, although this we already knew. "Let me speak." He looked at Braxton, his long hold on his brother's face a silent command.

Braxton cocked an eyebrow. "I'm not saying a word. Hope this plays the way you think it should."

"Trust me."

Yeah, Braxton didn't. Trust was high priced or hard won, and Annyon had neither paid out nor earned it. He still thought the camp was a misunderstanding. A communication snafu. Or maybe he just thought his intellectual world was separate from all of the ugly. The elitists who could not possibly be held responsible because they were too busy massaging their big brains to be evil.

I knew why Annyon had made his mother cry. Like Braxton, Annyon had tried to reason around reality, because reality didn't stand within reason.

We followed Annyon past the rubble that had once been the glory of our nation, through streets populated with downcast faces, fearful-paced footsteps, and suspicious glances. Our little group was a misfit in the shuffling crowd. Purposeful strides moving toward the epicenter of the viral exposure. We stuck out like a red blot on a grayscale image.

Yet we were not stopped.

There was an air of mystery that thickened as we drew nearer the hospital, and it took a moment for me to realize the source of it. We were the mystery. And the people were desperate enough to let the mystery move freely among them.

Fear had buckled them, creating a vacuum for hope.

But that was on the street, not in the trenches, and our destination held a different kind of people entirely.

A man with an automatic weapon waiting

across his palms stepped in front of Annyon as we came to the prison-fenced perimeter of the hospital. “This area is closed,” he barked, his eyes dull, expression neutral.

“We are aware of that,” Annyon said. “But my team has vital information. You need to let us pass.”

“Closed,” the man repeated, staring past Annyon at nothing in particular.

“I’m Annyon Luther.” Annyon swayed his head so that his face intercepted the man’s emotionless stare. “Lead researcher for the virology department. I have information that is pertinent to the new outbreak of smallpox. Let us pass.”

“Never heard of you.”

Irritation lined Annyon’s face. “I’ve never heard of you either.”

“Doesn’t matter. I speak on the authority of President Asend. I have my orders, and you’ve got nothing. I suggest you stand down.”

Skye and Tristan stepped forward, flanking Annyon, who checked left and then right, his stance becoming iron. “I’ve got this under—”

“Science boy says let us through,” Tristan rumbled, his bulk pressing against his Jackals uniform. “So let us through.”

The soldier settled an empty glare on Tristan but said nothing.

Skye inhaled, and in less than a heartbeat of time, she struck at the guard with a solid side kick, landing a cracking blow at his knee. His leg buckled, but his torso turned, bringing the nose of his gun around to her. Tristan's coiled muscles snapped as he reached for the weapon. Both large hands gripped the stock and muzzle, and in a fluid move that looked well practiced, his elbow landed a hard clap against the other man's face, sending him stumbling backward toward the wire fence.

In less than sixty seconds, Tristan and Skye had gained control of his weapon and of the situation.

Braxton filled the space by Tristan's side, his arms folded over his chest. "These impressive combat skills have been brought to you courtesy of the Party's special program for abandoned youth. And we are all the better for it."

Clearly sarcasm hadn't been completely driven out of his personality. A smile nearly slipped past my irritation with him.

Sprawled on one hip, heat simmering in his glare, the guard pressed two fingers near his ear. "Breach at Capitol Hill gate. Repeat, breach—"

Tristan settled aim on the man, and Skye leaned over him, her fingers pinched on a coin. "No one's listening, Party boy." She stepped over him while Tristan kept his aim trained, and

Braxton held him still with a knee in his chest. Skye inserted a needle through the soldier's uniform, into his thick shoulder, and pressed the plunger until the clear fluid in the vial drained. "Don't bother getting up. We can find our way from here."

In a fluid move, Braxton rocked back to his feet and stood. Tristan waited, holding his fire-ready stance while we filed through the gate. My heart hammered, my thoughts spinning with dizzying fear.

"What did you just do?" Annyon barked a low whisper to Skye.

"He'll be fine. Useless for a few hours, but fine."

Braxton picked up his pace to match Annyon's. "Persuasion. Modified to go IM."

Jude. Not the declawed kitten we thought he was. This was his fighting back...not to kill, but to neutralize.

"I told you to let me handle it," Annyon said.

Skye tipped a glare at him, stopped abruptly, causing him to nearly fall over her, and swept her hand toward the door of the hospital. "By all means, oh great one. Show us where you keep the blanket of death."

His face colored with heat, and his eyes smoldered, but he said nothing. Instead, he strode to the door, pressed the red button on the security box, and said in a monotone voice, "Annyon Luther, research department."

The light on the box blinked. Red. Red. Red.

Green.

Braxton clapped his shoulder with one hand. "Our lucky day. Guess they still like you, brother."

Annyon's mouth stayed pressed into a hard line.

Not one of us spoke as Annyon nearly stomped his way down the desolate hall, bringing us closer to the damaged part of the hospital. Yellow caution tape flashed at the end of the corridor, and I wondered if we'd traveled into the viper's pit for nothing. He stopped twenty feet from the blockade, which was backdropped by the fragments of the collapsed wing of the building, turned left, and did his voice-recognition security-code thing again.

The door opened, and we entered a room divided by tempered glass floor to ceiling.

Braxton looked the space over, folded his arms, and said, "We meet again, oh lab of the cruelly warped."

"Shut up." Annyon brushed past him, moving toward the desk in the corner on our side of the glass division.

"Just stating the truth."

"We had our reasons for the research."

"I hope yours weren't the same as Charlotte's."

Skye stepped between them. "As much as I'd love to see this brotherly match go down"—she looked to Braxton, her mouth tilted in a smirk—"my money would be on you, li'l Luther. We have the tiny issue of a growing epidemic out there, not to mention the distinct possibility of military pressure being dispatched our way at any moment. So..." She motioned to the lab.

Though his sour glare didn't change, Annyon nodded. "I need to make a call. My lab isn't set up for..."

He'd retrieved the All-In-One that he'd apparently left on his desk the day Braxton had come for him, and he sent out a call before he finished his thought.

Tristan stood post at the door, and Skye squeezed past him, mumbling something about watching the hall. Braxton took a place between the door and me. I felt his gaze on me and was tempted to turn to him, to look for traces of the boy he'd been. But then he'd study me back, looking for evidence of the girl I once was.

I ached for him to find it. Was terrified he wouldn't. The labyrinth of all that was lost seemed to grow thicker. Finding my way out seemed more impossible than it had before we'd left the Refuge.

"Dr. Hilton needs to see you."

I started, pulling my chin up toward Annyon, who had apparently finished his phone call.

Braxton was at my back. "Who is Dr. Hilton?"

"The department head. I told you—"

"What will he want with Liza?"

"Only to see if what I'm saying is so." Annyon strode toward the door. "After that, I'll have full access to the production lab. Your presence won't be necessary anymore."

Show my scars, and that was it? Was this really going to be that easy?

"Do I have your word, Annyon?"

Braxton's thoughts must have been traveling the same direction.

I put a hand to his arm, telling him without words to stop speaking for me. "I'm ready," I said to Annyon.

I thought I caught a flicker of Braxton's mouth. Almost like he was going to...grin. Like he'd found what he'd been watching for.

***

Braxton

I heard it in her voice.

The nameless strength that made her short declarations say so much more than her few words. Jude had been right. She was saved for a purpose. She'd survived for a reason. I had a feeling our world was going to change, and the girl who would bring it about was hiding under a hoodie.

I really hated that horrible sweatshirt.

She would lose it soon enough. Eliza was coming back from the dead. Life was warming her words and the tiny glimpses of a smile she'd let slip. Warming her heart. And when she was restored, she would stop hiding. She would see her scars as marks of victory. They would become beacons of light and hope rather than reminders of pain and shame.

She would see herself the way I did. Maybe then she could forgive me...

My thoughts danced around that hope as we marched through the eerily vacant halls, Annyon leading us, drifting on the confident swagger that came with his ridiculously high level of education. Eliza scampered behind him, looking like a hooded hobbit creeping toward her mission. The trio of redeemed sellouts followed on a sharp edge of caution.

"What do you know about this Dr. Hilton?" Skye asked, her whisper intended to stay between the three of us in the back.

"You know as much as I do. Head of the department. Need his approval before Annyon can work in whatever lab he needs to work in."

"Your brother is rather...ignorant for such a

smart guy," Skye said.

A thread of irritation wove through my head. Annyon and I weren't exactly buddies, but he was my brother. "What does that mean?"

"He really thinks he can reason his way through all of this." Skye hiked an eyebrow, and I knew she was thinking about the scene at the gate outside. "Like he's some kind of snake charmer and the sultry sound of his voice is going to lure everyone into his way of thinking."

"Clearly that hasn't worked on you."

Skye's sassy smirk poked against one cheek. "I'm not mushy minded, and neither is anyone else who is willing to aim an automatic rifle at his gut."

"Noted." I dipped my chin but didn't suppress the wicked grin tugging on my mouth.

"What does that face mean?" Skye hissed.

I chuckled. "Maybe his charming ways *have* worked on you..."

She rolled her eyes. "Idiot."

Another laugh moved my chest. "Come on, Skye—"

Her hand smacked hard against my jacket, shushing me as she stopped and tilted her head to listen down the hall we'd just left.

I heard it too. Feet. Several of them. Marching. Growing louder. Moving quickly.

"Guess the guard at the gate wasn't as useless

as you thought," I whispered down to Skye.

She ignored me, and Tristan clicked his weapon into fire-ready mode.

Skye issued orders like it was as natural as breathing. "Annyon, get Eliza to the doctor."

"But—" Liza's soft argument died before she had it out.

"Go." Skye snapped. "Now."

"It's okay, Liza," my brother said, taking her hand. "We're almost there, and I can lock down the hall once we get there. If the Mortal Kombat trio there can keep them back long enough, they can book it to the hall, and we'll all be safe."

Clever. Must be a Luther thing.

"Go." I fired a glare at Annyon before settling one quick glance on Eliza. If only I could see her face... "We're right behind you."

Her head bobbed, and she broke into a run. We turned to shuffle backward, trailing them as we watched for the oncoming attack. Annyon moved faster than I thought he would, given his nerd status. Then again, he'd been an athlete. Back in the long-gone day.

Liza was the one I was more worried about, but she blazed along beside him, moving with enough momentum that when he said to turn right, she skidded, reaching for the wall to steady herself before she could make the corner.

"They're clear," I shouted, standing in

between where Annyon and Eliza had turned and the end of the hallway where Tristan and Skye held in a combat-ready stance.

Both pulled back, breaking into a sprint toward me. The hollow pounding of boots against the hard white floors rumbled so close it seemed the soles of my feet could feel the enemy coming.

"Come on...come on...come on..." I muttered, as if it would help.

Skye bolted toward me. Tristan's long strides nearly kept pace with her, but he spun around to face the other way just before he reached me and the turn that would take us into the hall Annyon could lock down. His weapon tracked the vibrations coming toward us as he yelled, "Go! I've got this."

Still in motion, Skye grabbed my arm, nearly dragging me to the safe zone. I ran without looking where I was going because I was focused on Tristan.

"Run, Tristan! Just run!"

He didn't turn toward me. "Once you're safe."

I tried to fight against Skye's momentum taking me around the corner. There was no reason for Tristan to wait. No reason for him to stay behind...

"We need you safe, Luther. Let Tristan do what he knows he needs to do."

"You don't need me!" I wrestled away, nearly free.

Her grip dug hard, and I found out why no one in the Pride had ever won a challenge against Skye's authority. Even with my bulk and her diminutive size, she ripped me back into the safety of the locked-down hall and pushed me against the wall.

"He's clear!" she shouted over her shoulder.

The echo of a rifle drowned out her call. I cringed, my body coiled, and I squeezed my eyes shut.

"Tristan?" Skye called.

Shouting answered, an array of voices, angry and threatening, and none of them Tristan's.

My heart slowed, its harsh squeeze dizzying and painful. "Tristan!"

Skye's hand shook as she pulled it from my elbow, and I detected a hint of a wobble in her voice when she yelled toward the opposite end, where Annyon and Eliza hid. "Lock it down."

As if electricity had zapped my backside, I launched back to my feet. "No!"

"Do it!"

I made a move for the entrance where Tristan should have been. A hand gripped my jacket and ripped me backward. Another round of gunfire echoed in the next corridor.

A buzzer rang like a death toll. The hazard

lights fastened to the ceiling rolled yellow, orange, yellow, orange. Two steel doors peeled away from the brick walls, folding together. Closing us in. Shutting Tristan out.

God...

"Tell Luther he's not the only one who can hit what he's aiming for."

That voice...the tone dark. The words laced with anger.

A dark face flashed in the narrowing gap of the doors, pain etched in the folds of his drawn brows. Tristan glanced at me, then looked back down the hall, fired a shot at whoever it was coming for us, and then dove in between the doors.

One. Two. Three.

The steel trap clanked shut. The lock clicked secure. Tristan slid across the floor, blood soaking through his jacket at his waist.

Skye scrambled toward him. "You're shot," she said, the nearest to panic I'd ever heard her voice.

"Just grazed." He pulled back the open flap of his jacket and lifted the T-shirt hem to show the wound that had split the toned brown skin of his abdomen.

Skye fingered the spot just above the gash, making his muscles suck inward and his breath catch. After a low, contained groan, he pulled in another controlled breath and looked at me. "Did you hear what he said?"

"That he hit you? Yeah."

"No..." Tristan glanced back to the locked doors.

I followed his line of sight. A familiar face, one packed with rage, filled the small square of tempered glass encased in the door. He looked like his brother, feral and soaked with hate. Just like he had when he'd killed Hannah.

"Maybe he meant—" Tristan said.

"No." I cut him off. "He didn't. He just missed the kill shot and is too arrogant to know it."

I glared back at the boy whose mind didn't belong to himself. His glassy eyes stared back at me.

Quinn Sanger had sold us out. Again.

twenty-two

Braxton

"This is good news, but it might be too late." Dr. Hilton's study didn't leave Eliza's exposed face.

I read her posture. It said she was done with the display.

"Too late?" she asked.

"The outbreak has already breached the containment perimeter we'd set. There's another epicenter, though we're not sure how the virus moved so quickly and so far away."

"Where?" Annyon said.

"Glennbrooke, Indiana. There are whispers that Kasen has contacts there, but the White House is staying pretty tight lipped about it."

Home. Seemed strange that after everything horrible that had happened there, I still thought of it as home.

Eliza's eyes found mine, and we both calculated how the virus had moved.

A strained pause filled the lab.

"How bad is it?" Tristan asked.

Dr. Hilton swallowed, shaking his head. "Glennbrooke is on lockdown. No one is allowed out. The LightRail only stops to drop off medical supplies. Hospital is a quarantine zone, but the last I heard, black dots have been appearing in resident windows too. It's spreading faster than we had hypothesized, and nothing is stopping it."

"We can stop it," Eliza whispered.

There she was again. My heart lurched at the brief glimpse, filling with anxiety and pride all at once.

She looked at me, her face still exposed, so I could read the uncertainty in her eyes. I held her gaze as I held my breath. Her bottom lip slid beneath her teeth, a subtle show of her insecurity. I nodded, the best I could do to answer what I thought was a plea for strength.

Her chin edged up, and her expression frosted, as if I'd just offended her. As if she'd resented me offering her support, even though I was sure she'd silently begged for it.

"We can go." She reached for the hood that hung down her back. "You can get us through with a medical aide pass, so they'll let us off at the Glennbrooke station, and we can take whatever antibodies you can manufacture in the next twenty-four hours."

"You're wanted," Annyon argued, apparently finally convinced by the recent gunfire that this wasn't a peaceful ambassadorial mission.

Diplomacy was dead. Our lives were truly on the line.

"We slipped into DC." Skye stepped beside Eliza. "We can slip out." She paused, turning to study the girl beside her. "If you're sure. They don't deserve—"

"I'm sure." Eliza's answer seemed both wispy and bold. As if she was clutching her conviction even as her fear and resentment were tugging her away from it.

She was choosing to chase the darkness.

Dr. Hilton nodded. "I don't know if I have any leverage left with the system—perhaps they don't know that I'm locked in here with you as a willing accomplice. But if I can get you passes, I'll do it. You can be gone by the end of the day tomorrow." He glanced at Annyon and dipped one more nod, a silent courtesy, excusing himself from our awkward little party.

Annyon turned his eyes to Eliza, a fresh

expression of respect settling on his face. “You’re sure?”

Her hesitancy said *no*. But then she nodded.

He made eye contact with each of us, the same silent question pressed in that connection. Three solemn nods responded.

“I can’t leave the lab.” Annyon pushed a hand through his hair and settled his look back on me. “We have to keep producing the antibodies. Dr. Hilton won’t be able to do it alone, not at a pace that will be of any use.”

“What does that mean?” I asked.

“Someone with a little bit of medical knowledge will have to take the lead.”

Eliza. Pretty obvious.

“But it will demand...decisions.”

“What do you mean, decisions?” The lined regret carving Annyon’s face didn’t give me the warm fuzzies.

“Not every case will qualify for the antibodies.”

“Yeah, no.” I stepped nearer. We weren’t the cold hand of the Party. “We’re not playing Dr. Death here, brother. Not a chance. If someone’s got GMS smallpox, then they get treated.”

“It’s just not that simple, Braxton. This disease is highly aggressive. Not all of the cases will have a viable chance, and we can’t waste the—”

I cut off his stoic medical jargon. “They’re

people, Annyon. Stop referring to them as cases. You sound like a freaking Jackal. They're *people*."

His face flushed, and a moment of steely silence dropped between us. "Okay." He swallowed, nodded. "You're right. They're people, and that makes this hard. But the cold fact is we won't have enough. Eliza has enough medical knowledge, not to mention firsthand experience with the disease, to know who is beyond recovery. She will have to make the call."

That chilled space of silence returned, spreading wider the gap that existed between all of us. Eliza remained statuesque, the only evidence of her emotions buried deep beneath the blasted hood she'd drawn back over her head.

The girl I'd glimpsed just moments before was gone again. I missed her. In that moment, the time I'd first taken a fist for her back in junior high replayed.

"Say it, Church Girl," Hulk had demanded, a concoction of mocking and intimidation making his voice somewhere between sadistic and pure evil.

A solid beat of tension, and then, with a steady look locked on the beast, she'd said, "No."

Pure courage. No one had ever stood up to

Hulk like that.

Only Eliza Knight.

I waited, begging in the wordless tension for that girl to reemerge. To pull back that stupid hood she'd been hiding beneath and to stand.

She didn't make a sound.

"You can't ask her to do that." I stepped in front of Liza, glaring at Annyon. "You know that's not fair."

Annyon's unwavering gaze was apologetic but unyielding. "I don't have a choice." His eyes flickered to a spot over my shoulder and back to me again. "Someone has to make the call, and I can't go. Is there anyone we can trust more than Eliza to do what is right?"

The silent message *You be the strength she needs* was heard between the two of us, spoken in his concentrated look, the pity he shot Eliza with one more glance, and the regret tugging on his brow.

She didn't want my strength—wasn't much in the offering anyway. These days, she didn't want anything from me. But Annyon didn't understand because he didn't know the details.

I wasn't Eliza's backbone, never had been. But I could walk beside her in the silence. If that was what she wanted. Or maybe that was what she needed, even if it wasn't what she wanted.

"I need you to do this, Liza." Annyon's

attention went back to the small girl behind me. "Take Braxton and the others. They'll make sure you're safe. You can do this."

No answer.

"Liza?"

"Yes." Her voice didn't carry the conviction her loaded one-word answers had been weighted with before. But she'd said it.

I looked over my shoulder, not sure what I'd find in her reaction. Beneath the shadow of her hood, her look seemed stormy and lost. Then her eyes lifted and clamped on to mine.

I was swallowed in the strength of that swirling vortex. The storm consumed us both, pulling us into a squall that would certainly change everything, not only for the two of us but for everyone. If we survived.

And on the other side of that? I didn't know. I couldn't see past the darkness.

* * *

Eliza

This time, someone's life would be in my hands. The other side of the equation wasn't better.

We stepped off the LightRail in Glennbrooke, and doom tainted the air. Once upon another happy life, this had been home. Now it was one of the last places on earth I wanted to be. Actually, when I was honest with myself, most of the time I resented that I was still on earth at all.

Why did you let me live? I would whisper the thought to that strong, voiceless Presence. *I don't want to do this. Any of it. It's too hard.*

The streets were strained with a taut silence, the sparseness of people a testimony to the crushing pressure of destruction wielded by the smallpox epidemic. Businesses that had only ever closed on Christmas day had their doors locked up tight, window coverings drawn as if to mourn a death that was as certain as it was slow and torturous.

Braxton and Tristan lugged the cooler of life between them, their pace slower than normal because Tristan's "scratch" gunshot wound was still tender. Skye walked beside me and carried the weapon she and Tristan had acquired from the guard they'd disabled with Persuasion. Seemed over the top and conspicuous. Our little entourage met no resistance as we moved up Main Street, past the business district, and through the neighborhood that lay between Main and the hospital.

A haunted emptiness gripped the town. Yards were a silent space of loneliness. No kids ran, chasing balls. Bikes lay abandoned on sidewalks and drives. Transportation stops sat in mourning solitude, now without purpose. No people going to work. No buses to pick them up.

Death hovered, black and yet gleeful, a promise no one doubted even as they tried to hide from it. People stayed behind closed doors—many of which held the condemning silk of the black dot. The quarantine sign that really didn't say *stay away* as much as it said *sentenced to death.*

I'd survived smallpox. Yet I still wore that hopeless black dot over my heart. I ached to remove it...

The sensors on the automatic doors had been disabled at the hospital. We were required to push a buzzer and wait for someone to let us through. A person, fully armored in a medical hazmat suit, shadowed the other side of the glass door. Male or female, we couldn't tell. Didn't matter much.

"Symptoms?" the dry voice cut. Tired. Despondent.

"None." Tristan answered, his commanding presence carrying through his voice. "We're here to help."

Long space of nothing, then, "We have limited suits. I can't let you in."

"We don't need them," Braxton said. "The girl in the hoodie is a survivor. The rest of us have been vaccinated."

An exhausted snort of disbelief answered. “There’s not a vaccine. And there are no survivors.”

“There is, and we were given the vaccine three weeks ago.”

The suit stepped closer to the glass door, allowing us a glimpse of the face behind the mask. I knew this person—she was a nurse and also part of the hospital administrative staff. My dad had visited with her every now and then, but I couldn’t remember her name.

“Look, kid.” The nurse sighed. “This is bold of you, and I’m impressed with your generosity. But this isn’t the old smallpox, and however it’s been genetically modified has allowed it to short circuit the old vaccination. It doesn’t work. No one has survived, and whatever you were given won’t protect you. Go home and stay alive.”

My mind went back to the village on the Vacant Plains. Our safe place. The one where I’d wanted desperately to stay.

But I wasn’t saved to hide in my safe place...

Neither Braxton nor Tristan responded, and Skye, standing behind me, cleared her throat.

My cue?

I took a half a step forward. “I survived.”

The mask moved nearer, the eyes behind it searching me.

“Liza...” Braxton let the rest hang between us,

but I knew what was at the end of that.

Let her see. Show her your scars.

As if there were cords tethered in my core, my body tightened, and I felt a scowl tug my eyebrows together. I was a circus freak. My mottled skin made me a novelty of revulsion. Someone to stare at and back away from all at once. It'd happened at the hospital in DC—Dr. Hilton, who had studied and understood what smallpox would do to a person, had that same horrified *don't come near me, freak* stare.

Even in the village, people had frozen, their eyes unable to fall away from my damaged complexion, their self-control unable to smother their looks of disgust. I'd become...

Someone like Jude. The misshapen man who hid in a cave because the world couldn't handle what it had done to him.

Let them die then...

The slithering hiss of words wove through my mind and then plunged into my heart. It felt cold and terrifying and every bit as condemning as the lethal smallpox gripping this town.

Will you choose me?

There was life in that question. An offer of hope that reached past the black dot enclosing my heart. But reaching to grip that...

The woman in the hospital stepped backward. "Look—"

I moved closer to the door—nearly nose-on-glass close—cutting the nurse off before she could shoo us away again. My fingers felt thin and frail and clumsy as I pinched the edge of my hood, my hands quivering as I lifted it off my sure-to-be bed-head-quality, two-inch-long butchered hair. But I forced the covering back, and as the air touched my skin, unfiltered by the thick cloth, gooseflesh rippled down my neck and over my shoulders.

A soft touch of light warmed the places I usually kept hidden, and a hand, large and comforting—and yet alarming at the same time—spread over one of my shoulders, meeting the goose bumps with an equally energizing sensation.

The woman on the other side of the glass studied me, her eyes round, the posture of her shoulders indicating she'd drawn a sharp breath.

"How..."

"She was the only survivor," Skye said, her voice clipped. "One of thousands of victims who had been intentionally exposed before the accidental release happened in DC. You don't deserve her help, but she's here. Let us in."

The nurse's expression shifted from something like amazed hope to insulted, and she scowled as she stared at Skye.

"Or..." Skye moved forward, her movement

forcing me to step back. Thank goodness. "We could leave, and everyone in there can die. Your choice."

I saw why Skye had been given full leadership of the Glennbrooke Pride. She and Hulk had quite a bit in common. Except Hulk was a Progressive, and somehow Skye was not.

An exaggerated pause between Skye and the woman was pulled tight by their unwavering stares.

"She's your only hope right now," Skye said.

I shivered. I'd lost most of my hope. Stuck in the shadow of memories that anchored anger. How could I be someone else's hope?

The woman drew in one more deep breath and then nodded. The sound of a buzzer filled the tense space, and then the lock inside the door clicked. With a soft swoosh, the glass barrier slid to our left, allowing us inside. Still masked, the nurse looked us over, evaluating each one of us as if she had a reason to be scared.

"The Party sent you?"

"We're here to help." Tristan took over again. He pointed to the cooler on wheels that he and Braxton had been lugging. "Dr. Luther, a leading researcher in viral diseases, produced the antibodies your patients will need to survive."

The nurse nodded toward me. "From her?"

"Yes," Tristan said.

A pause lingered between them again. Then, "I've not had any word from DC about this."

Tristan raised his brow. Skye set her feet in a defensive stance. I let my gaze drop to the floor, hiding behind the shadow of the hoodie I'd settled back into place.

Braxton stepped forward. "Dr. Luther is my brother. I have his contact in my All-In-One. Would you like to speak with him?"

"The only Luther I've ever heard of was from here in Glennbrooke, and he was a rebel. He died for his violent crimes."

I felt Braxton ripple with anger behind me. He stayed silent though.

Skye, however, had enough. "Look, Captain Cautious. Let's just leave politics out of this, okay? You have people dying in here, right?"

The woman's lips pressed into a line.

"Do you want our help or not?"

Apparently the threat of imminent death overrode even the grip of the Party. With a small nod, she stepped aside, allowing full access to the wide hallway leading to the patient wing.

Tristan and Braxton led, the cooler carried between them. Skye waited for me to follow them.

The woman who let us in didn't follow our little parade.

***

Quinn

You must save her...

The voice—Hannah's—was so real, so near. I jolted up, searching for her in the dark.

Not there. Dead.

Sweat trickled along my hairline, and my heart hammered. I felt the bed beneath me—mine, not the mushy cot in the tiny, stale room I'd occupied in the village. The sheets tangled around me were slick and soft, woven from fine cotton and silk. A deep inhale filled my nostrils with the scent of lemons and chamomile, not dust and old wood. I was home. Had been for four nights.

Yet homesick.

Another night terror had gripped me, and Hannah's whisper had jerked me from the sequence of fire, screams, her betrayal, and then mine. She'd looked at me through the lifeless sheen of her beautiful brown eyes. Blood pooled beneath her head.

You must save her...

Her lips hadn't moved, but that was Hannah's voice. Her plea.

Tremors rippled through my body as the sweat cooled against my skin. I squeezed my eyes shut and saw Eliza's face. The rough craters of her scars tugging sympathy from my heart. The soft, silent pleading in her eyes perfectly matching Hannah's.

I swiveled against the bed, my feet landing on the solid, plush carpet. One fist gripped the sheet still tucked around my waist, and the other forked into my hair. I leaned forward, anchoring my elbow near one knee, and fought to contain the shaking of my limbs.

Mother's displeasure at my lack of information grew daily. She continued to fish, more strategically and insistently every day, for more detailed information about the location of the Refuge. Her determination had slipped past normal and invaded the territory of obsessive madness. If she knew what I'd done at the research hospital...

My nightmares had become stronger. As did the reality of the woman I called mother. Behind my closed eyes, her face glared. Fire smoldered in her eyes. Her perfectly smooth, creamy skin began to melt, sloughing off the face I was familiar with and exposing...

I shuddered, forcing my eyes wide open.

The demon stayed in my mind. With both palms, I pushed on the sides of my forehead. "Out!" I growled into the chilled darkness.

The image faded. Slowly.

You must save her...

The message was softer, less clear. Understanding blurred. Reality became once again unclear.

Whom was I supposed to save?

twenty-three

Eliza

The hours blurred together, and so did most of the patients. Each in various stages of the smallpox infection, they were miserable and alone, tugging on my sympathy and my resentment at the same time. I'd known this illness. Many others had...and those who had died in the Quarantine often couldn't even get a drink of water to sooth their blistering tongues.

I pushed away the ugly comparison as I replaced the used protective gloves from the last patient with a fresh pair. Glancing at Braxton, who had disposed of the antiviral vial we'd emptied and retrieved a new one, I used my elbow to push on the door latch and my shoulder to leverage open the door.

Two steps in the room, and I froze.

Him.

I backed away until I bumped into someone.

A hand wrapped around mine, strong and steady, yet gentle. Braxton refused to give up on me, even while I treated him with disgust. I was grateful and mad about that all at once. He respected my space, until he knew I couldn't stand on my own, and then he'd do this—take my hand, silently calling the old, stronger version of myself to rise from the shadows.

I'd never needed him this much. That terrified me, because as much as I wanted to let go of the knowledge that he'd let me down, I couldn't.

He'd betrayed me.

The reality of that stamped hard against my heart, every pulse thickening the dark spot that continually expanded in my soul.

He'd betrayed me. We could not get past that.

I could not get past it.

I pulled my hand away from his, but his other palm warmed the opposite arm, holding me steady. His hold on my arm began to itch. With a strong shrug, I pushed his hand away. The look on his face...

The twist of pain rung harder inside. But it was his fault. All of this between us was his fault.

“I don’t need you, Braxton,” I hissed, not recognizing my own voice. “I don’t want you here.”

He winced. “I know.”

Not the boy of my school years. Humble, broken. This version...he broke my heart and tugged it nearer with those whispered two words. I fought against the pull.

“Then why are you here? Go. Back to DC. Back to the Refuge. I don’t care. Just stay away from me.” My voice broke, and tears I didn’t want to submit to forced their way onto my cheeks.

“I can’t.”

“Why?”

Nothing. Everything. His expression spoke where his words did not. I knew why. It wasn’t supposed to hurt like this though. Control evaporated, and everything between us boiled through me. A wild rush. A thunderclap.

I rushed at him, and when my hands collided with his chest, every drop of my strength went into that shove.

He barely stepped backward. A tear slipped over his eyelid, falling against the side of his nose.

I love you.

If he said what was written on his face, what would I have done? Folded against him and sobbed? Slapped him? And then slapped him again?

My fists, clutching the front of his shirt, trembled. *I* trembled.

Slowly, Braxton raised one hand, and with the tiniest brush of his thumb against my cheek, he traced the trail my tears had made in the crevasse where my nose met my cheek. “I won’t let you do this alone.”

The wild fury calmed, leaving behind the mournful sense of a landscape destroyed by the ripping power of a colossal storm.

I was lost. In my mind, I sat in the middle of a place that had once been familiar and beautiful. It felt empty.

Braxton’s fingertips skimmed my face, the shudder of his touch an ache we shared.

And yet, I was alone.

“Why *him*?” I seethed, glaring at the young man stretched across the hospital bed. He lay deathly still, his breathing shallow and labored. His skin riddled with the furious claim of the pox.

But I’d recognized him. So did Braxton. It wasn’t fair.

“Why would God do this?”

Braxton’s breath rattled through his chest. “I don’t know.”

His tone was soft, sympathetic, and

affectionate, and yet unyielding. I wanted it to be harsh. To speak the release I longed for. *You don't have to do this, Eliza. He deserves this death. You don't have to save him.*

The old Braxton would have not only said those things, he would have insisted on them. And the old Eliza would have told him he was wrong.

Another ripple of tears quaked through me. Where was that girl? Braxton was waiting for her, refusing to give up on her.

But she was dead.

"I can't." Venom dripped from my voice, and I pushed away from his hold. My spine grew rigid. I turned to look at the bulky form dying alone in a hospital bed. My glare sizzled from deep within, the darkness that had been growing in my heart splurging over the bits of light struggling to survive.

"Liza..." Braxton touched my hand, his fingers soft and pleading.

I pushed him back. "No. You can't ask this of me. I won't do it." I turned my glare on him. "Hulk can die. I won't save him."

***

Braxton

She leveraged another shove against my chest

and then ran.

Who could blame her? How could God let this happen?

I pressed my back against the brick wall lining the hallway so I wouldn't have to look at Hulk and slid to the floor. He'd taunted her since we were kids. The bully. The beast. He'd targeted her once the Party had taken over, hell bent to see her broken.

And she had broken.

So had he.

We had been right. Hulk had been in DC when the explosion had released the virus. Charlotte must have sent him away when she realized what had been done. But it'd been too late. He'd been exposed. And now here he was, dying alone. No one to mourn his cruel life. No one to care if Eliza interceded for him or not.

I cared though. Something in me knew this decision of hers would chart a new course for her future. The one she was choosing was dark and lonely, and my heart ripped thinking of her chained to that path. The other was steep and difficult, and I resented that it was so unbelievably hard.

But there was life beyond the hard. And if the old Eliza were here, and I was in her place right now, stepping onto the path she was choosing, I knew what she would have done.

She would have fought for me to live.

***

Quinn

"You failed." Mother's snapping voice jolted me from my study. "I put my faith in you, son, and you failed. Now they've gone to Glennbrooke."

"Glennbrooke? What's in—"

She cut me off with a fireball glare. Didn't matter. I knew what and who was in Glennbrooke.

"You were handed an opportunity to eliminate both Eliza Knight and Braxton Luther. Do you realize what you let slip through your fingers? You could have ended this rebellion. Ended. It."

"I'm not sure that this all rides on—"

"That is because you have no understanding. All of this has been set into motion since your—" Mother snapped her mouth shut.

"Birth?"

Her jaw went rigid. The blaze in her eyes, the fury of her expression...*possessed* came to mind. I'd never seen her composure unravel like this. Not once.

"What is it about her that makes you afraid, Mother?"

Silence.

"Is she right?" I stood, my daring tone low as I stepped toward her. "Was she right to resist you and your Party? Do her scars testify to the truth about us?"

Mother straightened, and the wild look on her face froze. Transformed. Went back to the locked self-possession of the woman who had always controlled my life.

"Son." She reached to cup my face. I leaned away, but her fingertips still grazed my chin. "My delight and hope."

A familiar numbness oozed from the top of my brain, spreading over and through my head. It dripped down my spine, diffusing into my chest, slowing my heart. Making my thoughts blur.

I'd fought through this fog only once. Only for Hannah. One. Time. She was worth the struggle.

She was not here.

The warmth of a palm against my cheek drew my tired eyelids closed.

"My hope and my delight..."

I stumbled backward and sank into the chair I'd abandoned only a moment before.

"You will not fail me again, will you?"

My fists clenched. I'd fought through this once...

It'd never been this strong.

Had it?

"You'll find them in Glennbrooke."

The rebels were in Glennbrooke. Eliza. Braxton...

The hand was now on my shoulder, and a thumb pressed a satisfying trail up my neck, ending at the base of my skull, where the circles began.

My muscles gave way to the sensation.

No. Fight through it.

The circles continued, and my head fell forward. White beauty enveloped me, my Nirvana in a world that didn't make sense.

"Just rest now, son." The kneaded circles stopped. A light graze of fingernails over my neck set a shiver of gooseflesh over my shoulders. "I know you won't let me down. My delight and hope."

twenty-four

Eliza

You will carry his death. There will be no turning back.

The warning ribboned through my head in Jude's voice. He'd never said that—we'd never discussed the possibility of finding Hulk near death.

But it was something he would say. I couldn't ignore it. Him. Because Jude, more than anyone, would understand.

What would he do if he came face to face with Charlotte? Or Kasen? He had the brains and the ability to inflict any kind of retribution he chose on them. And yet he chose...

What?

To be a doormat?

Jude was no doormat. He commanded respect by his deep ways of thinking, loving. By protecting those who needed protection. Giving mercy.

Chasing the darkness.

I had run from the hospital, unconcerned with sanitation procedures. The town had already been exposed. Sentenced to death. My chasing into the night wouldn't change that one way or another. My feeble lungs burned. My legs wobbled and stumbled. Every part of me contrasted gravely against the girl I had once been.

She is dead, God. The girl who is left cannot do what you are asking.

My chaotic escape ended at a black spot of emptiness in the middle of a quiet upper-middle-class neighborhood. A vacancy of waste where we had once lived. Dad, Mom, Hannah, and me. And Braxton.

We looked like the home that had burned to the ground. Unrecognizable scraps of useless dirt. Left where they were to rot. Useless and ugly.

You were not saved for this either.

There by the oak tree that had been sacred once upon a dream, my legs buckled. I felt like a flimsy stuffed doll, landing on the cool spring grass in a heap of despair. The heels of my palms pressed into my eyes, and a single sob rippled through me.

"The darkness is too dark," I whispered to the Voice.

The Voice did not whisper back.

***

Braxton

I lowered beside her, across from the blank spot that had once been her home. Her little body hardened. The broken girl shelled up again. Locking me out, herself in, along with all the hurt and fear and anger.

Our tree reached to the heavens at our backs, the life we once knew burnt and crumbled before us. So much time had passed behind us—not measured by days but by tragedy. We'd been upended. Our lives looked exactly like the charred site of the Knights' home.

At some point, we needed to start rebuilding.

Eliza remained stiff beside me, refusing to look at me. Her back straight, chin stubbornly set away from me, and the rest of her face hooded by that blasted sweatshirt.

"Did you come to talk me into it?" Her voice snarled with harshness, so very un-Eliza. But she was talking, not ignoring me. Not stuffing away the monsters I knew she wrestled with.

"No."

In the gray shadows of the closing evening, I saw her chin shift. Maybe tremble. "You're supposed to."

"You've never needed me to tell you what to do."

Her shoulders rounded, and she hugged her knees to her chest. The muffled sniff told me what was really going on under that hoodie, and when she lowered her head, tucking her face into her arms, my heart cracked a little more.

"I can't do it, Braxton."

With a breathy whisper, the traces of my Eliza began to return. Kind. Honest. Good.

"It's too hard. Why would God ask me to do this?"

I didn't fight the burn of tears. "I don't know." Trembling, I reached for her nearest hand.

She didn't jerk away.

The gray shadows fell thicker, and in the curtain of this moment where there was only us, fighting the past, struggling against the pain of mistakes and betrayal and resentment. Eliza turned her palm until it pressed against mine and held on.

Tiny trembles registered on her shoulders, confirmed by the unsteady pressure of her hand in mine, and the occasional sound of her sniffing was all the movement or sound between us for several minutes. Still, I held on.

"You're so much like him." Her whisper softened the falling twilight.

A knot slipped around my chest, tied by the complexity of emotion in her voice. Wonder and resentment and pride and still more resentment all in one breath.

"I always saw him in you, you know?"

"No, I didn't know that." But somehow, it didn't surprise me. She always saw the best in me. Even when, really, it wasn't actually there.

"Does it bother you?"

A weak smile tipped my mouth. "No."

She turned her head, laid her cheek against her folded arm, and looked at me. I could feel, more than see, the questions in her stare.

"Dad and I are good now," I said.

I still wished I could have another moment with the man I'd spent most of my teenage years resenting. To tell him that I loved him. That he'd always been my hero—and that I had wished more than anything we could have found a way to be what we had been when I was a little kid. Pals. It still hurt that we'd lost that, but I was pretty sure that pain wasn't one sided. Dad had been just a man. A good one—but not perfect—and one who'd found the demands of life could swallow even the best of intentions. I got that now, especially sitting next to the person I'd cared about most and hurt the deepest.

I wished desperately for reconciliation. With him. With her.

"He'd be proud of you."

My breath shuddered as I drew it in, deep and long. Lifting a shoulder, I dipped my face into my sleeve to swipe the tears off my face.

"You are strong enough, Liza." I squeezed her hand. "You're the bravest person I've ever met."

She shook her head. "You always thought that. But the truth was, I knew you were behind me. Every time I stood my ground, you were there, at my back. Taking the blows for me." She sat up again, staring back at the remains of her home. "I wouldn't have been that girl without you being that boy."

"I'm right here with you, Liza."

She tugged her hand away, and defeat sagged through her. "I can't, Braxton. I just can't. Hulk took my life. Everything. Including us."

"We're right here." I rubbed my thumb across her shoulder. "Together."

Another shake of that hoodie I hated more and more.

"We're broken." Her words cracked into the heavy night. "I'm broken."

God help me, impatience and frustration rose in a powerful tide. I came off the ground and moved to squat in front of her, gripping both her shoulders. "The girl I know never depended on her own strength to do what she knew was right. And she didn't depend on me either. She found the resolve in a deeper well, and *He* never let her down."

She tried to pull away. It was my turn to shake my head, and my hold tightened. The shoulders beneath my palms tensed, and I saw the rise of her chin beneath that blasted hood. It was enough to tug at another wave of boldness in me. I leaned in, one hand capturing the lift of her chin. "You are still Eliza Knight." Heat became the undercurrent of my voice. Of the moment.

She froze, but I couldn't see the reaction in her eyes. With the hand that had been holding her shoulder, I tugged on that stupid thing hiding her face until it fell to her back.

Her hand curved around my wrist, and I thought she was going to shove me away. She didn't. The pressure of her grip strengthened, and though slight, I felt the weight of her face as she tipped it against my palm. The lines of her expression twisted, reflecting the battle I knew waged inside.

I didn't know how else to fight for her. "Stop hiding under this damn thing. It's not you, and you're shriveling up in the darkness."

She started to cry.

I did too.

***

Quinn

The stallion pounded through my split brain again. Hooves beating an angry demand. Nostrils flaring. Eyes blazing. He circled me. Stopped, reared, and then faced me head on. Flames flew near his muzzle as he snorted his contempt at me, and then he lowered his head, pawed the ground, and charged. Straight. At. Me.

I couldn't move. The ground thundered beneath me, and the heat of the flame bursting from his muzzle hit me in waves of intense warning. But I was stuck, and he wasn't stopping.

Take the bit.

The bit, as always, suddenly appeared in my hand. The metal was sharp where it should have been blunt, the chain studded with pointed metal pieces. It burned against my palm.

The brute kept barreling toward me. Two more heartbeats, and his solid hooves, powered by fourteen hundred pounds of pure, furious muscle, would strike me. Drive over me. Kill me.

Take the bit.

I lifted my hand with the bit in my fist. The taste of metal saturated my tongue as heat scalded my mouth. Pain seared through my cheeks right before a flow of warm goo oozed over my lips. I touched my fingers to the corner of my mouth, the spot that felt ripped by a razor.

Blood.

Well done, my hope and my delight. Now, do not let me down.

The stallion vanished. Instead of standing in a ring facing a possessed animal, I stood in a well-lit hallway, staring at Eliza Knight. My arm moved, lifting something heavy.

Eliza looked at me, her hood slipping from her head. Her cratered scars smoothed before my eyes. Her hair became long and wavy, like Hannah's had been. She said nothing, but a single tear wove over her smooth cheek, followed the outline of her jaw, and settled on her chin.

Don't let them tell you who you are.

My hand quivered, and I looked down to see what my grip held. A gun. Military issue automatic rifle. The kind I'd carried to the research hospital. The one I'd used to graze Tristan's belly—just as Braxton had done mine. The type that had been used against my skull, knocking me unconscious while Hannah turned away.

Do not let me down...

The shaking spread through my arm and shoulder and rocked my whole body.

Eliza.

Hannah.

Mother.

I lowered the gun and began to turn away. A knifing pain tore through my mouth. Warm, thick moisture coated my tongue and trickled out of the small space between my lips. The shot of pain stopped my retreat, returning my head to face Eliza again.

Do. Not. Fail.

White light pierced my mind, and in the next moment, there was only darkness. And excruciating pain.

And a gunshot.

I wished with everything in me that I'd felt the bullet tear through my own flesh.

But as I woke up, my head buried deep into my sweat- and tear-soaked pillow, I finally knew what was true.

I didn't have a choice.

twenty-five

Eliza

Braxton stayed with me as the night drew longer. His back against our oak tree, he simply sat in my silence. Not letting me go through the night alone. Waiting for the light to pry through the darkness.

I didn't slip my hood back over my head as I crawled closer to him. He covered my hand with his, tipped his head back against the fire-blackened bark of our tree, and shut his eyes. Grit burned in mine, salt from our shared tears, dirt from the ground I'd acquired in my fingernails. I studied the silhouette of this young man who now possessed the strength and character of his father, and a sprout of gratitude warmed in my chest.

He and his dad had finally found peace. I wished it had happened while Pastor Luther had been alive, but knowing that Braxton had reconciled with his father at all made me happy for him.

Maybe I wasn't dead after all.

His thumb slid over my wrist and palm, and then he gently tugged me closer. I didn't resist. When my head settled against his chest, his fingers danced through the pixied growth of my hair, sending a calming shower of tingles over my scalp and shoulders. I shut my eyes, and as the rise and fall of the chest beneath my head became slower, deeper, restful, I let the lull of this rare moment—free of the past—rock me into a peaceful sleep.

The first since Hulk had pushed me into a railcar.

I don't know how long we stayed that way. Morning had not yet awakened when my eyelids fluttered open. But I felt a new lightness in me, even without the sunrise, as I shifted away from Braxton. His arm slid off my shoulder, where he'd held me, and I began to scoot away. His quick intake of air was followed by the light touch of his fingers to my neck.

I shivered and melted all at once.

"Liza?" His whisper had the raspy quality of a

man not quite awake.

I took the hand that had touched my neck, folded it between my palms, and brushed a kiss to his knuckles.

His arm went slack, and I tucked his hand against his chest, in the warm spot where my head had been. Crawling, I backed away again and was nearly ready to stand, when his quiet voice caught me.

"Please forgive me..."

My throat closed over, and tears burned my eyes. Even in his sleep, he asked only one thing from me. Still, I wrestled...

I narrowed the small distance I'd put between us and found that I trembled.

"I'm trying, Braxton." Careful not to wake him, I feathered a touch over his lips with my shaking fingertips. "Honest. I'm trying."

His long inhale paused, and the breath he exhaled quivered. I pulled away again, pushed to my feet, and crept over the ashes that had been my life. Every stride took me closer to facing the boy who had burned it to the ground.

***

Quinn

I'd only flown in a military chopper one other time. I'd been angry and scared then too. But this time...

Two other carriers flew in formation behind us. An entire unit of soldiers, sent to take down four young rebels, armed with only one military rifle and the power to change the status quo.

The pounding inside my skull actually burned. Vertigo swept over me more than once, and before we landed, the officer in charge, who answered to me on this mission, squinted a critical look beneath my hat and asked, “Sir, will you be okay?”

“Fine,” I growled. “I’ll be fine when we have boots on the ground.”

“Ah.” He nodded. “Chopper flight is an acquired taste. It won’t be long now. We’ll land directly at the hospital, so you’ll have to make a fast recovery.”

Like that was in my control. Wouldn’t happen anyway. My problems had nothing to do with the flight. I nodded and gripped the strap to my seat belt.

“You’ll recognize the targets?” Commander Lewis asked.

I clenched my jaw. “Yeah. They’ll be the only ones not near death.” I wondered if he wondered about that. If he stopped to think about this situation at all.

Maybe he just took the bit and didn’t bother with the other details.

"What are your orders, sir?"

My orders, from my mother, via the president himself? Shoot to kill. On sight. It was intriguing that Commander Lewis didn't have the same details.

"When we find them, wait for my command."

"Sir?"

I leveled a look on him, one that dared him to argue with Kasen Asend's nephew. Or whatever I was.

"Wait for my command," I repeated.

He nodded.

Perhaps I'd just failed my last test.

* * *

Eliza

Two steps into his room. That was all the farther I got.

Shivering in the semidarkness as the early morning sun made a weak and unconvincing attempt to creep through the shaded window, my heart throbbed, and a chill crawled over me. I glanced at the tube of antibodies I'd taken from the cooler Tristan and Braxton had carried in and then looked back to the body lying on the other side of the room.

He should die. Hulk had been a bully since forever. He'd made my life...

I squeezed my eyes shut, clenching the vial in my left palm. My teeth sank into my bottom lip so deeply that the flesh split and blood oozed onto my tongue.

"I can't..." I whispered.

This burden is too heavy, the Voice answered.

I nodded. "Please don't ask me to save him. I can't."

That is not the burden that smothers you.

I stilled. Listened. Ached to understand, to not feel this ugly mass pressing me into the shadows.

He waited until nothing else could distract me. Until He had my heart's undivided attention.

It's too heavy, Daughter. Let me have it.

My vision blurred into a hot, watery mess, and my breath became shallow and quick.

Eliza...

The anger. The...

Hate.

He asked me to let it go.

I wanted to.

I couldn't.

It was mine.

I'd earned it.

I hated it.

Let Me have it.

Sweat made my palm slick as I squeezed that tube of life to death. I shut my eyes again, my lips quivering and my face wet.

"Help me..." I whispered a wobbly cry, true from the depths of my heart. "Please..."

A small spark of warmth ignited in my middle, not the consuming blaze that threatened to destroy, but a gentle light. A hope.

Strength. That was not my own.

The spark grew into a flame. I opened my eyes again, blinked until I could see the dying young man. My feet moved forward, though the determination to walk wasn't my own, and when I reached his bedside, my hands went to work as if powered by something else.

"Who...are...you?" The broken words were pushed through Hulk's cracked lips as I began mixing the antibodies into the bag hanging on the IV pole.

I stopped and turned so that he could see my full face rather than my profile. His eyelashes fluttered beneath the swollen pox that had nearly reached his eyelids. His look was agony, but I couldn't tell if he really saw me.

"You know me," I said softly.

Three labored breaths drew in and out of his chest. He swallowed, the act making him wince. "Are you killing me now, Church Girl?"

The resignation in his voice softened my hardened heart more. "I am not."

His mouth trembled. "Why?"

I searched for an answer. It fell from my lips

before I comprehended it. “Because I don’t want to live in darkness.”

Truth. I gripped it, and the flame inside me burned brighter.

* * *

Hulk stayed quiet while I finished mixing the second dose of antibodies and rehung the bag. In the few hours that had passed since I’d given him the first dose, his breathing had grown stronger and more even, his fever hovered at a safer 101 degrees rather than nearly 104, and he’d gained some color in his pocked face.

He would live. His recovery would be a fraction of what mine had been, and when he was on his feet...

God, what have you asked me to do? This man is evil...

I hoped I would be gone before he was out of that bed.

I turned to go, but Hulk spoke again before I could step away.

“You saved me?” His voice rasped from lack of use, but it no longer carried the wispiness of death.

I looked over my shoulder at him, and our eyes met. Tears glazed his.

My breath caught. I was actually startled to see

his emotion. "We'll see, Hulk." Four steps carried me away from the tamed monster to my escape.

"Eliza." He caught me again as I reached for the door handle.

I didn't know he knew my real name. And once again his brokenness pierced me.

"I hate that name."

Mine? No...his. Hulk. It wasn't his real name—it'd been something he'd been branded with.

"Okay." I nodded. I hadn't liked Church Girl much either. "I'll check on you soon, Garrison."

twenty-six

Quinn

The choppers beat the air with a thundering announcement of our landing, a certain warning to our four targets. My divided mind warred over that realization, one part seething at our lack of stealth, the other part relieved that they'd have a chance to run.

I couldn't live with the insanity slicing my thoughts and emotions anymore. If I found a way to die, could I see Hannah again?

Dressed in combat uniforms and hooded with hazmat masks, soldiers filed out of the chopper bellies, wielding their weapons as if the four we sought were beasts from the pit of hell. Not minimally armed kids who were probably saving the infected people in the hospital.

You must save her...

The divide in my brain tamed to a low burn, insanity stepping down, allowing clear thoughts to settle. Hannah would want me to find a way to live outside of my mother's grip.

She was not with me, exerting her power of manipulation. I could do what needed to be done.

The unit commander stepped off our aircraft in front of me, and I followed. The platoon assembled, the men looking to their commander, who in turn looked to me.

"Orders?"

We'd been over this. Another chance to say what he seemed to think I ought to say?

"Leave the sick alone. Do not lift your hoods or make skin contact."

He lifted one brow. "And if we find the Knight girl and her rebel leaders?"

I held his challenge. The gathering around us grew tense, their silence flaring the divide in my brain.

Don't let me down.

"Sir, the Knight gi—"

"Shoot to kill." A blaze of pain flared through my skull. I tried to hide my flinch. "But only on my command."

The soldiers eyed first me, then their leader. His stoic stance and concrete expression neither undermined my instructions nor endorsed my role as leader. It likely wouldn't either way. I wasn't military. I had no business being here, being in charge. Except that Charlotte Sanger made it happen.

She'd made all of this happen. And what happened there, this night, would determine not only my future but the future of the Party. Of the nation.

How could one girl's life become that valuable?

Her scars...

Her life.

Eliza Knight was a living indictment on the Party.

Commander Lewis switched his rifle to *fire* and turned back to his men. "You have your orders. Spread out. Find them. Don't get sick. Keep the coms clear unless you've found one. Clear?"

A chorus of "Sir" punctured the air.

"Don't die."

Another unified "Sir." And then they were off, boots pounding the sidewalks in a staccato rhythm of foreboding.

I followed, my footsteps unequal to their determination or training.

The halls of the hospital felt like a mausoleum. The chill of death slithered past us, twining over our shoulders, feathering against our necks and hands. Every soldier felt it, their postures tense. The fog of their breath against the masks we wore puffed thicker, quicker, the deeper in we tread.

I wondered if this sensation had permeated the Quarantine where Eliza had fought for her life. Where so many others had died. Had the darkness been this thick? The hopelessness felt like a coating of oil, suffocating the life within.

The halls split, and so did the unit. The scuffs of their boots on the floor didn't sound as confident as they had outside. Patient rooms dotted either side of the passages, and soldiers fanned out, checking behind each closed door. Only the moans of the sick broke the monotony of silence, an occasional plea for *help* or to *just end this* salting the mournful stillness.

But no rebels. Maybe the four had heard us.

"You." A sharp tone carried over the com tucked near my ear. "You're not sick. And you're not protected."

Silence. Adrenaline surged through my veins, and I stopped, waiting for the location.

"Southwest wing. Room 111," the same military voice called. "Two here. I've got 'em."

"We're unarmed!" The shout echoed through the halls.

"Sanger?" Commander Lewis's voice followed,

this time over the com.

"I'm on my way. Do not fire."

My steps turned into a jog, but my mind raced. What would happen now? If I saw Eliza, would it be like Hannah? Would I only see the hate? Would I feel the ripping of the bit in my mouth? The fire splitting my mind, separating reason from instinct? Would I feel the flames consume everything else but the thirst for her death?

Whom would I fail when I saw Eliza Knight?

A semicircle of soldiers formed in front of me as I approached room 111. Pinned against the hall, Braxton stood in front of a smaller frame—certainly Eliza. Shielding her as he held her to his back.

"You don't understand," he pleaded, "we're helping. We have the antibodies to save them—"

"Shut up, boy," Commander Lewis barked.

"No. You need to hear—"

Lewis backhanded him. Braxton had enough training in his background that he didn't go down, though Lewis's strength was far from small, but his loss of balance was enough for two other soldiers to lunge at him from either side. Their momentum forced him face forward to the ground, and his struggle, though impressive, was not enough to push them off.

Which left Eliza Knight alone against the brick

wall.

"Don't hurt her!" Braxton yelled, his words muffled because one uniformed knee kept his head pinned to the floor. "She's not a threat—and she hasn't done anything wrong. You can't hurt her."

"Sanger!" Lewis barked, drawing my attention back to the girl—our target. She shook, though she stood straight and looked at me without shame. And without the cover of her hoodie.

Her eyes—large and brown and very much like Hannah's—caught mine and held. I'd never seen that kind of determination before. It glowed from inside her, but not like the madness I saw in my mother. It was like—

Nothing I could describe. I knew in that moment why Mother feared her so much. She possessed something powerful. The light of hope that chased away the darkness. A beacon of freedom that drew rather than demanded. That was gentle and warm and...beautiful. It was real. It unraveled me. And for that moment while her gaze held mine, I felt my mind become whole.

Lewis stepped between us, severing whatever had just happened in that connection. The fire, the darkness, the pain in my head and my mouth, they all clamped down on me again, and I reeled in the confusion.

I ached for that touch of light again.

"She is our target, Sanger. Make the call."

I tried to look around him again. He moved so that I couldn't. "Make the call!"

"We have the other two." A group of soldiers marched behind us, and I glanced back to see the squirrelly Little Ninja and Tristan's bulk being dragged between four men.

"Quinn, what are you doing?" the Little Ninja spat. She struggled against the tie that held her hands locked behind her back, and when one of her guards shifted to still her, she shoved her bony shoulder into his gut. He doubled over with a grunt, and the other guard whipped her around, slamming the Little Ninja into the wall.

Time blipped in my mind, and I saw Hannah crashing against those solid bricks.

"No!" I shouted, lunging for her.

Lewis's large hand gripped my shoulder, ripping me back. "What are you doing, Sanger? We have them. We can end this. Now. Give the order."

Do not fail. Her voice slithered in between my ears, prickling the hairs on my neck and triggering that flare of white light that always preceded the vision. The explosion. The horse. The pain.

I felt it...like a knife inside my mouth, a blade against my tongue. It tugged the other direction. My head followed.

Eliza Knight...

Do not fail...

Something heavy and cold lay in my hand. I lifted it. Gripped the muzzle with my other hand...

"Quinn! Please, Quinn, you know the truth. Please don't—"

The sound of fist against flesh ended Braxton's pleading.

My heart rate slowed. The ringing in my ears rattled my brain. The burning pain of a blade against my tongue was nearly unbearable.

You can end this, son. My delight and hope.

Was she really speaking? Or was she that deep into my head?

It didn't matter. I couldn't fight the burning demand. I didn't have a choice.

A figure, massive, though slumped and weak, suddenly stood between me and my target. I blinked, my vision blurred and unsteady. When it cleared, I found a young man, larger than any I'd ever met, staring back at me. His face and muscled arms were riddled with pox, his lips white and cracked.

He stood in front of Eliza. Just like Braxton had. But his sweaty and rumpled shirt...

He was a Jackal.

"Are you Quinn?" His deep voice rumbled.

I didn't answer.

"Did *she* send you?"

His question didn't make any sense.

"Come on, Hulk."

Braxton couldn't see us with his face pressed against the floor, but he'd clearly recognized the voice. "She saved you. She had every reason to let you die, but she saved you."

"Please, Garrison." Eliza's whisper slipped from behind the Jackal.

My head snapped back. "Garrison?"

"Yeah. And you're Quinn." Anger tightened his voice.

"Garrison? What's going on there, Lewis?" Mother's voice buzzed behind my ear. Her real voice—not the one that murmured through my head.

"A Jackal just stepped in the way, ma'am."

"Garrison?" Her snap bit like a viper's. "Give him a com."

Lewis nodded to one of the soldiers beside me, and she rested her firearm long enough to toss her com to Garrison.

"Hulk." Mother's commanding address came over the sound waves. "You're alive."

"You care," he answered, all snark. "That's charming."

"I didn't know..."

"I was with you when the explosion happened. You knew. You did nothing. You were going to let me die with everyone else. One less mess to hide. Yes?" Hulk mimicked my mother's manner of speech perfectly. As if he was well acquainted with her ways.

It all clicked. Our frequent visits to Glennbrooke, our second home at the state center, only an hour's LightRail ride away. Her obsession with the Jackals...

Everything Jude had claimed was true.

"Hulk," Mother began in a voice that gave me chills.

"Garrison," he growled. "My name is Garrison."

Silence stretched for two heartbeats.

"Okay, Garrison. All is not lost. You are the pride and power of the Party. Finish this last task, and all that was promised will finally be yours."

His glare shifted from me to Braxton and back again. "I've heard that—"

"Finish this now, Garrison, and you will have what you've always wanted."

I watched with horrified amazement as the bulky man in front of me transformed into a child. His face twisted with confusion and longing, the expression of a five-year-old who had lost his parent and was desperate for a place to belong.

"Please, Garrison..." Eliza's cracked whisper

drew a sideways look from him.

"You are the pride and power of the Party." Mother spoke with the tone she used on me, only she told me that I was her "delight and hope."

Hulk blinked, and I recognized the slow glazing that melted over his eyes.

Memory manipulation? Could she have twisted it further...

"This is the last task, all I ask of you, and all that was promised—"

"Stop." My shout echoed in the tense hallway. I felt all eyes lock on me. "Stop it, Mother. Stop lying. Stop using us."

Mother paused for only a breath. "Begin with Quinn, Garrison. He is a traitor. He does not deserve a place with us."

Hulk's eyes flickered, rage registering behind what had been a blank expression. The man-child who had only moments before stood hurt and searching vanished, and Hulk, the pride and power of the Party, took on terrifying life.

She'd taken my brother from me and had turned him into a monster. Charlotte Sanger was the insidious woman Jude had implied her to be. And she was certainly not my mother. Not now. Not ever.

But she had control over the man snarling in front of me.

Hulk reached for the weapon carried by the soldier nearest to him, snapped it away from the man, and trained the muzzle on me.

I mirrored his position. "Don't do this, Garrison. She will never give you whatever it is you want. She will only use you."

"Shut up, you spoiled, selfish brat." He stepped closer. "You always had everything. I got nothing. It's about time she sees that you're useless."

"You knew about me?"

"Did I know I had a brother? Yeah. I knew about you."

Hulk took another step nearer. I slid one step back. "She's manipulating you. She did it to both of us. You have to see it now. She left you to die—"

"No!" Spit flew from his mouth as he snarled. "I was the one she really wanted. You were just the presentable one. The one our father wanted."

"Our father?" I shook my head. "I've never known my father."

"You see him every day, you idiot." A wicked amusement cracked his death glare. "You mean you didn't know?" The laugh he bellowed bounced throughout the hall. "Not as smart as all those tests said you were, eh?"

The gun in his hand began to swirl in a

mocking circle, taunting me as if this were a child's game of pin the bullet in the brother. A game I was destined to lose. I wouldn't pull the trigger, and he wouldn't miss.

"Is that what she's promised you?" I worked to keep my voice steady. "That you could see our father?"

The circle game ceased, and he gripped the weapon like he intended to use it.

"Think she'll do it? Or will she whisper those magic words over you again, and you'll have another task to complete. Just one more."

Pain and rage mingled in his eyes.

"Do you still see the explosion?" I asked, my tone low. "Do you hear the woman—our real mother scream?"

His jaw trembled.

"Hulk." Mother's voice edged near panic. "End this. Now. And then take care of the Knight girl."

He looked to his right, at Eliza.

"Shut her out, Garrison," I said. "She's controlling you. But you can fight it."

The glaze fell over his eyes again. He was slipping, fighting. Not understanding what he was fighting. I watched as his eyebrows drew down, pain withering his face. He squeezed his eyes shut, and the corner of his mouth twitched. He winced.

The horse. The bit. He saw it. Felt it.

"It's not for the animal," I said, daring to close the gap between us. "I know what you see. Don't take the bit."

I remembered the one time I'd fought through that vision. For Hannah, when we were living at the state center. The horse circled me, snorted flares of fire, stopped, pawed the ground, and then charged. In my hand, I held the bit, and the voice hissed "take the bit," just like it always had.

I always did, and the dream would stop. I would be safe. And under the control of the bit. Except that one time. My hand had opened, and the bit had fallen to the ground.

The beast charged me. I felt the punch of his great hooves cave into my chest, and my heart stalled as if it had been crushed. But then...

He was gone. I was fine, sitting across from Hannah in our dining room, angry that my mother was sending Hannah away.

How had I forgotten that?

"Garrison." Eliza crept from the place she'd pushed herself along the wall, her shaky hand reaching for my brother.

He startled, looked down at her as if seeing her through a soapy film, and then at his gun. His stance went rigid again, and I reached to pull her away. She held up a hand, stopping me and showing him her scars at the same time. Letting go of his gun with one hand, he stretched a finger to trace the pocks that dimpled the skin on her arm.

"Because of me," he said, and then with the same hand, he covered his beating heart, and clarity seeped into his eyes. "Because of you." The gun in his right hand lowered to his side.

My grip on my weapon loosened, and my arms trembled.

"Neither will engage, ma'am." Lewis's report snapped over the coms, and the audience I'd forgotten about came back into my narrowed view. All weapons were trained on me.

Charlotte's voice was sharp ice. "Take them all down."

Garrison and I pivoted in unison, our weapons repositioned.

"You do not take orders from Charlotte Sanger." I met the eyes of every soldier glaring back at me. "She is not your commander in chief."

"Sir?"

Lewis spoke, but his question wasn't aimed at me.

I scowled. "Lower your weapons."

Not one soldier moved.

"Sir? Your orders?"

Was Kasen—

"Give the command," Charlotte demanded.

The weight of silence deepened.

"Sir, we need a—"

"Do not engage." Kasen's timid response cut off Lewis's request. "Lower your weapons."

"What?" Charlotte's shrill voice was the opposite of timid. "We will lose everything we've worked for. Everything! Take them down."

"I cannot." Though defeat underscored his words, Kasen spoke with authority. "You can't take my sons from me again, Charlotte. I cannot let you do it this time."

"You donated DNA and nothing more. That was the agreement."

"Quinn has his mother's eyes. Garrison favors me. You promised me they'd be safe. I did everything you asked so that they would be sa—"

The report of gunfire jolted through my shock. Garrison and I both turned inward, huddling around Eliza.

"Sir?" Lewis tapped his com. "Sir, what just happened?"

Silence.

No one wanted to say what we knew had just happened.

* * *

Eliza

It was over. For me, anyhow, the nightmare was over.

Hulk—Garrison—was alive, and he and Quinn had saved me. Hannah had been right. Quinn was good. He sought the light and found it.

The unit of soldiers pulled back, leaving us in their panic to get back to the choppers, back to DC. Pandemonium was about to unleash nationwide. Charlotte Sanger had just shot the president.

The Party would fold on itself and the country...

Braxton scrambled to his feet, oblivious to the blood that had smeared from his nose, over his cheek, and down to his jaw. Quinn and Garrison parted, letting him get to me.

His arms nearly crushed me as he pulled me against his chest, his fingers curling into my stubby hair. "You're safe." The words wobbled off his lips.

I pressed my forehead into him, wrapping my arms around his shoulders with a fierceness that equaled his hold. "For now."

"No. It's done, Liza."

I smiled as a tear slipped over my eyelid, and I shook my head against him. "We weren't saved to stay where it's safe."

He pulled back enough to look at me. "What does that mean?"

I glanced to Garrison and then Quinn. "They'll be lost. The country, it's broken. We still have work to do."

Braxton studied me, his smirk a remnant of the boy I once knew. But when I thought he'd launch into an argument, he only tugged me closer, securing my head against his chest once again.

"I knew you were still in there."

I was pretty sure his sigh was a prayer. Of thanksgiving.

twenty-seven

Braxton

Eliza walked for a distance, her path taking her toward the scar where the camp had been. Still black, but a green fuzz had begun to poke through the sooty dirt, a bright contrast pushing life through what had only been destruction. I watched as she continued until she came to the edge of the burnt earth. She stopped, scanned the place of her nightmare, and then lowered to the ground.

An urge to run to her nearly had my feet moving, but I controlled it. She'd asked me to come with her to the camp, but once we were out of the van near the camp remains, she'd walked away from me without an invitation. If she needed a moment alone, or more than that, I didn't want to interfere.

She sat motionless, her gaze on the scene she'd known much too well. Was she reliving the humiliation, the terror? For a moment, I wished Jude's memory manipulator didn't have such catastrophic side effects. If we could take away the yuck that certainly lived in her mind...

But then, if we'd removed that, her choice to save Hulk—Garrison—wouldn't have been so profound. The freedom to choose...

To love. To forgive.

It was as profound as it was difficult. In a world that leaned more toward darkness, that kind of light meant life. Everything. And Eliza Knight proved who she was by what she did, even when it was unbelievably hard.

Emotions billowed inside me. This girl.

I loved her. And she'd chosen to love me back. How could that be?

Without explanation, it simply was.

I couldn't keep the distance between us anymore. We could sit in silence, if that was what she wanted. Only to be near her, that would be enough. When my footsteps took me to the place where she sat, she simply looked up at me, squinting against the sunshine casting warmth onto my back, and let a small smile lift the corners of her mouth.

These little miracles. Lowering myself to the ground at her side, I tucked that grin tight against my heart.

Liza turned back to the scar carved into the earth, and after a sigh that I couldn't read, she leaned her head against my arm. I studied her face, and from my angle above her, I detected a mix of emotions, but hate was not among them.

She continued to watch the land.

"What do you see?" I was a little bit afraid of the answer.

She didn't hesitate. "A big house." That little smile lifted her mouth again. "And gardens. Trees. A big park, with lots of trees and benches and places to gather or to simply sit alone."

"Only one house?"

"No, many, but a big one where the Quarantine was. Brick, so it will not be easily broken. And many windows, so we can see in and out."

"Sounds beautiful, Liza."

She resettled against me but said nothing more.

"Who lives there?"

I felt her long draw of breath and then the slow controlled exhale. "Jackals. Girls from the Pride. Quinn. Garrison. Anyone who has lost everything after the Party fell. Anyone who needs a place to recover, to find real hope."

I blinked as my throat swelled. "Will they be stuck here?"

"Never."

The depth of Eliza's heart. Did she know how well she reflected the heart of God? Suddenly, I needed to know...

"Liza, how did you do it?"

"What?" She tipped her chin to look up at me.

"Hulk...me? How—" My throat closed over the words.

"I didn't." She sniffed, sat up, and ran her fingers over the flaky dirt. "It was like nothing I'd ever known. I told God I couldn't do it. Even when I was standing in Garrison's room with the antibodies ready to push through his IV, I said I just couldn't. But then this feeling overwhelmed me. Like light, only I could feel it, and strength, only it wasn't mine. And I let go..." She glanced back at me.

"The anger?"

Sniffing, she nodded.

"You had every right to be mad. To hate us both for what we did."

Her jaw worked, and her face drew tight with emotion. "I thought so. But I wasn't winning anything. I was losing more, and that was awful. But the anger held me, like a rope coiling tighter around my heart, and I couldn't seem to get out of it, no matter how much I wanted to."

"But you did."

She shrugged, as if she didn't really understand what happened either. "In that moment of light and strength, He said to let Him have it—that the anger and hate were too heavy for me and He'd handle it." Her eyes came back up to find mine, and her small pause held meaning that words couldn't explain. "It was harder than I can say."

Easy to believe. I still was astonished by it.

Her gaze held steady. "I don't want to live in the darkness anymore."

"Me either."

She slid her hand into mine and leaned her head against my arm again. I surveyed what had been Reformation Camp, summoning a vision of Eliza's much prettier version—her house of Hope and Recovery. What I saw was breathtaking.

"It's pretty close to the refugee village," I said, wondering if she'd already thought of that.

"It is."

"Will that be trouble?"

So much resentment still festered. A nation transformed had become a nation destroyed. There was still a lot of hard waiting in front of us. Rebuilding a divided country from the ashes of bitterness and distrust and hate was going to be a bit like trying to construct a castle out of dry sand. With some gunpowder thrown in.

"There might be difficulties, but Jude believes it's a good idea."

Should have known she would have talked to him about it. I imagined his smile—the crooked, awkward version of Jude's peculiar smile that had become something of an inspiration to all of us.

"We'll learn to bridge the gap," Eliza said, her attention once again directed toward her vision.

Quiet breathed between us, letting me toy with the thoughts churning through my mind. She believed in hope, lived it. I leaned to breathe in the soft sweetness of her hair, thankful that she'd ditched the hoodie. Her fingers wove tighter through mine, and I couldn't let the questions inside me remain unsaid.

With my free hand, I grazed her jawline and tipped her face back up to mine. Her eyes searched me and held, and suddenly inhaling and exhaling felt like new activities I hadn't mastered yet.

"What about us?" I swallowed. "Where does that leave you and me?"

A sellout Jackal and a broken refugee. Both desperate for hope.

Her eyes softened. Her smile made my mouth thick. "We're the bridge in the middle, Braxton."

"Together?" A single word, but it meant so much. My nose neared hers as I whispered.

Her eyes fluttered shut the moment our faces brushed. "Together," she breathed.

My heart surged, but I paused, giving her a chance to move away. Instead, her hand slid against my jaw and curved around my neck. She kissed me. And kissed me again. The third time, I kissed her back, drawing her closer until it seemed she and I melted together.

My mouth tingled when she pulled away, and a beautiful flush warmed her face, but she didn't duck from my gaze, and her thumb smoothed over my lips. I pressed them against her forehead.

"Together," I said again.

She nodded and locked both my hands in hers. "We'll keep charging the darkness. Together."

THE END

If we are thrown into the blazing furnace, the God we serve is able to deliver us from it, and he will deliver us from Your Majesty's hand. But even if he does not, we want you to know, Your Majesty, that we will not serve your gods or worship the image of gold you have set up.

—DANIEL 3:17–18 NIV

WILL YOU STAND?

About the Author

J. Rodes lives on the wide plains somewhere near the middle of Nowhere. A coffee addict, pickleball enthusiast, and storyteller, she also wears the hats of mom, teacher, and friend. Mostly, she loves Jesus and wants to see the kids she's honored to teach fall in love with Him too.

www.authorjenrodewald.com
fb.me/authorJRodes

Made in the USA
Coppell, TX
19 May 2022

77961728R00213